SAVAGE BRATVA KING

AN FORCED MARRIAGE DARK MAFIA ROMANCE

RUTHLESS MAFIA KINGS

VIVY SKYS

Copyright © 2025 by VIVY SKYS

All rights reserved.

No part of this book may be reproduced in any form or by any electronic or mechanical means, including information storage and retrieval systems, without written permission from the author, except for the use of brief quotations in a book review.

1

GIANNA

I watch my suitcase trundle off down the ramp towards the waiting aircraft, the flight sticker flapping from the handle like a miniature flag and turn around to face my friends.

"Aw, come here." Mika pulls me into a hug, the fake fur of her leopard-print jacket tickling my nose and making it even harder to hold back the tears. "I wish we were coming with you, Gi."

I wish they were coming with me too, but that would mean introducing them to my family and telling them the truth about my fiancé, neither of which is going to happen. Not while there's breath in my body, anyways.

Cartier goes next. She already has tears in her beautiful big eyes, and I deliberately turn away, stare at the luggage still waiting in line, owners already carrying the stress of the coming flight on their shoulders. "Gi…" Cartier holds my arms and forces me to look at her. "You know you can tell us anything, right?"

I force a smile. "Sure."

"Only…" She sucks on her top lip and eyes me up like I just told her I'd arranged for a shipment of horror novels to land in her apartment after I've gone. "I don't know. Call me cynical, but you don't look like a woman who's flying back to Chicago to get married."

I tip my head back and laugh.

Mika stands next to her, shoulder to shoulder, ganging up on me.

I haven't told them much about Seamus. My fiancé.

I've shown them photographs. If they realized that none of these images were of me and Seamus together, they didn't say it out loud, and neither of them is known for their discretion and diplomacy.

Mika once told the guy in the grocery store near where we worked that I was the only twenty-three-year-old virgin in the world, and I deserved either a medal or for some adonis to come and sweep me off my feet and show me what I was missing. All with a smile on her face that promised it was in my best interests.

I did almost kiss a dark-haired adonis once. In a nightclub. I was drunk—not so drunk I didn't know what I was doing but steaming enough to tell the adonis that he was pretty kissable. The girls rescued me with a glass of water and a reminder that my fiancé was waiting for me in Chicago, and I'd be plagued with guilt in the morning.

And, of course, I didn't stop them.

"Pre-wedding nerves," I say.

"Wow, that's what you're going with." Mika's eyebrows do

this funny dance that I've never been able to master. "Who are you and what have you done with the real Gianna?"

"Stay, Gi." Cartier's tone is serious. "Who will get drunk with Mika next weekend if you're not here?"

"And who will tell Cartier it isn't real life when she finishes the tear-jerker she's currently reading?" Mika elbows Cartier in the ribs and earns herself a playful punch on the arm.

We're the three musketeers. We've worked together at the women's refuge in Montenegro for the past twelve months. We've helped people like Rosalie, whose husband beat her so badly when she told him she was pregnant with his child that she miscarried, her injuries leaving her unable to carry another child to full-term. We've cried together, made each other laugh, and generally picked each other up off the floor each time we try to stitch a broken woman back together.

They should be there when I walk down the aisle towards my future husband, but it's because I love them that I'm leaving them behind.

"We have Internet in Chicago, you know."

"Like you're going to take time out from humping your new husband to speak to us."

Mika laughs, the sound throaty and contagious, as someone's case splits open behind us, and a man mutters, "Shit!" under his breath.

Mika and Cartier watch with bemused smiles as the guy crouches beside his luggage and starts shoving his stuff back inside. "And that right there is the reason why I travel light." The lie just rolls off Mika's tongue; her clothes take up more space in the apartment than mine and Cartier's combined.

Instinct kicks in, and I leave my friends gaping while I help the guy pick up his T-shirts and sweaters and boxers which I try not to think about when I touch them. Just a regular suitcase filled with regular stuff, and not a designer label in sight.

He glances up and smiles briefly. "My girlfriend gave me a strap to wrap around my case, but I couldn't find it when I was packing."

"Is this it?" I pull out a heavy-duty, green nylon strap from the bottom of his case that's either for his luggage or some kind of weird fetish.

His shoulders slump as he takes it. "Where did you..." His gaze drops to the tangle of clothes. "I packed it, huh?"

"I think that's about it." I stand and go back to my friends as he calls out, "Thank you!"

"Good Samaritan to the rescue." Cartier links her arm with mine and drags me towards Customs.

"No way I was touching his tighty-whities." Mika flexes her fingers and takes my other arm.

"Well, this is it." I pull my arms free and turn to face them, a sense of cold dread puddling inside me.

Since the day my father requested my return to Chicago, I've tried convincing myself that if I think the worst, then the reality can only be better. Can't it?

I mean, Seamus isn't an ogre. Well, he isn't green, and he doesn't live in a swamp, but he isn't exactly unpleasant on the eye; he just isn't the guy I'd have chosen for myself. If choosing for myself was an option. The real problem is that I'm not in love with him.

I'm not in love with anyone else either, so it isn't like my heart is breaking at the thought of vowing to love him till death do us part. But one day, I might've fallen in love with someone else. I might've met my soulmate in a dog shelter in the Greek islands, or while feeding sharks in the Bahamas, or at an elephant sanctuary in Thailand, but all these opportunities have been snatched away from me before I've even had a chance to experience life.

Because of our family.

Family first and always, even for the youngest daughter.

Even for the youngest daughter who has expressed her desire to stay out of the family business. I guess an alliance with the Irish mob means more than a career spent working with vulnerable women and animals. I can already picture Seamus's response when I tell him that I want to set up a women's refuge in Chicago. "*Yeah, right. Oh, you're serious. Like you want me to care about people?*"

"Stay in touch, Gi." Cartier pulls me in for another hug.

"There'll be fucking hell to pay if you don't." Mika buries my face in her faux-fur coat. "We'll be on the first plane to Chicago to whip your sorry ass straight back here."

I'm going to miss this banter and laughter and friendship.

"I will. I promise."

And I mean it, I do. I'm just not sure how Seamus will feel about having my colorful friends come to visit his rambling mansion, or how I'll ever explain my reservations to them when they see the kind of wealth I already have and am marrying into.

I walk away from them and don't look back. I flash my fake passport at the guard working the security gate and head through to the departure lounge with the sinking realization that this will probably be the last time I ever see my friends.

I find an uncomfortable plastic seat and wait with every other economy class traveler for the digital board to announce the boarding gate number. My father protested about me traveling cattle-class, but this is the only time he has ever lost an argument since my mom died. Even my sister Mel fought in my corner and convinced him that blending in makes perfect sense. Who's going to notice a young woman traveling alone wearing a patchwork coat picked up from a thrift store and practical footwear?

I keep my head down. I sense excitement, anticipation, homesickness and anxiety oozing from the pores of everyone around me. Everyone has a story. But I'd wager that none has a story quite like mine. It doesn't make me extraordinary though, does it?

The women we help at the refuge are extraordinary. They're survivors. They've been defeated, destroyed and systematically dismantled piece by piece by men who would rather speak with their fists than their tongues, and yet they get back up and they keep right on fighting. Because the alternative is lying down and giving up, and they refuse to let violence win.

Ha! if they only knew...

When the gate is finally announced, I shuffle onto the shuttle bus to the waiting aircraft, file on board, and find my seat. I'm next to the window. It means that I can stare at the clouds without having to pretend to be asleep to avoid making small talk with the person in the next seat.

Who almost lands on top of me while he's trying to stow his carry-on luggage in the overhead compartment. "I'm so sorry." He uses the back of the seat to regain his balance, a smile appearing on his face when he recognizes me from the check-in area.

"Hi." I raise my hand in an almost-wave and gesture at the open locker above our heads. "At least your bag stayed intact this time."

"Well, so far, so good." He stands in front of his seat so that other passengers can pass him by and gets his arm stuck in his jacket as he tries to shrug it off. The jacket gets shoved in the overhead compartment, and the bag comes back out. He rummages around inside it for a packet of Swedish Fish and a book, zips it back up, and then finally sits down.

It's exhausting just watching him. He's the kind of guy who seems to be fidgeting even when he's apparently sitting still.

"Candy?" He rips open the packet spilling colored fish into his lap. He mutters to himself as he picks them up, and when I decline, says, "I can't say I blame you. I don't really like them myself, but my ears pop if I don't suck on something during take-off and landing." His cheeks grow inflamed when he realizes what he said. "If I don't suck on candy, I mean. If I don't have something to keep my mouth occupied."

I can't help chuckling.

He raises his hands in mock surrender. "I'll shut up now and let you enjoy your flight in peace."

"I'm not sure that enjoy is the right word."

He wrinkles his nose and peers around at the other passengers trying to get comfortable in the cramped space assigned to them. The man across the aisle stretches his legs underneath the seat in front of him. The woman behind me pulls the laminated information from the seat pocket and reads it. Everyone handles the impending flight in their own way.

"Lucky bastards who get to travel first class, huh?"

I smile. It could've been me, and sure, it would make the flight more bearable, but ultimately, it would change nothing. I'd still be leaving behind the life I chose for myself and going back to a life I didn't ask for.

"They're probably sipping champagne from crystal flutes right about now," he continues, popping an orange fish candy into his mouth.

I look at him properly for the first time. He has unruly brunette curls, a round face that might be kind of cute, like the goofy best friend in a romcom kind of cute, and hazel eyes with puffy circles underneath. There's no spark of attraction there; we're just two people who happen to be on the same flight back to the States.

"Do you read thrillers?" He turns his novel around to show me the cover when he senses me looking at him.

"Not really. I'm more of a cozy mystery kind of girl." It isn't true but hiding who I really am is so ingrained in me that I don't even have to think about my responses to questions.

"Nothing that gets your pulse racing." He smiles. I don't think he even registers the innuendos every time he opens his mouth to speak.

He rests his head back against the seat and closes his eyes, and I turn away to peer out of the window at the activity taking place around the aircraft. I'm excited to see Mel and Lucian when I get back. We have a lot of catching up to do, and even though things haven't been the same since she married Xander, my big sister will always be my best friend. My ally.

If anyone will understand how I feel right now, it's Mel. Because her marriage to Xander was arranged too. Even if he is the love of her life.

I'm grateful when the doors close, and the aircraft starts taxiing along the runway. Once we're in the air, there's nothing I can do about it. No going back. No point in churning through what ifs and maybes. This is my life now, and I might as well start accepting it.

I shut my eyes and allow my mind to wander. I think about my family, and the home I grew up in. My bedroom with its pale gold and ivory walls and the king-sized bed. The gardens and the pool and the tennis courts, and the way we still dress up for the evening meal because it's what my mom always wanted.

But the wealth and the comfort and the trappings seem to fade when I think about my life in Montenegro with Mika and Cartier. Sure, we saw some terrible sights. We saw women bleeding internally from injuries dealt out by their husbands. We saw burn scars and self-inflicted wounds, and broken bones that had healed awkwardly. But we also saw spirit and determination and bravery, and we compensated for these sights by laughing hard and having fun in our leisure time.

Leaving it behind is the hardest thing I've ever had to do, but I remind myself that those women didn't get a choice either, and they still fought back even when they had nothing left to fight for. Who am I to complain about a life of enforced luxury when so many women have to rebuild their lives from scratch?

My travel companion is quiet for a while. I hear him turning the pages of his book. Then, when the flight attendants come around with drinks and snacks, he stands up and retrieves his bag from the overhead locker.

"Do you play cards?" His voice jolts me from my reverie, and I open my eyes to find him holding a deck of cards in his hand.

"A little." I think about messy drunken games with Mika and Cartier, the three of us sitting cross-legged on the living room floor of our apartment with a bottle of Tequila and a mountain of potato chips.

"It'll pass the time. What do you say?"

I smile. "Sure." It will take my mind off Seamus for a short while at the very least.

We play a few games of Rummy. Andy—he tells me his name while he deals out the first hand—doesn't even complain when I win every round. So, when he suggests a game I've never heard of, I go along with it. He was right about one thing: it's better than sitting there counting the seconds and tracking the flight path on the screen in front of me.

The games get sillier, and noisier. Andy orders a gin and tonic for each of us, which takes the edge off the uneasiness in my stomach.

The first gin and tonic leads to another, and then a third. Andy is determined to win a game and laughingly tells me that there's a saying that goes, Lucky at cards, unlucky in love. He doesn't talk about his girlfriend, and I'm grateful because it means that I don't have to talk about Seamus.

But I should've eaten at the airport. I barely touched the on-board meal of meatballs and pasta, the smell making me feel a little queasy, and by the time I'm on my fourth gin with hardly a splash of tonic, my head is spinning.

I rub my face with both hands, and guzzle water from a plastic bottle. Alcohol doesn't normally affect me, but then it isn't every day I'm flying home to meet my fiancé, the man I'm being forced to marry. I've let it get to me more than I realized.

"Gianna? Are you okay?" Andy's eyes are filled with concern, his eyebrows almost meeting in the middle.

"I need to…" I squeeze my eyes shut. Try to stand up. "…go to the restroom."

The plane lists sideways, and I land heavily back in my seat. Bile rises in my throat.

"Sit down, there's a good girl." Andy leans across me and fastens the safety belt around my waist.

"No." I shake my head. "I need to get up…" I can't remember why I need to stand, or where I wanted to go, but the situation suddenly feels off-kilter.

"You're not going anywhere, Gianna."

Andy feels off-kilter. He isn't smiling. His eyes are cold and hard, and I can't be certain, but did I detect a faint accent when he spoke?

I try to raise my hand to call the flight attendant, but my arm feels like it's weighed down with a bucket of sand. "They won't help you," Andy says before the world goes black.

2

LEONID

I'm in a meeting at the Rudesian club discussing the expansion of my golf resort when my right-hand man Sergei arches an eyebrow from the doorway.

"Excuse me, gents." I stand and follow Sergei from the room, my phone passing into the palm of my hand in one well-practiced movement.

My office at the resort overlooks the golf course, and I stare out of the window at the businessmen in their golfing slacks and Under Armor shirts, and wonder, not for the first time, what enjoyment they get out of pushing a tiny ball into holes in the ground.

"Pakhan?"

I recognize the voice instantly. It belongs to Ivana, one of the two young women on my team, and one of a very small group of people I would trust with my life.

"Speak."

"We have been intercepted again." Her clipped voice buzzes through the speaker like a fly trapped inside a closed window.

"Casualties?" Outside the window, a heavy-boned man with a hefty paunch resting on top of his pants shuffles his feet and practices his swing.

I focus on the arc of the metal club as Ivana's voice buzzes in my ear. "Five fatalities. Some wounded. They've been removed as required."

The golfer hits the ball, the club resting on his shoulder as he watches its progress. "Who led the attack?" The question is unnecessary; I already know the answer.

"Xander Amory."

The leader of the Sicilian mafia in Chicago. The man who is single handedly trying to destroy me because no one ever explained to him that it is healthy to have rivals. It stimulates the brain, keeps you on your toes, promotes business transactions that might otherwise be ignored. Xander has decided that there isn't enough room for both of us in this city, and I'm taking him at his word.

With one difference: I am going to win. And when I do, he will be sorry that he ever started this bloody war.

"Retreat." I hand the phone back to Sergei.

The golfer is moving on, the caddy dragging the clubs along behind him. "Chyort voz'mi," I curse in Russian. I inhale deeply, my diaphragm expanding with the air in my lungs.

The Sicilians are relentless. Their attacks have become an almost daily occurrence since the failed attempt to kidnap Xander's wife and son, but this one was expected. It was a distraction while I set the wheels in motion to retaliate, and Xander swallowed it hook, line, and sinker. It was more than just a distraction though, which is why only a handful of people are aware of my intentions.

"Inform the men that the meeting has been adjourned."

Sergei waits for me to continue. His olive-skinned face is a mask of serenity, but I can see the tension in his shoulders. You do not get to spend so much time in close quarters without learning one another's tells, although if asked, he would remark that mine are not quite so obvious.

"It is time for the Sicilians to understand who they are dealing with, is it not?"

Sergei nods, a glint of amusement in his eyes. "Everything is in place."

I am tired of being on the fucking defensive. That is not who I am. It is not how the Ivanov family works. But this time, I feel the cold burn of revenge coursing through my veins. The failed kidnap attempt was a hiccup, nothing more. But hiccups only serve to make the warrior stronger, more determined, more lethal.

I face Sergei, the man who has been by my side since we were teenagers. The man who is like a brother to me. The man who knows when I'm about to sneeze before I even know it myself.

"No fucking mistakes this time."

His mouth curves into a smile. "Yes, boss."

I wish I could reciprocate the gesture, but Xander has been a thorn in my side for far too long, and the thorn will sting on the way out. "Ramp up security and double the patrols." Sergei responds with a curt nod. "And, Sergei, I wish to be informed the instant the asset is delivered to my door."

"Of course, boss."

He enters the boardroom, and I hear him dismissing the men who stack up their papers and leave in silence. I wait for Sergei to carry out my orders before leaving the resort, nodding at regular customers, and greeting the patient wives with wide smiles on my way to my waiting Cadillac. These people put dollars in my bank account, but I'll never understand why so many of them have trophy wives, beautiful women who are content to be seen and not heard.

Maybe this is the reason why I have never married despite the pressure from my parents to extend the family bloodline. I will not be content to marry a woman who stands by my side, smiles in all the right places, and provides my guests with the kind of hospitality worthy of a Michelin starred restaurant. I want a woman who is prepared to stand up and fight for what she believes in. Sure, I want that belief to be in me, but I want a woman who will tousle me in bed rather than be submissive. I want to look at her and know that I have met my match as well as my soulmate.

It is a tall ask. Impossible, some might say.

Marco opens the rear door of the sleek black Cadillac as I approach. He's a short solid man with clear blue eyes and thick hair that had turned silver-gray by his twenty-first birthday. He has been driving me for over a decade now, so I don't need to tell him where we're going.

The casino is busy. I navigate the VIP entrance, stopping to kiss the cheek of a regular Hispanic customer, and ignore the way her fingertips brush my sleeve, while her eyes slant suggestively. Some might see it as a perk of the position, but I never mix business with pleasure, especially when that pleasure will bring another mafia family knocking on my door.

The bartender has a drink waiting for me in the private lounge. Negroni. I peer over the balcony at the main area, at the losers with hunched shoulders gambling away their inheritances, at the wealthy Asians who throw money at the table knowing that eventually some of it will stick, at the winners who allow themselves a small gloating smile before they chance their luck again.

Chance is a peculiar concept. A possibility. Events beyond a person's control. And yet so many people risk their entire lives on the flip of a card.

Unfortunately for Xander Amory, I leave nothing to chance.

We always knew that it would come to this. My family is the wealthiest and strongest Russian contingent in the United States. Xander Amory heads up the Sicilians. He has loaded his chips on the side of war, and I'm not a man who shies away from the front line.

I swallow the Negroni in my glass and signal for another.

I was five years old when I saw my first corpse. *FIVE YEARS OLD.*

I heard raised voices coming from my father's study. The anger in their tones wasn't what dragged me barefoot from my bedroom; in my father's line of business, tempers often frayed at the edges, and deals got destroyed by a wrong word or an imagined slight, or a bullet in the back of someone's fucking skull. No, it was the cold menacing threat behind them, and the ominous silence pervading the rest of the house.

I crept downstairs, my heart thumping inside my chest. I thought my father or one of his men might hear it, but no one was standing guard outside the door to his study. My toes sank into the thick pile carpet on the stairs in anticipation of what I might find when I reached the bottom. But nothing, literally nothing, could've prepared me for the sight of my father firing a bullet into the skull of his right-hand man.

My stomach lurched sickeningly at the same time as my body seemed to turn to ice. But I must've groaned like a ghost or squealed like a pig because my father turned his head and looked at me, the murder weapon still in his hand. Then he calmly rose from his seat, stowed the gun inside a drawer, and closed the door behind him as he came to me at the bottom of the stairs.

"Come, moi syn." He placed his warm hands on my shoulders, turned me around, and guided me back to my room. When I was tucked up in bed with the comforter pulled up to my chin, he said, "Never allow love to cloud your judgement, Leonid, because heads turn for far lesser things."

I nodded. I had no idea what he was talking about, but suddenly, with the firing of that single bullet, the man who had been my role model, my comfort blanket, my shelter when the rest of the world was raining, had taken on a ghastly appearance. My papa was gone, and in his place was a man whose footsteps I was destined to fill. That night, I fell asleep with the image of my uncle, a man I'd known my entire short life, sprawled on the floor of my father's study with cold, vacant fisheyes and blood trickling from a hole in his head.

In the casino, I gauge the time by the fuzziness slowly wrapping itself around my brain from the Negroni. This coupled with the increasingly charged atmosphere from the casino bowl below has never let me down yet. The evening is still relatively young when Tamara enters the private lounge, collects her favorite tipple, Applejack and soda, and joins me at the table in the corner by the balcony.

"We have secured the asset, Pakhan." She sips her drink and watches me coolly from beneath raven-black bangs.

Tamara and Ivana are identical twins, but few people realize it at first glance. Tamara's curls, wide smile, and smoky eyes give her a soft appearance and an almost childlike quality that most people are instantly drawn to. Especially men. Ivana on the other hand wears her hair cut short and spiky, the tips dyed lurid green, the strange look accentuated by the elongated green flicks at the corners of her eyes and the battered Doc Martens that I've never seen her without.

I rescued them twenty years ago when they were just little kids. They'd been trafficked from abroad, arrived on American soil in a filthy container that stank of piss and shit, several of the adults with them already dead. My father had been tipped off that the cargo was entering our port along with another shipment that we were expecting, both of which had been made known to the police commissioner.

They were just a couple of scared little girls with wide green eyes and grubby faces, and the sight of them made me feel nauseous. What kind of sick bastard would abduct kids and sell them into the sex trade? My father said that they were probably sold by their own parents, and that was the fingertip that pushed me over the edge.

While my father handled the shipment we'd been expecting, I relocated the girls to our safe house and saw to it that the sick fucker who shipped them here would never touch a woman again.

My mother cleaned them up, fed them, gave them clothes to wear and moved them into a guest room in our home. She cared for them, but I was the one they looked to as their savior. Their superhero. Some kind of fucking demi-god in a gold loincloth and wielding a jewel-encrusted sword.

They still do, even though they know the real me.

Sergei would kill to protect me. But Ivana and Tamara would kill themselves if they believed that it would keep me alive.

"Where is it?" I swallow my drink in one mouthful.

"En route to your home." She watches me coolly. "Do you want me to see that it is settled?"

"Where is Ivana?"

"At the safe house. She had to lose another man."

Fuck! The body count is rising. This asset had better be worth its weight in gold or I might be forced to go in harder and lower.

"No, ask Ivana to arrange a little welcome party."

No point going in soft with the new asset; she needs to know that we mean business, or she'll get too comfortable, and we'll have nothing left to barter with.

Tamara inclines her head. "As you wish."

She is under no illusions that I wish her sister to be welcoming when our new guest arrives. They shared a womb. They know each other's thoughts without speaking the words out loud. She might not like the way her sister operates, but she understands that they are both simply doing what needs to be done to survive.

Her glass is empty, but she doesn't move.

"What is it?"

"Your father has requested that you dine with him tonight."

"Has he now?" I sit back in my seat and signal the bartender to fix me another drink.

"Are you not going?" Tamara blinks her pretty green eyes at me.

As if I could ever refuse? She said it herself; my father requests my presence at his home tonight. Attendance isn't optional.

The bartender places our drinks in front of us and removes the empty glasses.

When he is out of earshot, I face Tamara. "I'm going. Perhaps dinner with my parents is exactly what I need before I greet the new asset personally."

I do not have to run my business decisions by my father before I carry them out, but he still has his finger on the pulse of every mafia family in the city. He will know the losses we have incurred at the hands of Xander Amory, and he will expect me to retaliate … with interest. This evening's meal will not be a warning for me to back off but rather a reminder that I need to marry and produce an heir.

"And you're coming with me." I clink my glass against hers and down it in one.

3

GIANNA

Dim lights. Walls a nondescript color that might once have been white. Dark blackout curtains.

I push myself into a sitting position, my breathing growing shallow as my head reels, and bile rises in my throat. "Don't be sick. Don't be sick. Don't be sick," I whisper to myself, but it's a close call. My head is pounding, my tongue sticks to the roof of my mouth, and my throat clicks when I swallow. I feel like I polished off an entire bottle of Tequila on my own, which Mika would never have allowed.

Then I remember...

I left Mika and Cartier behind in Montenegro.

It starts coming back to me in frantic flashes of light. The aircraft. Andy. Silly card games and little cans of gin and tonic. It was lighthearted, fun, a way of passing the time until it wasn't. It all turned dark when I tried to stand up and leave my seat.

An image of Andy's cheeky grin and geeky awkwardness pops into my head, and I lean over the side of the bed and retch. Nothing comes out, but my head feels like it's going to explode.

He fucking drugged me.

The suitcase splitting open, his girlfriend telling him to strap it together, the Swedish fish candy… It was all just a smokescreen, and I fell for the oldest trick in the book.

I force myself back into a sitting position and drag my legs over the side of the bed, slowly, supporting my head with one hand as if that will stop it from toppling off my shoulders and rolling away. I survey my surroundings. It's a small room. I'm on a single bed that isn't completely uncomfortable, but there are no other furnishings. A basement maybe?

I have no idea if I'm in Chicago or another part of the country, but I need to get out of here before whoever abducted me comes back. Because if they don't kill me—which is extremely feasible given my family name—my father will for insisting that I travel alone.

"Stupid," I mutter to myself, my voice hoarse. "Stupid. Stupid. *Stupid*."

Gripping the side of the bed, I force myself to stand up. My legs feel like Jell-o, and the room rocks as if I'm still on the aircraft, but I stand there, swaying unsteadily and wait for the motion in my head and stomach to subside.

There's a door. I make my way slowly across the room and wait there, straining my ears for any sounds outside the room. But all I can hear is the blood gushing through my veins, and the dull thud-thud-thud of my heartbeat. Holding my breath, I reach for the knob and turn it, panic clawing its way around my insides when I realize that the door is locked.

"Help!" Survival instinct kicks in, and I rest my cheek against the solid door, praying that someone might be walking past and hear me. "Let me out!"

When no one comes, I start pounding on the door with my fists, yelling until my voice cracks and almost disappears.

Pulse racing, and my breaths coming in shallow gasps, I go back to the bed and sit down heavily, forcing my head between my spread knees to stop myself from passing out. When the dizziness passes, I sit up straight and take stock of the situation.

I have no idea where I am or how long I was unconscious. I go to the window, draw the curtain back a little, and let out a small sob when I realize that there's just a wall behind the dense fabric. I was right. I am underground, which means that my only escape route is up, and up is where the people who abducted me will be waiting.

I take deep breaths, in through my nose, and out through my mouth, and wait for my pulse to regulate itself.

Then I make a mental list of bullet points in my head. *I'm not dead heads* the list. Sure, Andy drugged me, but he was only the go-between for whoever is holding me here, and they want me alive. I'm no use to them dead. Which means that they need something from my family. Or perhaps from Seamus.

I shake my head and try to picture my fiancé's reaction to the news that I've been abducted. He'll either be so enraged that he'll retaliate alongside my family, or he'll congratulate himself on catching a lucky break.

Probably the latter.

So, if this isn't about Seamus, then these people want something from my family. Right about now is when I wish that I'd taken a bit more interest in the family business, but I do know enough to understand that this is a power struggle. They hold me until they get what they want, and if they don't get it... Well, that won't bode well for me, will it?

So, what do I do? I take myself out of the equation, that's what. If they don't have me, they have no leverage, and both sides will be forced to resolve the power struggle another way. The difficult part is going to be finding a way out without getting myself killed in the process.

I think about all the women I've worked with in the refuge. They all found themselves in far worse situations than this, and they all made it out the other side. Sure, they had the scars to prove it, but I'm a Sedric, and I'm no one's pawn.

I'm so lost in thought that I don't realize anyone is coming until I hear the key turning in the lock. I stand up, staring at the door as it swings open.

A young woman is standing in the doorway, feet planted wide in Doc Marten boots, arms folded across her chest. She can't be much older than me, but it feels like we're worlds apart. The green-tipped spiky hair, the green flecks on her eyelids, and the black leather outfit are almost designed to make her intimidating, but it's more than that. There's a mark under her left eye; is it a tattoo? But there's also something in her demeanor, in the way her chin juts forward and her top lip curls at the corner that shows that she's a woman who is used to being in control.

"Who are you?" I face her squarely and wish that I wasn't so hoarse.

"Your worst nightmare."

Her smile bares her top teeth like a dog on the attack. I'm sure that's a line from a movie, but I can't think of which one right now. Probably one of the action movies my brother Daniel used to love when he was younger.

"Where am I?"

The smile morphs into a sneer. She would be beautiful if she wasn't quite so aggressive. "You're exactly where you need to be."

"Why am I here?"

She steps closer. I can smell her exotic perfume and something else. Danger? "You ask a lot of questions for a little printzessa." There's a hint of an accent when she speaks, Eastern European maybe. Or Russian.

"Who are you working for?"

The smile is back, and I can see her pointed canine teeth. "That would be telling, and I'm in no mood for small talk."

"Why not?" The question comes out before I can even think about it. But if I think we're going to get acquainted and become lifelong friends, I'm mistaken.

"It's been a long day." She pauses, and her eyes glitter in the dimly lit room. "If you want to find out how long, just keep on talking."

My eyes flicker to the door behind her. She left it ajar when she came in; all I have to do is get past her.

I don't waste a beat. Head down, I lunge at her, the top of my head colliding with her diaphragm and sending her sprawling backwards. Her spine hits the door, slamming it shut, and I groan inwardly. That wasn't supposed to happen.

Like a cat, she springs to her feet, grabs my hair, and hurls me across the room.

Covering my face with my arms, I roll across the bed and crash into the wall, my shoulder taking the full force of the collision. But I'm not giving up that easily. I jump off the bed and try to dash past her to reach the door, a low animalistic howl erupting from somewhere deep inside.

Her fist connects with my jaw and blinding white pain explodes inside my head. I crumple into a heap on the floor, cradling my head in my arms. I remind myself to keep breathing, in and out, in and out, while the pain creates a Fourth of July display behind my eyelids. When I can think straight again, I move my lower jaw from side to side, and almost cry with relief when I find that nothing is broken.

"Game over. Get up."

I open my eyes to find her Doc Martens in front of my face. Sliding my eyes sideways, I can see that the door is shut, and she is standing between me and freedom.

I drag myself onto my feet slowly, buying myself some time while trying to figure out my next move. I can see the gun tucked inside the waistband of her leather pants. *Fuck!* She might not shoot to kill if I try to escape, but I have no doubts that she will shoot me, and I stand a better chance of escaping without a bullet wound.

Upright, I realize that we're about the same height and build, but I sense that this woman is pure muscle. Okay, so I have to try talking my way out of here.

"Do you know who my father is?"

She scoffs and furrows her brow. "I know."

"So, you know that he will get me out of here and there will be serious repercussions."

Serious repercussions? What am I, a kindergarten teacher?

Her half-smile tells me that she's had the exact same thought. "Bring it on, baby."

What the actual fuck. A sliver of ice trickles down my spine. I'm alive for now, but these people obviously want war.

"Who are you working for?"

She shakes her head slowly. "You still think that you can ask the questions?"

"No, I just want to know when the person in charge around here is going to be brave enough to show his face."

I can see that I've hit a nerve when her eyes narrow. She slides a slim dagger from her jacket pocket and licks it, taking her time, enjoying the effect it has on me. "Pakhan is taking care of his personal affairs. He will come to you when he is ready."

"Pakhan? What does that mean?"

"It means the man in charge, as you put it."

"So, he has me kidnapped, keeps me in his basement, and doesn't even have the decency to come and speak to me himself. He can't want me that badly."

Her mouth contorts into another unpleasant smile. "He doesn't want you at all, printzessa. You are simply a means to an end."

She walks to the door and hesitates, turning around to face me, confident that I won't dare to attack her a second time. "There is a bathroom through there." She indicates a second door next to the bed that I hadn't even noticed. "I suggest you freshen up before Pakhan returns. He likes his women clean."

She locks the door behind her when she leaves, and I realize that she didn't even tell me her name.

In the compact but clean bathroom, I splash my face with cold water and check out the purple bruising blossoming across my jawline. I'll have to be more careful next time, perhaps even find something in the room to use as a makeshift weapon. She made it obvious that she isn't afraid to use violence, but I still believe that she's under orders to keep me alive.

The question is: whose orders?

Checking out my reflection in the mirror, I barely recognize the woman staring back at me. My hair is matted from sleep, my face is pale, and my eyes have the haunted look that I saw in the faces of the women who came to the refuge.

"Come on, Gianna, stay strong." I force myself to smile. "You're a Sedric, and don't you forget it. This pakhan likes his women clean, so clean is what he's going to get."

I scrub my face until it glows. The mottled bruising on my jaw is growing darker by the second, but I intend to wear it like a medal and show him that it will take more than a bruise to keep me down. I strip off my clothes and wash as best I can with the facilities provided.

When I go back to the other room, a crisp white dress trimmed with tiny black gems has been laid out on the bed for me. I approach it with caution. It isn't the pakhan choosing my clothes that bothers me, it's that I never heard someone enter the room.

4

LEONID

My parents' palatial property should still feel like my childhood home, but it has been many years since I've been able to appreciate its splendor. Decades. Tonight, it feels like the kind of place I need to enter, carry out my duties, and leave again with as much haste as is acceptable without appearing disrespectful.

As always, I stand on the threshold, straighten my suit jacket, and run my fingers through my thick black hair.

"Here. Let me." Tamara stands in front of me and straightens my tie, poking the dimple with her index finger, her lips quirked up in a lopsided smile. "Almost perfect." She stands back to admire the view.

"Almost?" I arch an eyebrow.

"A smile would help, Pakhan." She forces my lips upwards with her fingers, and I immediately drop it again.

"I will smile when I have something to smile about."

"Says the man who has everything."

She stands aside and waits for me to step inside first. The conversation is over, and as usual, she had the last word. It's a skill that both sisters have perfected over the years, and one which irritates me more than I have ever let on. To anyone.

In the foyer, the polished marble floor gleams like a mirror, reflecting the light bouncing off the heavy crystal chandelier hanging high above our heads. The walls are polished wooden panels, each object on display chosen for its jewel-like vibrancy and history. Two Fabergé eggs, one in sapphire blue with an elaborate golden filigree design, the other in gold and silver. There are goblets and plates, imperial statuettes, and glossy feline ornaments studded with diamonds. My mother's personal collection, and the only part of the house in which my father has no input.

My mother makes a grand entrance on the sweeping staircase wearing a floor-length ivory gown, the collar encrusted with tiny shimmering gems.

"Leonid." Her face lights up as she approaches me and presents her cheeks for me to kiss. "And Tamara. Look at you. You grow more beautiful with every passing day." She pinches Tamara's cheeks leaving behind the imprint of her fingernails on the pale flesh.

"Thank you, Mama." Anyone else would've had their hand batted away before it came anywhere near Tamara's face, but she accepts my mother's greeting with reverence and respect.

We have never spoken about what fate might've befallen them had I not discovered the twins in the shipping container that day. But they remember enough. That kind of childhood can never be erased.

"Leonid." My mother's eyes glitter. "Your father—"

"Is right here."

My father emerges from his study, a fine mist of dirty-brown smoke from his stogie clinging to his immaculate black suit. It is the aroma that I have always associated with my father. His hair is gray but still thick. His face is craggier than it used to be, the grooves on his forehead like ruts on an unmade road, but he is still a handsome and imposing man.

I incline my head in his direction. "Father."

They did not demand my presence at dinner for my pleasant company. Invitations to the Ivanov home are extended solely at the head of the family's discretion, and usually when he has a demand or a warning to deliver.

He leads the way to the dining room where the table is set for four. My siblings are either not invited, or they have made their excuses to be elsewhere tonight because they know what this is all about.

Crystal bowls filled with ice contain tiny dishes of caviar, fish roe, and chopped egg yolk; a silver platter is filled with various types of homemade bread sliced into perfect miniature triangles. Valentina, my parents' maid, fills our glasses with water, and my father dismisses her with a wave of his hand.

Tamara dutifully keeps her head down. My father is the first to help himself to food; once he has filled his plate, the rest of us are free to eat. I've lost my appetite, but I spoon caviar onto my plate and take some sourdough bread from the platter before filling a smaller glass with ice-cold vodka.

My father chews slowly and swallows. It is a habit that he has carried with him since he took over as Pakhan from his own father, this unhurried enjoyment of food as if every morsel might be his last. I scoop caviar onto the toasted bread, stuff the whole lot into my mouth, and swallow without tasting it. I am a busy man, and I have no time for unnecessary foreplay.

He washes his food down with neat vodka and sits back in his seat. I can feel his anger emanating like molten lava from his pores. "Talk to me, Leonid."

Tamara continues to chew her food, but her hackles are up like a cat sensing the approach of a ferocious dog. She wouldn't dare to disrespect me or my father, but she and Ivana have spent their entire lives in fight-or-flight mode. It's a tough habit to crack.

"We lost more men today." I refill my vodka glass and study the clear liquid. I can feel the burn before I raise it to my lips. "So, I am doing what I do best: I am ensuring that I am the winner in this war against the Sicilians."

My father's expression is neutral. His movements when he raises his eyes from his vodka glass to me are slow and purposeful. "By abducting the youngest Sedric daughter." He blinks slowly like a lizard basking in the sun. "Did you or did you not just say that we are at war with the Sicilians?"

"Correct, father."

"So, please explain to me what the fuck you are doing." His tone is neutral too, low and measured leaving the emphasis on his words.

"She is Sedric's printzessa." I match his tone. "She is also Xander's sister-in-law. Melissa will do whatever it takes to protect her baby sister from the way of life they were born into, and what Melissa wants, Melissa gets. Or so I've heard."

My father processes this information. "The plan?"

"The plan is to make sure that I deliver baby Sedric to her brother-in-law, shall we say a little more tainted than she was when she arrived."

My mother gasps out loud. Tamara suppresses a smirk that no one else notices.

"Tainted?" My father grips his glass so tightly I wait for it to crack. "Fucking tainted? This is your plan to win the war?"

"She is a bargaining tool. Leverage. No more than that. She is pledged to the Irish contingent. A potential ally against the Sicilians if I choose not to corrupt her completely."

"Leonid." My mother releases a sigh and rubs her left temple the way she always does when she is trying to resolve a minor problem in her head. "We did not raise you to be the kind of man who corrupts innocent women."

"What kind of man did you raise me to be?" I swallow at the look of disappointment that flashes into her eyes.

"A leader," my father interjects before my mother can respond. "A fighter. A pakhan worthy of the family name. Not a lowlife who bargains with little girls."

It's a low blow, and Tamara instantly bristles. I can't see her hands beneath the table, but I instinctively know that they are balled into fists. She and Ivana were little girls when I saved them from a way of life that would've seen them dead before they were thirty, and I would rather slit my own throat than barter with their lives.

I wipe my lips with a crisp white napkin. "Is that all, father?"

He motions for me to remain seated. "What do you intend to do with this *printzessa* once you are finished with her?"

"I will return her to where she belongs, naturally. Once she has served her purpose."

"This isn't a game, Leonid." He narrows his dark eyes at me. "I trust you have thought about the consequences of your actions."

"No, this isn't a game. This is war. Didn't you teach me never to turn a blind eye to an angry poke? I know what I am doing, father. My eyes are wide open, and if the way to checkmate is by taking the opposition's printzessa, then that's what I intend to do."

"Checkmate, printzessa, eyes wide open…" My father waves a finger in the air in a circular motion. "You say that it is war, and then you talk about games." His accent is more prominent when he is angry. "You put all of us in danger to soothe your pride."

"This is not about my pride. This is about putting Xander Amory in his place."

He shakes his head. "In my day, this would have already been resolved. And do you know why?"

I can take a pretty good guess, but I keep quiet.

"Because I had a family to protect. Family comes first. Always." He inhales deeply. "I have chosen a bride for you. Maybe once you have a family to protect, you will stop moving pawns around a chess board and start acting like the leader I thought you were."

I refill my glass and swallow the icy liquid in one gulp. The burn doesn't even touch the sides. "I will choose my own bride when the time is right."

He dismisses my comment with a wave of his hand. "This is a suitable match. One that I should have considered long ago. The daughter of a powerful ally. It will strengthen our position, and then—" he makes an explosive gesture with his hands "—you will be ready to go to war."

"I am already at war, father. An Ivanov does not turn his back on his enemy and depend on his wife's family to back him up."

"Please, Leonid." My mother's voice is little more than a whisper. "Listen to your father. In time, you may grow to love your wife."

"Like you did with father?" The words slice through the air before I can think about what I'm saying. And right on cue, her face crumples.

Before I can apologize, my father's fist thumps the table. "Your mother and I have always loved each other. It is a shame that you are too stubborn to see that."

I glare at him. "Oh, I see it. Why do you think that I'm attacking Xander through his wife and her family? Melissa is his Achilles heel. His weakness. His blind spot. I prefer to remain stubborn and alive."

I stand, my chair scraping across the polished wooden floor. Tamara stands too, shooting an apologetic glance in my mother's direction.

"I wish that you would talk about Elena." My mother has an almost angelic look about her, but she always knows how to stick the knife in and twist until it bleeds. And fuck that name still hurts.

"There is nothing to talk about." I dig my nails into the palms of my hands. "It was over years ago."

"But you still feel it in here." My mother places a hand above her heart. "I worry about you, Leonid."

I circle the table and lean over my mother to give her a hug. "You have nothing to worry about. I am fine."

But she clings to my hand, forcing me to look her in the eye. "Never forget that love can also be a strength. It can give you something—*or someone*—worth fighting for."

I have never yet met a woman worth fighting for. Not since Elena. And she proved herself unworthy of that honor.

"I will bear it in mind, mother, but I doubt that person will be the daughter of a powerful ally, and I can guarantee that I will win this war without her assistance." I straighten and make for the door. "Goodnight, Papa."

He doesn't try to stop me.

Behind me, I hear Tamara saying goodbye. I imagine my mother embracing the younger woman and whispering in her ear to try talking some sense into me, knowing this is one that she will never win.

5

GIANNA

I PACE the room wearing the white dress my captor provided for me. I don't need to see the price tag to know that it's expensive. It feels different against my skin, like the designer wanted the wearer to feel caressed when she wore it. It's not quite the vintage clothes I like to root around the thrift shops for. I've always loved the thought of wearing a dress that might once have been worn and discarded by Marilyn Monroe, or Vivienne Westwood, or Judy Garland. It's like, wow, they don't make clothes like this anymore.

But I have to admit that this feels good.

It's just a shame it's going to be wasted on an asshole I haven't met yet because the loser sent a woman to do his dirty work.

I wander back into the bathroom and check out my reflection in the mirror. The fabric clings to my breasts and hips in a way that jeans and sweaters rarely do. So, my captor is a perv who wants to undress me with his eyes while he figures out how to dispose of me without spilling too much blood on the fancy carpet. Well, I've got news for him. I bleed plenty when I'm cut.

I go back to the bedroom and pace some more.

I should maybe think about what I'm going to say to the asshole when he finally shows his face, but it's hard to concentrate when I'm stopping every few steps to listen for sounds of movement outside the door.

Instead, I recite in my head the names of the women I met in the refuge. Maria. Evangeline. Hope.

Hope was one of the worst cases we saw. Her husband broke both her legs when she tried to leave him and then buried her alive on a construction site. She was filthy when she was discovered by the emergency services and taken to the hospital where she spent months healing her broken bones. But that's the thing with hospitals: they can fix broken bones, but they can't fix broken spirits.

Despite her horrific background, Hope was the woman who embraced every other victim in the refuge. She was the one who encouraged them to never give up hope. To believe that there was always better to come.

I sit down on the bed, tears welling in my eyes at the memories. And immediately jump up again, afraid to crease the dress before the asshole villain of the story decides to show his face.

Where the hell is he?

What's so important that he can't even come here and introduce himself?

Or is he hiding because I know who he is?

Fuck! I start pacing again, my thoughts scurrying about inside my head and tossing out random names. Andy was American, I think. The spiky-haired witch could potentially be Russian or Eastern European, but it doesn't automatically mean that the boss is Russian too. Is it someone my father knows? Or my brother Daniel. Or Mel.

Xander?

My breath hitches in my throat, while my heart is trying to run the 400-meter sprint faster than Gabby Thomas. No, Xander won't be behind this, not if he wants Mel to stay in his life. My sister would skin him alive if anything happened to me.

Seamus then? I've deliberately ignored any correspondence regarding my marriage to Seamus which, I'll hold my hands up now that I'm stuck in a basement without an escape route, was probably a silly move. But hey, I was just a gal enjoying her final moments of freedom before she walked into the execution chamber. Okay, I'm being melodramatic, but I'm not going to beat myself up over it.

So, maybe Seamus and this potentially Russian asshole are at war. Maybe he's holding me captive until Seamus backs down. Or offers him a reward.

Would Seamus pay to get me back though? I stop pacing and replay our nonexistent relationship in my head. Which takes about thirty seconds give or take a second or two either way.

I should've told Mel about the arranged marriage.

It hits me like a shopping cart at full speed that my sister would've been my only ally in the whole marriage-to-the-Irish-mob thing, and I didn't tell her because my father made me promise not to. But promises can be broken, right?

Mel would never have let this happen. She'd have fought father all the way to keep me out of the family business like we'd always talked about. Then, I wouldn't have been on the plane, and I sure as shit wouldn't be stuck in someone's basement wearing a dress that looked like it belonged on a runway.

"What the fuck am I even doing?" I mutter under my breath.

I reach behind me, unzip the dress, and shrug it over my shoulders. "I'm not being dressed up like a doll for some crazy-eyed Russian fucker who can't even be bothered to come and see me himself."

I toss the dress onto the floor, pull on my jeans and hoodie, and flop backwards onto the bed, staring at the ceiling. He doesn't get to tell me what to do. He might control the witch, but he doesn't control me. No none does.

But the dress is burning a hole in my brain from its crumpled heap on the floor, so I sit forward, pick it up, and smooth out the creases. If he wants me to wear it, he can ask nicely. Still, I fold it neatly and leave it on the end of the bed because it's what my mom would've done.

I lose all track of time. You don't realize how badly you crave daylight until it is gone, and then it's like your body is straining to get outside, to soak up the sunshine, and fill your lungs with fresh air.

I lie down and close my eyes. I sit up and stare at the stupid curtains hiding the stupid brick wall. I walk back and forth, back and forth, counting my steps in Serbian to keep up with learning the language widely used in Montenegro, and getting the numbers muddled inside my head. Then, on my hands and knees, I crawl around the floor trying to find something that I can use as a weapon against him if I don't die of boredom before he gets here.

There's nothing. I don't know how many people the asshole keeps imprisoned down here, but he seems to have gone to great lengths to make sure they can't hurt him. "Coward." My father always said you can't trust a coward.

On my back on the floor, I slide my head under the bed and try to unscrew the legs, but it's not that kind of bed. I feel the underside of the frame, but it's solid. In the bathroom, I try to break the pipe leading from the toilet cistern to the ceiling, but without something heavy to use, it's impossible.

I wash my hands again. Stare at my face in the mirror again. Unfold the white dress, and fold it back up again.

I know what he's doing. He's trying to wear me down by keeping me waiting. He thinks that he can come in here and find me a quivering mess who will beg for her life.

"Think again, asshole."

I eventually fall asleep and dream of smashing the unknown asshole's face with the pipe from his own toilet cistern while yelling at the top of my lungs, "No one puts baby Gianna in a corner!"

"Wakey, wakey."

I'm roused from slumber by something cold and hard tracing my sore jawline. Suddenly alert, I scramble back against the headboard, clutching the comforter to my chin to find the wicked witch of the west grinning at me with her dagger in her hand.

Fuck! That's the second time she's gotten into the room without me hearing her. What is wrong with me?

"Where's the pakhan?" My gaze slides to the door as if I might find him standing there watching me in my sleep. Which would be even more psychotic than the crazy woman with a teardrop tattooed underneath her eye.

"He's waiting for you."

He is?

"Well, tell him he can wait a bit longer. I'm not a morning person, especially when I'm woken up at knifepoint."

Is that a hint of a smile on her lips?

It vanishes almost immediately, and before I can react, she grips my wrist in her iron fist and drags me off the bed and onto my feet. The dagger is back. I can feel the tip drawing blood from my neck just below my jawline.

"This is what knifepoint feels like." Her breath is warm on my cheek. "But be warned, I am not a morning person either and I've not had any caffeine yet today."

I hold her gaze. My brother Daniel made me promise when I was a little kid never to look away first. We would have staring competitions until our eyes watered, and I always won, so I'm confident that the witch will tire of this game before I do.

Besides, she just told me that it's morning, and that her boss is ready for me. "I need to use the restroom first. I'd hate to disappoint him at our first meeting."

Her eyes drift to the white dress still folded neatly on the end of the bed, and I mentally fist-punch the air. *Yay!* She looked away first. Gianna one, witch zero.

"Get dressed."

"I *was* dressed, but I took it off when your boss stood me up. I don't normally give a guy a second chance, so he should think himself lucky that—"

I don't get to finish the sentence. She slaps my cheek with her hand, and man, does it sting. Hot tears prickle behind my eyes, and I force myself not to blink. I refuse to give her the satisfaction.

"You have one minute. If you are not dressed, I will drag you up the stairs naked, and then we will see what Pakhan thinks of his latest asset."

She releases me and stands by the door watching me closely while I step out of my clothes and into the white dress. My brain cells are reeling. While I would love to plot my revenge against the witch for daring to touch me, this will have to wait.

She called me an asset.

So, what, her boss thinks that he can keep me here indefinitely like some kind of plaything or a new car? My father will have something to say about that. I try to console myself that my family will rescue me any time now, but I've already spent at least one night in this basement, and here I am dressing for breakfast with the enemy because someone needs her morning coffee.

"Ready." I stand facing her while her eyes roam me up and down.

"Follow me."

She turns on her Doc Marten heels and opens the door. I don't need to be told twice. I follow her out of the room and into a dingy corridor where the ceiling lights give off a sickly yellow glow. We pass several other doors that, thankfully, remain firmly closed. All I need now is to peer inside one of the boss's dungeon rooms and find him getting his ass spanked by a dominatrix with a paddle.

Through a door at the end of the corridor, and we climb a spiral staircase. The air gets warmer the higher we climb, and I swear that I can already taste the sweet smell of wet grass and sunshine even though there's still no sign of a window. Then another corridor. This one has plush ivory carpets on the floor —*who in their right mind has ivory carpets?*—and creamy, silk-covered walls. No kids in this house, that's for sure.

There are no pictures on the walls. Nothing that will give me a hint about who my captor really is. Then, the witch enters a room and stands aside, waiting for me to follow her. I guess this is it.

Deep breath.

I find myself in an enormous dining room. A huge, polished table is in the center of the room, but my eyes are instinctively drawn to the floor-to-ceiling windows draped in sheer voile and the daylight streaming through them. Like a dehydrated nomad in the desert, I stare at the rays of sunshine and fill my lungs with air, and that shot of vitamin D is better than caffeine any day.

Someone clears their throat, and I'm jolted back to the moment.

A man in an expensive dark suit is seated at the far end of the dining table. His jet-black hair is slicked back highlighting angular cheekbones, a strong jawline, and amber eyes. He wears a platinum wristwatch, and I'd bet every cent in my bank account that his shoes are so shiny I could see my reflection in them. Everything about him screams money loud and clear, and I've grown up around wealth. But this...

He looks me up and down, his eyes finally settling on mine. "Kind of you to join us, Gianna."

Us?

I notice the other woman sitting at the table and do a double take. She could almost pass for the witch, only she's softer, her face framed by fat, round curls, and no visible tattoos. A man stands in the far corner of the room, hands behind his back, eyes hidden by black wraparound shades. Very intimidating.

"I'm hungry," I say, pleasantly surprised by how steady my voice sounds. "I thought a place like this would probably offer a decent breakfast."

Beside me, I sense the witch flexing her fingers. My captor catches her eye and gives a barely perceptible shake of his head.

"Sit," he orders in his rich baritone voice.

I could sit as far away from him as possible, but instead, I take the seat closest to him, his expensive cologne wafting my way, his eyes following my every move. So, I give him something to watch. I reach for a slice of toast from a silver rack and shove half of it into my mouth.

"You really should provide a kettle and some coffee sachets in the rooms." I make sure to speak with my mouth full. "Maybe some biscuits, you know, to satisfy the guests between meals."

The dark-haired woman sitting across the table from me flinches. What? Have they never heard anyone talk back to their boss before?

I swallow hard. My mouth is dry as driftwood, and I fill my cup with steaming coffee. Holding the cup to my nose, I breath in the aroma and study my captor from beneath lowered lashes.

There is something immediately striking about him. I mean, he's classically handsome, obviously tall and definitely broad-shouldered, but with those amber eyes… I can't look away. My pulse races away with a mind of its own, and I swallow a mouthful of coffee that is so hot it scalds my tongue, but I need the distraction.

He studies me coolly, giving nothing away. "I will remember that for future *guests*."

"Do you make a habit of drugging women on airplanes and locking them up in your basement? There must be a name for that kind of fetish, but I can't think of it off the top of my head." That's it, just keep talking, Gi, I tell myself. He'll be sure to let me go when I start to get on his nerves.

His plate is empty, I notice.

"What's the matter, not hungry?" I help myself to another slice of toast and load it up with crispy bacon and maple syrup. I can't remember the last thing I ate and I'm suddenly ravenous. Being held prisoner will do that to you.

Somewhere behind me, the witch must be baring her fanged teeth because he motions for her to be still.

"Are you going to tell me your name, or did I sleep through the introductions?" I ask.

His eyes flash. I mean, they literally flash, and a shiver of something—*fear, excitement, a warning to myself to rein it in*—travels down my spine. I honestly never knew flashing eyes was a thing until this moment and I'm stunned into silence, which doesn't happen often.

"Leonid Ivanov."

Another shiver passes through me, and my fork stops midway to my mouth. Leonid Ivanov. Even the way he says his own name is like a kiss of sunshine on a summer day.

Until I remind myself that this asshole had me drugged on an airplane, and fuck knows how I even got here. Did he not read the memo that you can't just go around doing that to innocent people?

"Why am I here?" My voice cracks like it thinks I should probably stop with the runaway dialogue right about now.

"Because I want you here."

"When can I go home?"

"When I say you can."

O-kay, so that's how he wants to play it.

"My fiancé won't let you get away with this."

"Your fiancé?" He arches an eyebrow and continues to pour his honey-coated voice all over me.

"Seamus Mulligan." I pause. "Oh, wait, did no one tell you about him? Yeah, he heads up the Irish mafia in Chicago. He won't let you keep me here against my will..." My voice trails off when I see the bemused gleam in his eyes.

"You think that your fiancé can take on my entire organization?" He sits back and sips his black coffee, but those amber eyes hold on to mine.

"Seamus and my family. Oh, and let's not forget Xander, my brother-in-law."

"Oh, I intend to do exactly that once I have taken Xander Amory down."

"I..." I shake my head.

I need to hold it together, keep up the bravado, not show him that I'm afraid because he will have already won. But now, I'm not only afraid for me, I'm afraid for Mel and Lucian and the rest of my family.

His eyes grow cold suddenly, and I shudder as if the sun just went behind a cloud. "What's the matter?" he asks, mimicking my earlier question. "Run out of steam so quickly? I must say, I had higher hopes for you."

I push my chair backwards, breakfast and coffee threatening to come back up. "I'm done here."

"Sit down." His voice slices through the air in the room, laced with something toxic instead of the honey I imagined before.

I turn around to face the witch who is already marching towards me. "I want to go back to my room." I see it in her eyes, the rising mountain of a man behind me as he stands up and towers over me.

I turn around slowly, clenching my fists, and willing myself to stay strong. I've already rattled him; now, all I have to do is keep up the momentum, and he'll be begging my dad to take me back.

"I said sit down." His top lip curls into a snarl worthy of a Rottweiler, and my insides turn to mush that has nothing to do with fear, and everything to do with his narrowed eyes locked onto mine.

I straighten myself to my full five feet and four inches and tilt my head towards the ceiling to peer up at him. "And I said that I'm done here."

A tic appears in his temple. "You are done when I say you are done."

"You don't get to tell me what to do. You have no idea what my family is capable of."

His mouth twists into a sinister smile and he laughs out loud. I don't hear anyone else laughing. "I have every idea what your family is capable of, but they will have to find you first."

"They will." I stand on tiptoes and still barely reach his shoulders. "They will find you, and they will make you pay for this."

And yep, I'm so forceful that he turns around, walks back to his seat, and ladles a heap of scrambled eggs onto his plate.

6

LEONID

"*They will find you, and they will make you pay for this.*"

Her words echo in my mind like a slap I didn't see coming. I am not afraid of her family. Her father is using his daughters as pawns to buy alliances that will strengthen his waning position. It is Xander I am interested in. Only Xander.

But I saw the fear behind her defiant eyes, and some irrational part of me came loose and wished, for her sake, that her family was stronger. They have allowed their little printzessa to slip through their fingers and they really should've taken better care of her because now that she is here, they will have to spill blood to get her back. Xander's blood.

"Sit."

I barely glance at her. In the corner of my eye, I notice the way Sergei steps closer, ready to move her himself if he must. Tamara and Ivana have been following the conversation with furrowed brows. Perhaps they expected an alternative outcome, one in which the printzessa cried and begged for me to let her go home.

It is true that the kind of disrespect she has shown me would have earned anyone else a warning they could not refuse, but Gianna is different. Perhaps it was the way her boldness flickered for a moment to reveal the fear lurking beneath the surface. Or perhaps I simply find her amusing, like a playful puppy with a squeaky toy.

Either way, my anger has cooled, and I am not ready to send her back to the basement. I am not done with her yet.

I suppress a smile when Gianna returns to her seat and sips her coffee.

The eggs are extra buttery this morning, just the way I like them. I am hungry after the wasted evening meal at my parents' property the evening before, and I have a good feeling about today. I might hold onto the Sedric asset a little longer than planned; she will certainly provide some entertainment that I hadn't counted on.

I study her face while I eat. Her thick strawberry blond curls make me think of mermaids sitting on rocks and luring sailors to their death. Her eyes are the turquoise of the Indian ocean on a clear day, and her lips...

"Boss?" Sergei's voice interrupts my reverie. "Do you need me to stay?"

I wave him away.

Mermaids and fucking oceans...

I down my black coffee and refill my cup. Why was she traveling economy class, unguarded? Does her family think so little of her that they would allow her to travel around the world unchaperoned? When this is over, they will have learned a lesson they will never fucking forget, but at what price?

My mother's words come back to me. "*You will learn to love your wife.*"

I loved Elena. Is that not punishment enough? Love is overrated. It is for people like Xander Amory and Gianna's father. It is for men who are prepared to live with the chink in their armor and ultimately lose the war.

"We were able to retrieve some items from the shipment, Pakhan, but the rest… We could not get to it in time."

Ivana has joined us at the table, her spine straight, eating directly from the tureens as she always does. Another habit that no amount of food will ever break. She eats quickly, shoveling food into her mouth without tasting it, her eyes alert to the slightest threat.

Gianna might be a mermaid, but Ivana is a serpent, poised to strike.

My fists clench. I expect to see a smug expression on Gianna's face, to hear her gloating over my losses, but she is silent, for now. Oblivious. And it occurs to me that she has no idea her brother-in-law is responsible for the war that has delivered her to my home. Of the good men I've lost. The millions of dollars that fallen into the wrong hands.

Months of planning blown to the wind. Shipments that were supposed to solidify our position, not crumble it.

Gianna is here for one reason only, and I must not lose sight of it.

"You are not eating." I set my fork down and meet her turquoise eyes that are still burning with anger in complete contrast with her calm, delicate features.

This is what makes her so fucking dangerous.

Perhaps I should've sent her to Pedro. The dark walls of the Russian prison would've quelled that fire.

"I am not hungry." Even as she says the words out loud, her eyes tell a different story.

"Do not lie to me, Gianna." I set down my fork and dare her not to look at me. But it seems that my new asset enjoys a challenge.

So be it. She will soon learn that I cannot be beaten. She clearly needs to learn that I am the one in control here, and that I always get what I want, and I can keep this up indefinitely.

Her family will never find her. Seamus—if he even cares enough to look—will never find her. For beneath the gleaming façade of my elegant property lies a fortress that would not feel out of place in an Agatha Christie whodunnit. Hidden passages, reinforced walls, secret tunnels; my little printzessa hasn't even scraped the surface of the places in which I could hide her if this is the game she wishes to play.

I pick up my fork and use it to point at her plate. "Eat."

"I'm. Not. Hungry." She faces me, and the fear in her eyes has been replaced by defiance.

It has become a battle of wills. Game on.

"Fine." I hold her gaze. "Ya tebya syem." *I will eat you.*

"Pakhan." Tamara's gentle warning does not even penetrate my thoughts.

I am focused. Gianna will do as I say, or she will suffer the consequences.

Gianna's furrowed brow as she stares right back at me does not make me gloat as it should. It's a low move, using a language she does not understand. But I am in it to win. I am captor, she is captive. I am Pakhan, she is Printzessa.

And corruption has never tasted sweeter.

She wants me to translate, but she will never ask. She is far too proud. A purebred mafia daughter. So, let's see her play the game her way.

She slants her eyes at me and when she speaks, her voice is hoarse but steady. "I'd rather starve."

I shove my plate away from me. The cutlery crashes across the table, and the coffee cup topples, spilling brown liquid across the pristine white cloth. Tamara jumps to her feet and mops up the spillage. Ivana doesn't even flinch.

I cover the distance between me and Gianna in a fraction of a second and turn her chair around to face me. I grip her chin in my fist, tilting her face towards me. "That can be arranged."

She winces as if in pain, but her eyes hold mine. There's a steely glint in the turquoise now, splashes of silver in the ocean, like the calm before the storm. Gianna tries to wrest her chin from my grip, and that's when I notice the mottled purple bruising crawling across her jawline and up into her face.

"Who did this?"

"I fell."

She's lying, daring me a second time to call her out on it. She's got spirit, I'll give her that.

"One more chance, Gianna." I could slice the atmosphere in the room with a knife, but at this moment, only the two of us exist. "Who did this?"

A glimmer of amusement reaches her eyes, lighting them up momentarily. "I told you; I fell."

Something snaps inside me, something dark, twisted, and familiar. I admire her balls, but no one plays Leonid Ivanov at his own game and gets away with it.

I grab her fork, sweep the lid off the tureen closest to me, and scoop up a bunch of scrambled eggs. "If you won't eat willingly, I will feed you myself."

Her eyes flash. Is she goading me? The woman is playing with fire, and people who play with fire always get burned.

I raise the loaded fork to her mouth, spilling eggs onto the dress she is wearing, as she clamps her lips shut. I grip her chin more tightly and push the fork between her lips, spattering more egg down her chin and onto her lap.

She holds my gaze, faint lines fanning from the corners of her eyes as her mouth stretches into a smile. She's fucking laughing at me.

Then, without warning, her lips part and she wraps them around the fork. Only, she doesn't just take the food, she drags it off the fork slowly, deliberately, her tongue licking the underside of the utensil in a way that's more unsettling than it should be. Her eyes stay locked on mine.

"Well, what do you know?" Her voice is husky. Seductive.

"Turns out I can be obedient after all." She moistens her lips with the tip of her tongue.

My grip on the fork tightens. What the hell is she doing?

"I want more, Leonid," she breathes. "Please."

She doesn't blink, and I'm mesmerized by the tiny slivers of silver and green in her eyes, my stomach lurching at the sound of my name on her tongue. Time stands still.

Then Ivana leaps from her seat, yanks the fork out of my hand, and spears more eggs. Before she can force it between Gianna's lips, I grip her wrist causing her to drop it onto the table with a clatter. I don't speak. I don't need to. Ivana backs off, hands raised in surrender.

This is my game. I'm the master, and the sooner Gianna learns that I'm not messing around, the better.

This time, I grab a handful of scrambled eggs with my free hand and shove my fingers into Gianna's mouth. Shock widens her eyes. Her shoulders tense up. Then she swallows and caresses my fingers with her tongue until it is all I can feel. Warm and moist and... My fucking cock twitches involuntarily inside my pants.

Before I can slide my fingers out of her mouth, her hand covers mine. "Are you enjoying this, Leonid?" She pronounces it Lee-oh-nid, dragging out the syllables. "How about we ditch the audience and go somewhere quiet, huh? Just the two of us?"

I am a man who is accustomed to always being in control. I know my limits. I can drink a bottle of vodka, no sweat, and if one more shot is going to tip me over the edge, I stop. But for the first time in my life, for one fleeting moment, self-control is the last thing on my mind.

Then, with a burst of anger, I remember who I am. And who she is.

I lean closer, so close our breaths mingle. "Don't push me, Gianna."

"Oh." Her bottom lip rolls out, and the tip of her tongue reappears, flicking between her lips and leaving them slick. "I was only playing the game. Perhaps you'd care to explain the rules again."

"*My* game. *My* fucking rules. Follow them or you will find out what happens to those who don't learn quickly enough." The cold metal in my voice isn't enough to tame the growing erection in my pants.

"Is that a promise?" she purrs against my lips, arching an eyebrow.

I release her chin, and she slumps back in her seat, the fight suddenly draining from her, and I realize with a spike of red-hot fury somewhere deep inside my chest that she thinks she has won.

"Take her away." I go to the window and turn my back on the room.

I don't trust myself not to cross the line and finish what Gianna started, and I know that if I do, the power will be in her hands. The weakness will be all mine. Just as I explained to my parents. She is my asset. *Mine.* And she will play by my rules no matter what it takes to break her.

"Pakhan?" Tamara's gentle voice reaches me, but I keep my eyes firmly fixed on the window. "What shall we do with her?"

I hear it in her voice, the uncertainty. My people need a leader, they do not need a man who buckles at the knees of a beautiful woman. It is the first time I have ever heard uncertainty in Tamara, and it is like a jolt of electricity through my veins.

"Whatever it takes. Just make sure that she remembers this lesson."

I hear them drag Gianna from the room and I don't look around.

7

GIANNA

"Where are you taking me?"

He turned his back to me. around. He strode to the window, barked the order, and didn't even look around at me. Asshole. If he didn't want me to play the fucking game, he shouldn't have started it. He knows who I am. He must've known I wouldn't fall onto my knees and beg him for mercy; it isn't how the Sedrics work.

The witch has my hair wrapped around her fist and is dragging me back along the corridor like a caveman. The woman is a maniac who clearly gets off on inflicting pain, and I refuse to show her that my scalp feels like it's on fire. So, I appeal to her sister. Her softer side.

"Where are you taking me?"

"Stop talking!" the witch snaps.

I stumble down the spiral staircase, my feet skimming several steps at a time, her grip on my hair the only thing preventing me from hurtling face-first to the bottom. My shoulder collides with the banister and a bolt of pain travels down my spine. On the bottom step, my ankle twists, and it feels as if she will rip my scalp from my skull as she yanks me back onto my feet.

Instead of taking me back to the basement room, we turn in the opposite direction. Or rather, she walks, and I try to keep up. More closed doors. The temperature drops. The further away from Leonid we walk, the more uneasy I become. My heart beats a dull tune in preparation for what's to come.

We stop outside a door, and the witch waits for her sister to unlock it. I breathe deeply, try to make eye contact, and she meets my eyes briefly. But all I see is pity in her dark eyes.

"Please," I say, finally succumbing to the panic unraveling inside my chest. "Take me back to Leonid. I'll apologize. I'll tell him that I've learned the lesson."

No answer. I did what he wanted, I begged, and I hate myself for it, and they're not even listening to me because they're following orders.

Something icy slithers down my spine. Whatever they intend to do to me, they will only stop if Pakhan issues the order, and he's upstairs in his luxurious dining room eating fucking scrambled eggs.

The witch shoves me through the door, and I slam straight into a second door. They both follow me, filling the cramped space, locking the original door behind us and unlocking the one in front.

The rush of cold air sends shivers through me. *This* is Leonid Ivanov's dungeon. This is where the man practices whatever unholy activities he enjoys when he isn't out there making millions and kidnapping the daughters of his mafia rivals. And the only people who know where I am are the wicked witch of the west and goth-Glinda.

The lunatic grips my wrist, and I'm grateful for the small win; at least with my scalp intact I can think more clearly. They're not going to let me go, and there's not a chance in hell of them listening to anything I have to say, so my only option is to fight back. Only, I have no clue what I can fight with until we reach our destination.

The doors are more solid here. If I'm lucky, they'll throw me into a dungeon and lock the door, but this hasn't exactly been my lucky day so far.

Does he know where they're taking me? If so, does this mean that for one brief second, I had the upper hand in his stupid little game? Because if that's the case, he intends to break me, but he has no idea that I've seen what happens to broken women. They reinvent themselves into a stronger version of the women they were before.

We stop outside a metal door, and the witch's knife appears in her free hand. "Try to run and see what happens." Her lips twitch at the corners, and I wonder if smiling doesn't come naturally to her. What did he do to her to make her so unhinged?

"We should use the hot room," goth-Glinda says. "Pakhan doesn't want her dead."

My pulse starts racing so hard I think I'm going to be sick. Every obscenity I've ever heard from my father's men springs to mind, but I remain silent. Yelling at them will let them know that I am scared. Better they have no clue what I am thinking—the element of surprise is all that I have on my side right now.

"Don't go soft on me now, Tamara." The witch cricks her neck from side to side. "The cold room will teach the printzessa a lesson just like Pakhan wanted."

I ignore the conversation and focus on the name. Tamara. It's better than nothing.

The door creaks open to reveal a dimly lit chamber with concrete walls and a low oppressive ceiling. The concrete floor is covered in slime and moss, and the air, when we step inside, is dense and damp. In the center of the room is a pool that sits flush with the floor.

I breathe in and splutter, the dankness clogging my parched throat.

But the sisters appear to be unaffected. Perhaps this is what they do for pleasure, come down here and swim around the cold pool for the sheer adrenaline rush.

Fear clamps around my chest like a vice, and I let it. Fight or flight. Without it, I don't stand a chance.

As the witch drags me towards the pool, the chill raises goosebumps on my arms and the back of my neck. I glance around for some kind of makeshift weapon that I can retaliate with. Anything. But with a mounting sense of dread creeping through my veins, I realize that all I can use to my advantage is the slickness underfoot.

She forces me to my knees. "Tamara, are you sure this is what Leonid wants?" I manage before her sister grips my hair in her fist and pushes my face into the water.

The shock is immediate. The freezing water feels like millions of tiny needles piercing my skin, and my body instantly reverts to panic mode. My muscles tense, and I open my mouth to scream. My eyes, my ears, my nose, my lungs... My entire body has been invaded by the icy liquid, and panic continues to flood my veins, making it impossible to think. My skin is on fire and frozen at the same time, and my brain is struggling to understand the agony.

I can't breathe. My arms thrash around in the water, trying to get purchase and push myself back out, but it's so deep, and my body is so cold that my movements are sluggish and futile.

She yanks me out of the water by my hair.

I don't have long. Water pours off my burning face and fills my eyes, and I choke more water out of my lungs. I scrabble around my whirring thoughts, trying to remember what I was going to do, but I can't think... Fear bubbles beneath my stinging skin, and I don't know how to contain it.

Too late.

My face is back underwater, and I don't have the energy to fight it. All I can do is think about the pain filling my skull. I close my eyes... My entire body is numb and trembling so violently that I fear I'll slide out of the maniac's grip and submerge myself.

But if I do, I'm taking her with me.

The thought appears from nowhere like a light being switched on.

She drags me out a second time. I can't feel my face. I can barely suck in enough oxygen to keep the blood pumping through my veins, but I cling to the one thing that's keeping me in the present.

I'm taking her down with me.

With a surge of adrenaline, I twist around to face her cold, dark eyes, and allow my body to go limp. An eerie warmth floods my body as I lean backwards, throwing myself into the pool, my hair still twisted around her hand.

I see it in her eyes. Shock. A perverse flicker of admiration perhaps. Then her hand hits the water, and she tries to free herself, but the momentum and the slippery ground is pulling her down with me.

My head and shoulders sink beneath the surface.

The shrieking panic is gone, and in its place is an irrational sense of warm, comforting peace. She didn't win. She didn't break me. If I get out of this alive, I will be stronger than she will ever imagine, and she'd better start running.

Then, I'm no longer in the water. I'm lying on the slick, icy ground, and someone rolls me onto my side, and hot liquid is pouring out of my lungs. I cough and splutter. I can't feel any part of my upper body. I can't even open my eyes to see what's going on because my brain is still trying to make sense of it all.

But I'm still alive.

I won.

"I said teach her a lesson. I didn't ask you to drown her like a fucking animal."

I recognize the voice. It's cold and powerful and dangerous, but somehow, I get the sense that it is on my side.

"Get out of my fucking sight, Ivana."

Ivana. Now I have both names. I store them away inside my head for later use.

Warm strong arms wrap around me. I feel myself being hoisted off the ground as if I'm as light as a feather. Then, my head is resting against a solid chest, and I can hear the *thump-thump-*

thump of Leonid Ivanov's heartbeat as he carries me out of the room.

He might've come to my rescue this time, but I will never forget that he gave the order, and a tiny spark of hatred ignites inside me.

8

LEONID

Tamara leads the way back into the main house, opening and closing doors in silence, leaving me alone with my thoughts, and Gianna in my arms.

After the twins left the dining room to carry out my orders, I sat back down in my seat, drank black coffee, sweet, and replayed the conversation between me and Gianna in my head.

Had I expected Gianna Sedric to be a meek slip of a woman who would take one look at me and promise to do whatever I asked? Was that really what I wanted? I needed to stick to the plan. Hold her here, spoil her for any other man, and then release her back into the wild like an uncaged animal.

What I hadn't expected was for her to swallow the bait and turn the game around on me. What did she grow up on, fucking Russian roulette?

She'd caused me to break my own goddamned rules. I'd shown weakness the instant she turned the seductive charm on me like a teenager yet to pop his first cherry. I'd taken my eye off the ball, and she'd snuck right in there as if she'd known all along about my intentions for her.

But it was the bruise on her jaw that had spurred me into action.

She lied about how she got it. I knew that she was lying, and rather than coerce the truth out of her, I let it slide. First sign of weakness, and she'd jumped on it with both hands like a passenger leaving a sinking ship.

She was covering for someone, and the only person who'd been alone with her since she landed was Ivana. Was she afraid of Ivana? The woman could be intimidating—hell, she even worried me sometimes with the intensity of her reactions—but that wasn't it. She wasn't protecting Ivana either. Which meant that those bruises were between Gianna and Ivana, and she wanted to inflict payback in her own way and in her own time.

But women like Ivana only understand violence. I'd warned her to back off; I'd disrespected her position in front of the printzessa; then I'd given her the perfect opportunity to release her embarrassment onto my captive.

Once the truth hit, I ran down to the basement, my feet barely touching the staircase. I didn't consider how it would look when I stopped them from carrying out my own orders. My thoughts, as muddled as they were, were solely for Gianna's welfare. Dead, she was as good as useless to me. I might as well pin a target on my back and hand myself over to Xander Amory with my hands above my head.

But when I saw her plunging backwards into the freezing water, something came untethered inside me. I barely registered Ivana sprawling face forwards on top of her. My vision was clouded red. I saw Gianna's face disappearing under the water's surface, and I reacted to save her.

My asset.

The pawn in my game to take down Xander Amory and his Sicilian mob.

Now, carrying her back into the house with her body curled against mine like a sleeping child, I feel more like her protector than her captor, and I don't understand how this has happened. Was this her intention? She knew exactly what she was doing when she licked my fingers, but my knowledge of the way women's minds work is limited to my relationship with Elena, and Elena would've seduced the Pope to get what she wanted.

Still, something tells me this is not the case with Gianna.

Or does she have me so fooled that I will believe whatever she wants me to believe?

I stop outside a guest room on the upper level of the house and wait for Tamara to open the door. She does, but not before her eyebrows disappear questioningly beneath her soft bangs first.

I follow her inside, still carrying my cargo in my arms.

The room is painted in shades of cerulean and turquoise, just like Gianna's eyes, and I realize too late the reason why I must've been drawn to this guest bedroom rather than any other. With daylight pouring through the window, it is warm and inviting, not exactly what I'd had in mind for my prisoner when I sealed her fate a couple of days earlier.

Without prompting, Tamara pulls back the comforter and stands aside while I settle Gianna onto the bed. The instant her body leaves mine, she seems to go into shock, trembling so violently I can hear her teeth chattering. I drag her wet clothes from her and pull the comforter up to her chin and tuck it around her. But it isn't enough.

"Fetch me coffee," I bark at Tamara. "Plenty of sugar."

The door closes softly behind her.

Gianna's eyes are closed. Her lips are tinged with blue, and her cheeks are pale, her veins visible beneath the surface like tiny meandering rivers making the bruises on her jaw look like an unearthly poison taking over her body. Another rush of anger fills me—not at Ivana this time, but at myself. Why does it affect me so badly to see her like this when I'm the asshole who wanted her broken?

"Gianna." I place my hand on top of the comforter, and she instinctively leans into it, wrapping her body around my arm without opening her eyes.

Her cheeks feel like ice when I place my knuckles against them, but her forehead is burning up. She's feverish, thanks to me. Violent shivers seem to rock her body in waves.

So, I do the only thing I can think of doing while I wait for Tamara to return: I lay beside her on the bed, pull the comforter over us both, and transfer my body heat to her.

I wrap my arms around Gianna and rub her the way a mother might rub a child wrapped in a towel to get them dry, and gradually, the shivering subsides. The pink slowly returns to her cheeks and lips, and her breathing regulates. Gianna tucks her knees up to her chest, instinctively keeping the heat in her core, and I can't help smiling at how fragile she looks, like a newborn baby.

I'm still lying beside her on the bed, the comforter pulled up to our chins, when Tamara returns with a pot of steaming coffee, and two small jugs of cream and sugar.

She hesitates inside the doorway when she sees us. All kinds of emotions dance across her face, and something I'm not quick enough to catch flickers in her eyes before she blinks it away. Jealousy? Sergei stopped teasing me long ago about Tamara's crush on me when I told him that, to me, she will always be the little kid I discovered in a stinking container. But my mother has hinted on several occasions that she worries the young woman's affection for me will be her undoing.

I don't want Tamara to love me. She is too important to me for our relationship to be destroyed by misplaced affection. So, making sure that Gianna remains under the covers, I ease my bulky frame off the bed and take the tray from Tamara.

"Why didn't you stop her?" I demand.

"I tried." She shrugs. "She was simply carrying out your orders, Pakhan."

"My orders were to see that she understood the lesson."

Her gaze slides to the bed and the pale face on the pillow, stringy-damp hair fanned out around her like a halo. "She understands."

Tamara might not always agree with her sister's methods, but she will always have Ivana's back. Even if it means choosing her twin over me. And I would not have it any other way. I give loyalty to my people, and I demand loyalty in return because without it, we are nothing.

I take her words on board and nod once to confirm that I understand also. "No one touches Gianna without my knowledge. No one harms her. No one so much as fucking looks at her the wrong way or they will have me to answer to. Including Ivana. Do you understand?"

"Yes, Pakhan." Tamara peers down at the coffee pot. "Do you want me to stay with her?"

"No. I will stay a while."

"But, Pakhan, the next shipment is due later today."

"I canceled it. What is one shipment when I have a war to win?"

Tamara goes to walk away and falters with her hand on the doorknob. "Do you know what lesson you were trying to teach the printzessa?"

Her voice is steady, calm, but laced with something else that I cannot quite place. She would never normally dare to question my orders. It seems that Gianna's presence is affecting her too, and I don't know if this makes me feel glad or uneasy.

"Yes. Do you?"

"You wanted to show her who is in control."

Something icy settles inside my gut, turning circles like a dog trying to get comfortable. "And you think I failed?"

"It is not for me to say."

She turns away from me again, but before she can leave, I set the tray down on the nightstand and grab her arm, spinning her back around to face me.

"Speak."

Tamara lowers her gaze to my hand on her arm. "When was the last time you laid a hand on me?"

It's an easy question to answer. "Never."

"So, why is it different now that she is here?"

The question unnerves me. "Nothing has changed."

"Don't you see?" She holds my gaze, searching my eyes as if she wants to see what's going on inside my head. "Everything has changed."

I release her arm. "You have no idea what you are talking about. I have secured the asset as planned. Nothing more."

"So long as you and the asset both believe this to be true, then we have nothing to worry about, huh?"

I shake my head. "Stop talking in riddles and say what you want to say."

"Alright, Pakhan." Tamara takes a deep breath as if psyching herself up for the punchline.

I might rule with a combination of fear and loyalty, but not with the twins. Never with the twins. I don't want them to fear me, I'm their savior. If they fear me, they will be able to walk away from me, and that means that my enemies will be able to buy them and encourage them on their way.

"Don't get too attached, is all I'm saying. One day very soon, you will hand her over to Xander or Seamus, and then what?"

The thought of Gianna and Seamus together makes my flesh crawl. It opens up something twisted and rotten inside me and makes me want to put my fist through a wall. He is not the man for her; she deserves so much better than the Irish pank.

"Then we will be exactly where we want to be." I pick up the tray and turn my back on Tamara, dismissing her from the room.

9

GIANNA

I'm on vacation somewhere hot and beautiful like Puerto Vallarta or Hawaii. I step out of the hotel and shade my eyes against the blinding sun with the flat of my hand. The sunlight makes golden ripples dance and shimmer across the surface of the pool, and I take in a deep breath, releasing it slowly as a sense of peace fills my chest.

This is paradise. I can feel it, I can smell it, and when I spread my arms wide, I can hold it in the palms of my hands. Why would anyone ever want to leave?

I navigate around the sun loungers and make my way to the water's edge. The heat on my bare arms and legs fills me with energy like a flower with its face turned towards the sky soaking up the vitamin D. It surges through me. Makes me feel alive.

Laughter reaches me from the pool. Kids are playing with a ball, tossing it to each other, lunging into the water when the ball is thrown wide. Warm splashes land on my arms and exposed stomach, and I laugh along with the kids. It's only a game. A bit of fun.

I sit on the poolside and swing my legs into the water. It's warm, but it still takes my breath away at first as my body adjusts. Turning my face back to the sky, I sit there for a while, listening, breathing, living in the moment. Nothing else matters but the heat on my arms and my feet swaying back and forth, back and forth, making ripples on the surface.

Time to get in and cool down.

But before I can lower myself into the pool, someone grabs my head from behind and plunges my face beneath the surface. I try to push them off me, but they're too strong. I open my mouth to scream, but no sound comes out, only bubbles. I thrash about, trying to draw attention to myself, waiting for someone to help me.

And the water is cold... So cold.

It sears the skin from my face. I feel like I'm on fire. My lungs are about to explode, but I'm not ready to give up, and rage flares inside me. Drawing on the last reserves of my energy, I tip myself backward into the water to get away from whoever is trying to drown me, sinking, sinking, knowing that I'm playing by my own rules, not theirs.

Then, just as I use up the last remaining dregs of oxygen in my lungs, strong hands grip my arms and haul me onto the poolside.

I'm shivering uncontrollably. I curl my body into the fetal position, unable to feel my frozen skin. Unable to even think.

All I know is the feel of the stranger's arms around me as they carry me to safety. Then blackness.

Someone helps me into a sitting position. They support my back with their strong arm and hold steaming-hot sweet liquid to my lips.

"Drink."

I swallow a mouthful of coffee, and it burns on the way down making me cough. They wipe my chin, make me drink some more, and this time I can feel it coursing through my veins.

My eyelids are heavy though as if someone has taped them down. I give up trying to open them and settle back in the comfortable bed. I don't know where I am or how I got here, but I know that if I stay, I'll stop shivering, and everything will be alright. Only the cold has seeped through to my bones. My teeth are chattering, click-clacking together and making my jaw throb.

Then someone lies down beside me in the bed, pressing their body against mine, sharing their warmth with me. The relief is instantaneous. I relax against them and finally drift off into a deep dreamless sleep...

I open my eyes with a start.

I'm in a room I don't recognize, in a bed I've never slept in before. My head is pounding, and my face is stinging, raw, like I just came inside from a wintry blizzard. I touch my cheeks with my fingertips afraid that they'll come away bloody, but they don't. I swallow, and my throat feels as though it has been scraped with sandpaper.

Sitting up slowly, memories come flooding back in vivid bursts, making my breath hitch in my chest and my pulse race. Breakfast with Leonid Ivanov. Forcing me to eat. Being dragged underground to the cold room by the two sisters. Ivana and Tamara.

A cold knot of hatred coagulates inside my gut at the thought of Ivana pushing my head into the freezing water. It all gets a bit hazy after that, but I remember promising myself that I will make her pay. I will make them all pay.

Pushing the comforter off me, I realize that I am in my underwear. A quick glance around the room, and there's no sign of the clothes I was wearing when I went to meet my captor, but I have no recollection of taking them off. Did he ... undress me?

I swing my legs over the side of the bed and stand up. My knees tremble, and my legs are shaky. But I force myself to examine my body from my toes to the top of my head. If Leonid touched me, I need to know. Not only because my father will kill him, but because my father will have to wait in line until I've finished with him.

There are no obvious signs. I touch myself between my legs, and I'm not sore or wet or swollen, and I would know, wouldn't I? But there's a gaping black hole in my memory after I entered the freezing water, and I don't like it. The only problem is, I can't trust any of them to tell me the truth.

I stagger unsteadily to the door, knowing it will be locked before I even twist the knob. I turn around and inspect the room. The bed is huge, the sapphire blue comforter is heavy, the drapes at the window light and floaty. There's a wardrobe pushed up against the opposite wall, but when I open the doors, I'm disappointed to find that it's empty. The drawers in the nightstand are empty too.

There's a kettle on the desk, and I smile to myself when I spot the coffee sachets and biscuits wrapped in plastic on the tray beside the white porcelain cup.

Another door. Another bathroom. But this one is much larger than the previous one, the walls covered in tiny cerulean, jade green, and silver mosaic tiles, lights are flush in the walls and around the giant mirror. There's a claw-footed tub in the middle of the room and a walk-in shower with a rainfall head.

I strip off my bra and panties and stand under the steaming shower, eyes closed, rinsing this day off my skin. A temporary escape. I use the jasmine-scented liquid soap to scrub every inch of my body; it does little to ease the knot in my stomach, but it does at least leave me feeling more like myself than I've felt since I arrived.

Then it occurs to me that Leonid had me moved from the basement to this luxury. Why? I clear a circle on the fogged-up wall of the shower cubicle with my hand and peer out at the fluffy blue towels on the heated rack, the bottles of lotion and moisturizer on the glass shelf above the basin, and the toothbrush and toothpaste in a silver holder.

Why is he treating me like a guest when we both know that I'm a prisoner?

Reluctantly, I turn off the water and wrap a thick towel around me, scrunching my toes in the fluffy bath mat. Is this room a sweetener to keep me quiet about what happened in the cold room? An apology? He ordered the maniac woman to teach me a lesson and now he thinks this will make it better.

One thing is for certain though: he wants me alive.

I walk back to the bedroom with the fluffy towel still wrapped around me and perch on the side of the bed. I have to be smart about this, try to stay one step ahead of my captors. I'm valuable to them, and that's my only leverage. I know I must bide my time, but I don't know if I can keep my mouth shut when he orders me to sit and eat like I'm a pet dog.

The key turns in the lock, and my muscles reflexively tense. I stand up, clutching the towel across my chest, pulse racing.

It's Tamara. Her eyes narrow, taking in the damp hair, my bare legs, and the towel, but her expression is unreadable. "You're awake."

"How long was I out?"

"Twenty-four hours."

Fuck! Another day has passed me by, and I'm still here. Why hasn't my father tried to free me? What are they waiting for? For Leonid Ivanov to make it easy for them? I don't know how I'm supposed to handle this situation alone, and the passing hours are chipping away at my resolve.

"I brought you some clean clothes."

She comes closer and drapes another dress across the end of the bed; the fabric is soft and velvety; the color is seal gray. My favorite. Lucky guess on the part of my captor.

I don't move.

She hesitates like she wants to say more. Sorry about my sister, maybe? I won't hold my breath for an apology; I don't even want one. I'll deal with Ivana my own way.

"It will be better for everyone if you do as Pakhan says."

"Everyone?" I can't help being cynical. Maybe it's because her nutjob sister tried to drown me yesterday.

Her expression softens, and I think I maybe see a hint of a wistful smile. "Trust me when I tell you that Pakhan is a kind man. The sooner you stop messing with him, the sooner you can go back to your life, and we can go back to ours."

Okay, so there are two things wrong with this statement. Firstly, she cannot seriously expect me to trust her. She's not the one who was drugged on a plane and is being held against her will in a house with a fucking dungeon.

And secondly... Why would she even care about me going back to my life?

She gives me one last lingering look before leaving the room and locking the door behind her.

I feel like yelling at her that I'd trust them more if I wasn't being held prisoner, but what's the point? While I was watching her, my brain was spiraling down its own rabbit-hole, thinking about the women in the refuge, and my father, and comparing it to my own situation. The women we helped were hurt because the men in their lives found their weakness and used it against them; in most instances, that was their children. My father acts the same way when it comes to his rivals.

Which is exactly what Leonid Ivanov is doing. He sees me as my family's weakness because Mel is protected by Xander. So, all I need to do is find Leonid's weakness, and I have a strong suspicion that she just walked out of my room.

Bingo!

When she said that we can all go back to our lives, what she really meant was that she can have Leonid back to herself. But does he feel the same way about her, and what would it mean for me if he doesn't? Would she turn against me and try to get rid of me herself? I have no doubts that, if necessary, she could be just as psycho as her sister, but where would that leave my captor? Right now, he needs to keep me alive, but a ways down the line, would he still feel the same, especially if it meant choosing between me and Tamara?

These thoughts are still churning around inside my head when I drop the towel on the floor and pick up the dress.

I freeze when I hear the key turning in the lock again. Did she forget to say something, like, *next time you try to seduce my boss I'll cut out your tongue*?

Clutching the dress in front of me, I face the door, expecting to see short black curls and dark eyes, but my heart leaps into my throat when I find myself staring at Leonid Ivanov's expensively clad chest.

10

LEONID

Something inside me uncoils and then scurries to tie itself back up in knots when I open the door to find her standing by the bed naked. My breath hitches. My cock instinctively rises to the occasion, bulging against my pants.

Tamara didn't warn me that I would find her undressed.

I glance back along the corridor, but Tamara has already vanished. Did she deliberately withhold this information? Is she angry with me for being too lenient with the printzessa, or is she still upset with me about our conversation the evening before? Because she believes that Gianna's presence changes everything.

I haven't seen Ivana since the cold room—she is no doubt releasing her frustration in the shooting range or on the first poor unsuspecting guy who offers to buy her a drink at the casino.

I'm here because I need to set the wheels in motion to complete the mission and return Gianna to her family. Tainted, as I'd so nonchalantly pointed out to my father.

Whatever twisted scenario my father might've painted inside his head when I revealed my intentions, he should know me well enough to understand that I would never corrupt the printzessa against her will. I am not a monster. Not that kind of monster anyway.

No, Gianna will come to me of her own free will. She will be unable to resist my obvious charms. She will succumb to my advances and beg me to take her, and that's how I will deliver her back to Xander and Melissa: panting, wet, and so desperate for me that no one else will ever do.

I mentally shake myself.

I'm an asshole, I won't deny it, but I'm not normally such a conceited, arrogant asshole who thinks women will fall at my feet and beg for me to fuck them in every available orifice. Sure, it has happened before. On several occasions. But I never take the women up on these offers because my cock shrinks far too quickly when I'm with someone who has no self-respect. He's a fussy fucker.

I already knew that corrupting Gianna Sedric would be a challenge. It was part of the attraction when I gave the order to kidnap her rather than her sister Melissa. But I'm starting to realize that perhaps I underestimated her, and this sends an unexpected buzz of excitement shooting through my veins that is better than any shot of Billionaire Vodka.

It has been a long while since I have experienced the thrill of anticipation, and I didn't even realize how much I missed it until our little game over breakfast yesterday.

Even now, standing there naked with the gray dress barely covering her breasts and pussy, she faces me squarely, her turquoise eyes locked onto mine. She is vulnerable, but she hides it beneath the veneer of Sedric pride. Perhaps she is more like her family than she realizes.

I allow my gaze to roam her body. I can see the swell of her breasts on either side of the flimsy fabric barrier, the curve of her pale hips, the dip of her waist. She has a tiny mole on her left hip, and I can already imagine how it would feel to track my tongue around it before making my way to her exposed sex.

My cock twitches, and I raise my eyes to meet hers. She still watches me coolly, as if daring me to come any closer. This should ignite my anger; she should, after all, be intimidated by me, her captor. But I still recall the way it felt when she pressed her trembling body against me beneath the comforter, like a wounded bird, and I want to know how it will feel when she comes to me willingly.

Her hair is still damp from the shower. I can smell jasmine and something else that makes my balls throb. Her natural smell perhaps. Or the promise of sex. Because with my eyes lingering on the inviting curve of her breasts, I'm struggling to think of anything else but taking her nipples between my teeth and nibbling on them until she groans with pleasure.

This is proving to be the most enjoyable mission yet, and it's all thanks to Xander Amory. Perhaps I should send him a thank you note with a lock of Gianna's hair.

My lips form a smile before I can stop myself.

Still, she doesn't speak, and I wish I knew what she was thinking.

"How are you feeling?" My eyes track the dark angry bruise on her jaw, and she instinctively juts her chin, still defiant, wearing the mottled stain like a trophy.

"Are you asking because you care?"

She could back away into the bathroom and get dressed in private. She could ask me to turn around while she covers her nakedness with the dress. But she does neither. It occurs to me that Gianna is perhaps still taunting me after her seductive display at breakfast, but if that were the case, she would drop the dress and show me what I'm missing.

No. Gianna Sedric is proving to me that I don't scare her. She is either very brave or very reckless. I cannot wait to find out which.

"Yes. You are important to me."

"So important that you ordered Ivana to torture me?"

"I ordered her to teach you a lesson in obedience." My conversation with Tamara slides back to the forefront of my mind. *So long as you and the asset both believe this to be true, then we have nothing to worry about.* "I am not here to talk about Ivana."

"What are you here to talk about?"

"You, Gianna."

Her expression remains impassive. "Me or my family?"

"You. I already know about your family, but you, my little printzessa, they have kept as secret as the crown jewels. Why is that?"

Her fingers subconsciously clutch the dress tighter to her breasts, and my cock clamors for more. That involuntary gesture tells me all that I need to know: they were saving her like a priceless filly to sell to the highest bidder.

She seems to be holding a debate with herself, the flickering of her eyelids the only giveaway that she is composing her response. Just when I think that she will come back with a sarcastic rebuff, she says, "Because I want nothing to do with the family business."

"Yet you are engaged to be married to Seamus Mulligan."

"I..." She chews on her bottom lip, and I can see the way her breathing grows shallow by the indentation between her collarbones. She is clearly not a happy printzessa.

This should make me ecstatically happy. It will be even easier to corrupt her than I had at first imagined because she doesn't want to marry Seamus. Or is it deeper than that? She doesn't want to marry into another mafia family. Whatever the origins.

My hands ball into fists. This I can relate to; her family has arranged her marriage, and all she can see ahead of her is a lifetime of bloodshed and obedience. For someone like Gianna Sedric, this would be the worst form of torture, worse than anything that Ivana could inflict upon her. For the second time during our short acquaintance, I question her family's intentions regarding their youngest daughter.

"Yes. I am getting married to Seamus."

"Do you love him?" The question takes me by surprise as much as it does Gianna.

She raises her chin, while her eyes still hold mine. "I don't see how that is any of your business."

"You are right, of course, it is none of my business. I am simply curious."

"In your capacity as my captor?" There it is that spark of feistiness that caught me by surprise at our first meeting.

The dynamics between us have changed since I carried her from the cold room, but she is still there, the Gianna who refuses to be broken.

"What else would it be?"

I step inside the room and close the door behind me. Still, she doesn't even flinch. With calculated movements, I cross the room and stand in front of her.

"Maybe you wonder what it is about Seamus that I find attractive."

"Indeed." I smile. I want her to open up to me. Familiarity breeds trust, and if this mission is to be successful, I need her to trust me enough to find me desirable. "Tell me."

"He is good looking, of course," she begins.

"Of course."

"And kind." I incline my head, waiting for her to come up with something I can believe. "And ... protective."

Protective? That's what she's going with?

"He isn't doing such a great job of protecting you right now."

The flash of silver is back in her eyes. "Maybe he didn't expect anyone to drug his bride over a game of Rummy and hold her prisoner in a fucking basement."

The thought of taming this wildness and molding it to my whim on every available surface in my sizable mansion makes my pulse race. No, Gianna is not destined to marry Seamus Mulligan. She needs a man who can tame her, control her, keep her in check while providing her with everything that her body desires.

I gesture to the comfortable room. "Basement?"

A flash of irritation sparks behind her eyes. "Does Seamus know where I am?"

"He will know when I am ready to tell him."

"And when will that be?"

"When I am quite certain that you have served your purpose." My voice is cold. "Because make no mistake, Gianna. I have allowed you into my home and provided you with all the comforts that you might need, but you are here for one reason only."

"Which is?"

"To help me win."

"Win?" She shakes her head, her damp curls tumbling forward over her shoulders. "Win what? What are you talking about?"

"You know I can't tell you that because then I would have to kill you."

Her eyes harden momentarily. "Isn't that what you're going to do anyway?"

"Oh no, printzessa. I have far greater plans for you."

I reach out and smooth her hair over her shoulder, my knuckles brushing the swell of her left breast. My cock reacts instantly, my blood pumping into my erection. I leave my finger there, the warmth of her skin making it tingle.

I search her face for some kind of reaction and find nothing. She is unreadable. But she doesn't slap my hand or pull away from me. She swallows hard, and that's when I can see the amount of self-control it is taking for her to remain so impassive.

"Plans?"

I feel her warm breath on my face. Her cheeks are still flushed and blotchy from the cold room, but her eyes are clear, her lips pink and moist, her chin tilted towards the ceiling. I vow to myself that when I am done with her, she will never look at Seamus Mulligan the way I want her to look at me. She will never beg him to fuck her. She will never beg him to let her come on his tongue.

I am torturing myself with these mental images, but I need this torture to fuel my resolve. Gianna is not one of the high-class escorts who serve my guests at the casino. She isn't someone I picked up in a bar after a few drinks. She is the daughter of a rival family, sister-in-law of the Sicilian pank who is systematically trying to take me down. I want her to want me. No more, no less.

And when that happens, her presence in my home will no longer be required.

I slide my hand beneath the gray dress that is barely covering her nakedness and cup her breast. Fuck it feels good. Better than I'd even imagined it would feel. She is warm, her skin silky-smooth from her shower, and I can feel the steady da-dum, da-dum, da-dum of her heartbeat.

Her eyes are still locked on mine as if she was waiting for this to happen, as if she knew that me touching her was inevitable from the moment I entered her room.

Her room? My room.

My balls are already heavy for her. I caress her breast with my thumb, gentle circular movements, exploring her silky flesh, her curves, the ripe fullness. She sways slightly, but her eyes give nothing away.

I move closer. Our breaths mingle, her heartbeat strong and steady beneath my hand. And oh, how I would love to spread her legs wide and slide my tongue inside her right now, to taste her sex, to feel her orgasm exploding over my face.

It takes every ounce of self-control that I possess not to snatch the dress away from her, drop to my knees, and suck on her pussy. But that would ruin everything. If I make my move now, I risk incurring her hatred rather than her desire, and this will have all been for nothing.

Patience, Leonid. I can be patient when I need to be.

"Did you touch me?" The whispered question takes me by surprise. "When you undressed me."

"You were unconscious."

"So?"

I locate her nipple with my fingertips and tease it, feeling a surge of pleasure in my loins when it instantly hardens. That's it, there's a good girl.

"So, I like my women conscious, Gianna. And believe me, if I had, you wouldn't need to ask. You'd be standing here, begging me for more."

I lean closer, and her pupils dilate as she peers up at me. Slowly, holding her gaze, I slide the dress from her hands and drop it onto the floor at our feet. I cup her chin gently, tenderly almost, and lower my lips to her mouth. Her lips instantly part and our tongues meet. She doesn't close her eyes, but instead, she tries to see right through me, as I fill her mouth with my tongue.

Then, when she responds, her own tongue licking my lips, I pull away. With a curt nod, I leave the room, locking the door behind me. I don't look at her nakedness. I want to. Fuck how I want to. But I need her to trust me.

She knows how easy it would've been for me to take advantage of her, and now she also knows that isn't what I want.

My win.

11

GIANNA

When Leonid leaves the room, I bend and retrieve the dress, moving on autopilot. I'm not even aware of my breaths sawing in and out. My thoughts are spinning like cotton candy, my pulse speeding like I just ran a few laps around my father's estate.

Because overriding everything else that my body is experiencing right now, is the memory of his tongue in my mouth. My lips are still parted. I can still taste him, feel him, smell his cologne lingering on my skin.

Should I have pushed him away? Should I have fought his advances and covered my nakedness with the dress or the comforter? I don't even know what caused me to react the way I did, but what I do know is that he wanted to make me feel vulnerable, and I would rather die than let him succeed.

On trembling legs, I make my way to the bathroom and peer at my reflection in the mirror. My face is blotchy, but that isn't what catches my attention; it's the flush on my cheekbones, the glimmer of something unrecognizable in my eyes, the plumpness in my lips. I touch my lips with my fingertip, tracing the feel of his tongue in my mouth. In comparison, my finger is cold and solid, and I quickly withdraw it, trying to erase the memory.

"What am I doing?"

My eyes travel down my naked body, lingering over my full breasts and stopping at my sex. He didn't even look at me. I gave him the perfect opportunity, but he turned around and walked out of the door without so much as a glance at my pussy, and my face grows hot with embarrassment.

He wasn't even tempted.

This should make me feel better about my situation—at least there is no chance of him taking advantage of me—but instead, I feel inexplicably ... disappointed.

What the fuck was I thinking? Did I think that I could seduce him, blow his mind with the most amazing sex he'd ever had, and then be allowed to walk out of his life leaving behind only a pleasant memory? Me, the twenty-three-year-old virgin whose experience of French kissing was gained from watching *Grease* on repeat as a little girl.

"Jeez..."

But still, I can't shrug off the feeling of anticlimax settling inside me. I would never confess this to Leonid, but my sex is still tingling from his proximity. I feel like the moth drawn to the glow of a lightbulb. My traitorous pussy, against all the red alerts flashing like beacons inside my head, was drawn to the promise of his touch, and his indifference is a stinging rejection.

I go back to the room, pull the dress on over my head, and sit on the bed, staring at the door, waiting for his return.

Why did he come? I cannot believe that he wanted to check I was okay. Is teasing me part of his game plan? My cheeks grow even hotter at the thought that I played right into his hands.

I replay what happened inside the cold room in my head—it's the only way for me to suppress the throbbing ache between my legs, focusing on the knot of hatred inside me for that woman.

Time slips slowly by.

My heart literally performs a somersault when I eventually hear the key turning in the lock and then slows to a serious thudding beat when Tamara comes in with a tray of food.

I stand anyway. "You brought food."

Her eyes slide up and down my body, noting the fit of the seal gray dress. "Pakhan is busy. He asked me to look after you." She sets the tray down on the desk and turns around to face me.

"I thought..."

I stop myself from telling her that I'd hoped to leave the room. That I'd hoped to get a second chance to eat with Leonid now that I've learned my lesson. That I realize that now Leonid is my only chance of escaping this situation in one piece.

"You thought wrong, printzessa." She narrows her eyes, and I get a fleeting glimpse of her sister that sends a shudder through my body. Tamara might be a little softer around the edges, but if pushed, I've no doubts that she is capable of the same levels of cruelty.

Once her footsteps have receded along the corridor outside the room, I go to the tray and check out the food on the silver platter. A spinach and ricotta omelet, perfectly folded in half, a tossed salad in a vinaigrette dressing, and a wedge of cheesecake drizzled in strawberry coulis.

I'm ravenous after the hours spent unconscious and the ordeal of the cold room, so I sit at the desk and clear the plates, washing the meal down with a can of soda.

Satisfied, I go back to the bed and sit down.

I don't know what to do with all this empty time. I am used to being kept busy, and I make a mental note to ask Tamara to bring me something to read when she comes back to collect the tray.

Time drags. I go to the window and peer outside at the clouds drifting lazily by in the bright blue sky. I watch the birds hopping across the lawn and nestling in the trees. The sparrows, finches, blue jays, and starlings. How I envy them the freedom to fly away when the whim takes them; they have no idea how lucky they are.

There is no one in the extensive gardens. Not a soul. I can't help thinking what a waste of land and a massive property this is when there are so many families out there without a roof over their heads. Then I remember that my family is just as guilty of amassing wealth and living a life of luxury, so how can I judge?

Subdued, I check out the window and almost cry out loud when it opens. Peering at the door over my shoulder, I open it wider and lean out. It's a long way down. If I jumped, I would break both my legs at the very least, and I can't risk being held here as a patient as well as a prisoner. There are no drain pipes near the window either, no ledges that I could potentially use to break my fall, and the ground beneath me is concrete.

Sighing heavily, I go back to the birds but leave the window open so that I can breathe the fresh air. I play a game I used to play as a child, mentally ticking off the different colors as they fly away and seeing which color is the most common. I list all the species I can think of, then, when I run out of ideas, I switch to listing dog breeds instead.

The sky turns a darker shade of blue, and violet starts to seep in from the horizon like spilt ink.

Tamara returns with another tray of food and removes the earlier tray at the same time. Her eyes linger on the open window, but she doesn't order me to close it, and I wonder if she'll return with a key to lock it, or if she is praying that I'll fall and break my neck.

"Tamara?" She hesitates near the door at the sound of her name, her expression giving nothing away. "If I'm not allowed to leave the room, could you please bring me something to read?"

She nods once and leaves. No wonder Leonid is so moody if his conversations are all so one-sided.

Day slides into night, and no one comes back. Not even Tamara.

I remove the dress, hang it up in the wardrobe, and climb beneath the comforter naked. But sleep eludes me. Instead, my brain resorts to tormenting me again with images of me and Leonid, his tongue in my mouth, his hands slowly removing the dress from my grasp.

What had he said? "*You wouldn't have to ask if I'd touched you. You'd be begging me for more.*"

My hands instinctively drift down towards my sex and part my folds gently. The tingling between my legs instantly resumes as if it had just been waiting for me to pick up where my captor left off. I slide my legs open across the silk sheets and insert a finger. It comes out slick, and I find my clit, rubbing it back and forth, back and forth, so gently it feels little more than the kiss of a breeze on a summer's day.

Then, I imagine how the scene would've looked to an outsider, me naked, Leonid fully dressed in his expensive tailored suit, towering over me with my head tilted back as he forces his tongue between my lips. With my free hand, I cup my breast the way Leonid did, squeezing my nipple until it hardens. I spread my legs even wider, my finger rubbing my clit harder.

What if someone else had entered the room and found us like this? What would Tamara have thought? Would she have been jealous, disappointed, angry?

How would Leonid have reacted?

In response to the theoretical question, my brain immediately plants an image in my head of Leonid with his face buried between my legs, his tongue deep inside me.

My movements become frantic. My breathing becomes ragged. And my orgasm comes hard and fast, my body jerking, and my thighs clamping around my hand as I curl into the fetal position and fall into a deep contented slumber.

I'm woken by the aroma of grilled bacon, scrambled eggs, pancakes and freshly brewed coffee. Dammit! I can't believe that Tamara snuck into the room again while I slept. The woman is like a fucking ninja. Has she never heard of knocking?

I sit up abruptly, the comforter sliding over my naked breasts, at the thought that it might have been Leonid instead. Would he have stood there watching me sleep? It's ever so slightly creepy if he did, but my pussy doesn't seem to agree with me.

I stand up and cross the room naked, stuffing a pancake into my mouth with my fingers and filling a cup with steaming black coffee. It isn't until I'm halfway through my breakfast that I notice the newspaper folded neatly beside the tray. It wasn't exactly what I had in mind when I asked Tamara to bring me something to read, but I unfold it and scan the headlines, my stomach lurching when I read the latest news from the White House and a smaller article about a shooting in a residential area.

No mention of me.

Not that I should be surprised. My family would never go to the press—it isn't the mafia way. My disappearance would imply a weakness in the Sedric camp; it would undermine my father's position and alert the other mafia families to an impending power struggle. But still, this media silence feels like another barrier to my rescue. I've been here for days, and to my knowledge, no one has tried to find me.

My breakfast sits heavily in my stomach.

I shower, wrap myself in a fresh fluffy towel, and wander back into the bedroom to find the tray removed and an oversized T-shirt folded neatly on the end of the bed. I use it to cover my nakedness, towel-dry my hair, and sit down at the desk a second time, scouring the pages simply for something to occupy my mind.

Another two days pass by with the same routine. Three meals a day are brought to the room with clean clothes and fresh towels.

If he's trying to torture me with lack of human contact, it's working. Never before has silence sounded so loud and angry like a tiger on the hunt for its next meal. Now, the thought of him cupping my breast in his hand and sticking his tongue down my throat makes me want to rip his limbs from his torso and shove them up his smoking-hot ass.

Then, on day four, Tamara comes in between meals and eyes up the T-shirt I'm wearing and my bare legs. "Here, get dressed." She holds out a silky chestnut-brown dress and waits for me to take it.

"Nah, I'm good." I shrug. I'm done playing Leonid's stupid mind games, dressing for him only to spend the rest of the day imprisoned within these four walls. "Brown isn't my color."

"You don't want to go for a walk? Fine."

She turns around to leave, and I blurt out, "Wait! I can go for a walk?"

She eyes me coolly. "I thought you were good."

I snatch the dress from her, before she can change her mind and go back to my captor with the news that I'm happy in my little prison. Dragging the T-shirt over my head, I don't even care about Tamara seeing me naked. I pull the dress on and slide my feet into my sneakers.

"Where are we going?"

"Don't get your hopes up, printzessa. We're going outside the house, that is all."

I match her stride along the hallway, grateful that she didn't feel the need to cuff my hand to hers or fasten a rope around my neck.

Outside is outside. Even if I am confined to Leonid's magnificent, landscaped gardens.

I spot the man in the dark suit at the bottom of the staircase, all bunched up muscles and thick thighs beneath the well-cut cloth. There's another stationed by the sliding glass doors that open onto the garden like they expect me to try and bolt when I can see the bulge of their guns beneath their dark suits.

I might be desperate but I'm not stupid.

My stomach twists when I recognize the man from the dining room when I was introduced to Leonid. I think his name was Sergei. He nods at Tamara and falls into step on the other side of me. I wonder if he has been assigned to me in place of Ivana, and the thought gives me a surge of renewed strength. If I'm right, Leonid is deliberately keeping us apart for my own protection.

"You have twenty minutes." Sergei's accent is clipped, his voice not quite as deep as Leonid's. "Don't even think about trying to escape."

"Why would I when the alternative is being held captive in such scintillating company?"

I walk slowly. If twenty minutes is all I'm allowed, I want to savor every moment. I tilt my face towards the sun, the rays seeping through my skin and warming my bones. The gardens are extensive, lush lawns leading down to a series of tennis courts, old-fashioned walled gardens, and what appears to be a maze. There are Japanese-style pagodas in lacquered red and black, and covered seating areas clothed in climbing roses, the whole expanse surrounded by woodland.

I gasp. I can't help myself.

I have always loved the gardens of my father's estate, mainly because it was my mother's favorite place, but this... This is something else.

"I'm glad that you find my home pleasant."

I didn't even hear him coming. My heart races, fueling my silent anger at being confined to my room for so long. "I wouldn't go that far."

I keep walking and am surprised when he replaces both Sergei and Tamara.

"Aren't you busy delivering ransom notes or organizing your next abduction or something?"

I don't need to look at him to hear the faint snort escape his nostrils or to sense the smirk on his lips. "I delegate such trivial matters to my men."

Ugh!

"So, what, you gave the order to have me kidnapped and then sat back with a bottle of Jack and waited for me to arrive?" I don't know why this bothers me so much. It's obvious that's exactly what happened.

"It was Negroni actually. I don't drink whiskey."

He heads down towards the maze, and my legs follow without me even thinking about it. "I based this maze on the hedge maze at Hampton Court Palace in England. Have you ever been?"

"I..." Deep breath, Gianna. I only have twenty minutes, and if he wants to talk about mazes, who am I to argue? He might lose track of time and let me enjoy my taste of freedom just a little bit longer. "No, I haven't."

He enters the maze and turns left. And I follow.

The dense silence shutting us off from the rest of the world is almost immediate. I try to peer through the seven-foot hedges, but it's impossible to see beyond the surface branches. I gaze up at the solid blue sky and turn three-sixty, but it's like being cast adrift on the ocean, and when we turn the next corner, I already feel lost.

"Do you know your way around the maze?"

I study his profile, the aquiline nose, the deep-set eyes and heavy brows, the narrow lips and strong jawline. Separately, his features are unremarkable, but thrown together, he would turn heads in a crowded casino. Not that I've ever been inside a casino. But there's something about him that makes me think of roulette tables, vodka shots, and women draped in diamonds and little else.

"No. That would be impossible."

We turn another corner, and then another, and panic that we'll be stuck in here until Sergei rescues us makes my pulse race. Is he deliberately trying to get us lost? Are Sergei and Tamara under orders not to come looking for us? And is it such a bad thing if they are?

I should be enjoying my extended period of freedom, but all I can think about is being trapped inside the maze with Leonid Ivanov knowing that no one would be able to hear me if I cried for help.

He stops and faces me, and it occurs to me that he is almost as tall as the goddamned hedges. He tugs a lock of my hair forward over my shoulder. "Are you afraid, Gianna?"

"Of getting lost in the maze?"

"Of getting lost in the maze with me." His voice is so smooth, it's almost hypnotic. Is this how he gets his women to be submissive—by hypnotizing them?

"Should I be?" I raise an eyebrow questioningly.

"It depends..." His knuckle caresses my cheek, sending shivers down my spine.

"On what?"

Something has shifted between us since the last time I saw him. I can't tell if he is testing my trust in him, or if my attempts to seduce him and get him to see me as an attractive woman rather than the sister-in-law of his rival have worked. Either way, my pussy is screaming at me to let him touch me and see what happens, while my brain is hardly putting up a fight.

"On whether you think you will find your way out before I do."

I lick my lips. "Is that a challenge?"

He smiles. And my heart does this funny fluttery thing that belongs in every rom com ever made. "I'll give you a head start."

"Are you serious?"

I mean, I know that Sergei is probably waiting at the entrance with his finger on the trigger of his gun, but even so, what if I managed to crawl out of the maze beneath the hedges or get so lost that no one ever finds me? I could spend all day hiding behind corners and running when I see them coming, couldn't I?

He inclines his head. "Sure. Why not."

"Okay." I back away from him, heading the way we came.

"There is one condition to this game, Gianna."

I stop, my blood gushing in my ears. Here it comes. The veiled threat to stop me from trying to escape. "If I find the way out before you do, I get a kiss."

12

LEONID

I watch her turn around and walk back the way we came. She doesn't question the condition as I expected her to. Does she think that she will find her way out of the maze before I find her? It doesn't matter either way. I'm already confident that she'll kiss me before long.

When I said that it would be impossible to know the way out of here, it wasn't strictly true. It would be difficult of course, but not impossible. I made sure to lead her to the middle of the left branch of the maze, but the question is, was she paying attention?

I wait between the hedges and gaze at the sky.

I can't hear her footsteps. The maze was designed so that, once inside, people could not call for help or go their separate ways and yell out instructions to each other. But I don't need to see or hear her to sense her determination to win.

She has been waiting three days for me. Three days left alone with her thoughts and the feel of my tongue in her mouth, wondering why I didn't take advantage of her. She will no doubt have experienced a cycle of emotions.

Shock.

Confusion.

Anger.

Perhaps even disappointment.

But above all, I will have already sowed the first tiny seed of trust within her heart against her will. I could've overpowered her, and she'd have been powerless to stop me, but I chose to walk away without even gazing at her nakedness.

I didn't need to see her pussy with my own eyes to know that it is beautiful. The swell of her breast in the palm of my hand was enough to tell me that nothing about Gianna Sedric's body could ever disappoint.

My cock grows warm and hard, and I force myself to concentrate on the matter in hand.

Do I allow Gianna to win today, or do I claim my kiss? If she wins and reaches the exit before me, it will reinforce her trust in me when I'm forced to forfeit the condition. But allowing her to win will also give her hope. It will provide her with a finish line, an arrangement that will end the day I return her to her family.

There is also the little matter of wanting to taste her again to consider.

But perhaps today's forfeit will make the inevitable reward that much sweeter.

I set off in the same direction as Gianna. I can't see which path she chose at each fork in the maze, but I can smell the jasmine scented body wash she has been using, and I can see the imprint of her footsteps in the spongy grass. I can see each wrong turn she has taken, and where she has backtracked on herself.

Smiling to myself I stroll leisurely around the maze, taking my time, and imagining Gianna coming to me naked, right here between the dense hedges, with the sun beating down upon her golden hair. And in the image, her legs are spread wide, and she has that mischievous glint in her eyes.

Even so, I'm waiting at the entrance when she arrives, slightly breathless, her cheeks pink with a combination of the day's warmth and frustration at getting lost.

She stops abruptly when she spots me. "I... How did you...?" Her eyes narrow, accusing me of somehow cheating. "You've got a plan of the maze on your phone, haven't you?"

"I can assure you that I haven't. What would be the fun in owning a maze with no secrets?"

Her eyes drop to my mouth, and she swallows hard. Then, she steps closer, her gaze never faltering, and my cock starts bobbing along to its own tune. It's a game, I tell myself. Only, I'm starting to lose track of my own rules. Either that, or Gianna is rewriting them as she goes.

She comes so close that I breathe in the smell of her, mingled with freshly mown grass and dewy leaves. Gianna is nothing like the women I meet in the casino. Or the trophy wives at the golf resort who flutter their eyelashes at me, praying that I'll give them the attention they so desperately crave while their husbands practice their swing. Everything about her is fresh and raw and honest, and I'm already rethinking this war against Xander Amory to include the Irish pank Seamus.

Her eyes hold mine. The turquoise is deeper in the shade of the hedges, like the ocean as the sun sinks behind the horizon, and it takes all my self-control not to order her to lie down on the grass and beg me to fuck her.

Her lips part, and I'm mesmerized by them as they come closer, closer, her pupils dilating until the turquoise almost disappears. I can almost taste her when I grip her wrists and hold her at arm's length.

What the fuck am I doing? I was supposed to secure the asset, hold her prisoner, and corrupt her as quickly as possible to get the job done and send her back to Xander. But here I am driving myself crazy by delaying the inevitable.

She blinks slowly, confusion dancing behind her eyes. "I lost," she says, her voice husky.

"I'm going to give you a second chance." I don't miss the flicker of mistrust in her eyes and wonder if I have perhaps misjudged this tactic, but I force myself to stay on track.

"Why?"

Does she want this?

"Because this is my game, and I can change the rules whenever I like. We'll try again tomorrow. Best of three. It will allow you time to think about where you went wrong."

She shakes her head. "Tomorrow, you'll take me a different way, and I'll be in the same position as I am today."

"You have my word that I won't."

"Your word?" Her eyebrows shoot upwards.

"Gianna, you and I both know that if I wanted to kiss you, I would."

I realize, too late, how that sounds when she lowers her eyes and sucks on her bottom lip. And I can't stop myself. I pull her closer, her hips pressed against the bulge in my pants so that there is no mistaking how much I want her, and I lower my face so that our lips are almost brushing.

"Same time tomorrow."

Then I release her and watch the curve of her butt cheeks beneath the dress as she walks back to the entrance.

"Gianna!" I call her back on impulse. I don't want her to think that I'm going soft in the late morning sunshine. "Tomorrow, the condition changes."

Her smile fades.

"Tomorrow, if I win, I get more than a kiss."

Her eyes flash, but she quickly recovers and tilts her chin towards the sky in defiance. "More than a kiss? How much more?"

"I haven't yet made up my mind." *Here is where I blow it*, I think to myself. "Do we have a deal?"

She nods once and walks outside to rejoin Sergei and Tamara.

The following day, Gianna is wearing a black and white polka dot dress with a full pleated skirt that sways around her hips when she walks. The dress has a low neckline that reveals a glimpse of her pale breasts, and she seems totally oblivious as she walks along between Sergei and Tamara.

For a couple of moments, I get to study her without anyone questioning why, and without her expression clouded by the knowledge that I am solely responsible for her captivity. She seems to glow in the sunshine as if she and the sun are connected in some way that no one else understands. Her long curls glint like molten gold.

Then she notices me and smiles, and that twisted serpent inside me uncoils just a little.

"Game on." She slants her eyes at me and moves closer so that Sergei and Tamara can't hear her next words. "I thought you might not show because you're afraid of losing."

"I never lose, Gianna."

Her lips quirk into a lopsided smile. "Fighting talk, huh?" Then, "Have you been out here all night learning the shortcuts?"

It's my turn to lean closer. "You will have to find out for yourself."

We step into the maze together. I can almost feel Sergei's eyes boring into the back of my skull, and I don't even want to think about what Tamara would like to do to the little printzessa. But I also know that, whatever happens, they will never question my methods or motives.

"Do you ever not wear a suit?"

"No. I have special wetsuits made for the shower."

She keeps her eyes fixed straight ahead, but I catch the smile tilting the corners of her mouth. The silk skirt swishes around her legs, and I can see the mound of her pussy through the flimsy fabric out of the corner of my eye.

I lead her deeper into the maze this time. When we eventually stop, she turns three-sixty trying to get her bearings.

"Ready?"

She takes a deep breath. "Do I get a head start again?"

"I will count to ten before I follow you." She walks off, her pace picking up, as I call out, "May the best man win."

"Or woman…" Her voice is like a light switch being flicked as she disappears around the corner.

I count to twenty. Gianna won't win because she wants it too badly. She is desperate to beat me, and desperation breeds panic and bad decisions. Her father should've taught her that the only way to win is to imagine yourself the victor, and the universe will do the rest.

Sure enough, I'm waiting for her just inside the entrance when she arrives, a fine sheen of sweat on her upper lip and collecting in her cleavage.

Her shoulders drop when she realizes that she has lost for a second time. "Did you cheat? You must've cheated. How did you get here without me seeing you?"

"I took my time, Gianna, like the tortoise and the rabbit."

"Hare." She shakes her head, her curls tumbling around her rosy face. "The tortoise and the hare."

"Come here." I hook my finger at her, and she walks towards me, her expression unreadable. "I believe you owe me more than a kiss today."

She moistens her lips with the tip of her tongue but, unlike over breakfast, this reaction isn't calculated. "I haven't kissed you yet. You might not want more when you realize that the reward isn't up to standard."

Does she really have no idea how beautiful she is? She is worth so much more than a bartered bride for an Irish mob leader who hasn't even put the feelers out on the streets of Chicago for his missing bride-to-be.

"Maybe you should let me be the judge of that."

The silence closes around us like a cocoon as she leans against me. Standing on tiptoes, Gianna wraps her arms around my neck and presses her lips against mine.

I know I can't force this. I'm not an asshole who goes around taking women by force—any man who does that deserves to get his cock chopped off and shoved down his own throat in a ball sandwich—but I need to do this at Gianna's pace, or the entire mission might as well be aborted right now.

But the instant her tongue slides between my lips, my body reacts. I entwine my fingers in her hair and crush her lips with mine. I push my tongue into her mouth, her soft groans only fueling my urges. I can't get enough of her. I want to be inside her, filling every part of her with me, blurring the lines between our bodies until I no longer know where my body ends and hers begins.

"Leonid..." She pulls away long enough to breathe my name against my lips before I smother them again.

I might be aching to dip my cock inside her, but I'm not so blind that I know she isn't squirming. She isn't struggling to get away from me. She wants this as badly as I do.

"We have a deal, Gianna."

"What do you want?" The question is barely audible above the blood pumping around my veins and into my cock.

I want all of her. I want to taste every inch of her. I want to hear her scream out my name when I ram my cock into her sex and then take her some more. But at the same time, I'm conscious of how precious Gianna is. She is more than an asset to be used against Xander Amory. She is more than a bored mafia wife looking for the kind of passion her husband reserves for gunning down any enemy that stands between him and his next billion.

When this happens, I want her to beg. I want her to desire me more than she has ever desired anything or anyone in her life. I want her to feel like she can't live another day without feeling me inside her.

I unwrap her arms from around my neck and lower my head to gaze directly into her eyes. "You can't give me what I want."

The instant I can no longer feel her lips on mine, I realize how much I miss them, but I tell myself this is the only way.

She blinks hard, tears collecting on her bottom lashes. "I don't understand." I can see faint teeth marks around her mouth from the violence of my kisses and resist the urge to lick them better. "I thought..." She's fighting the emotions inside her head.

Perhaps she came here today resigned to lose. Perhaps a tiny part of her wanted to lose so that she could see how far I would go. But I'm walking a fine line between needing her to want me and satisfying my own urges to bend her over and fuck her from behind, and I'm in serious danger of crashing and burning.

Fuck! How far do I go before my mission comes tumbling down around me?

It's one thing to tease her but outright rejecting her is a different thing entirely. At least that's what I tell myself.

Before I can talk myself out of it, I place an arm around her back and crush her against me, feeling her swollen nipples through my shirt. Then I slide my free hand beneath the voluminous skirt and find her naked sex. She's wet. My finger comes away slick as her eyes widen. But she doesn't pull away.

She doesn't fucking pull away.

"You're dripping, Gianna." My voice is husky, and she only nods, the movement so fleeting, I can't be sure I didn't imagine it. "Is that for me?"

Another nod. I can feel her heartbeat thudding against my chest.

I slide my finger inside her gently, probing, feeling her wet tightness swallowing my finger whole while I caress her pussy with my thumb. Her sex clenches around me, and I find her clit, rubbing her own slickness into it.

Gianna's breathing becomes ragged. She leans heavily against me, hiding her face, as my finger works back and forth, in and out, her juices flowing down my hand. I work her until she can barely support herself on her own two legs, and then I pull my finger out, holding her upright while her breathing regulates, ignoring the way my balls throb.

Eventually, I tilt her head backwards and hold my slick finger to her lips. "Taste it."

She licks my finger tentatively to begin with, watching me the whole time. Then she curls her tongue around me and closes her eyes.

"This is what I want, Gianna."

I turn around and walk out of the maze, nodding at Tamara and Sergei as I pass, and hoping that I haven't pushed her too far.

Tomorrow, I tell myself.

13

GIANNA

I don't know how long I stay inside the maze, leaning against the hedge, because I'm afraid that if I try to walk, I'll collapse into a sloppy mess on the ground. I can still feel his finger inside me. I can still feel myself dripping down the insides of my thighs, warm and sticky as if I've come unplugged.

How can he do this to me?

How can I allow my father's enemy to do this to me?

Leonid Ivanov must be almost twenty years older than me. He oozes the kind of life experience that I can't even begin to imagine. But ever since he rescued me from Ivana and carried me up to my room, it's as if I can no longer think of him as the enemy. I look at him and all I can see are amber eyes, strong shoulders, and jutting jaw.

I feel like an animal searching for a mate who will provide me with strong healthy children. My cheeks flood at the image of him impregnating me with his sperm.

Shit! I felt the bulge in his pants that seemed to go on and on forever, and imagine him filling me up, his cum overflowing and spilling out of me, and wonder what Mika and Cartier would think of me now. I remember Mika saying once that she viewed every man she dated as a potential husband, and I'd laughed because I thought she was joking. But she wasn't. "Don't you meet a guy and wonder what your babies will look like?" she'd asked.

Cartier and I had both said no.

I didn't have the heart to tell them that I'd be wasting my time anyway, because my father would eventually arrange my marriage to a potential ally.

But Leonid must secrete the kind of pheromones that are irresistible to anyone who meets him. Jeez, I can still smell myself. I cover my mouth with one hand and exhale, praying that Tamara won't be able to smell me too.

I shouldn't be attracted to him. This is the man who arranged my abduction and calmly ordered the wicked witch of the west to teach me a lesson; if anything, I should be repulsed by him. But somehow, one kiss, and my knees are still trembling, and I want to yell at him to come back and finish what he started.

"*I can't have what I want.*" That's what he said.

I dissect the statement, word by word. He can't have me because I'm an asset for him to barter with my brother-in-law. I'm his leverage. And if I'm no longer a virgin when he hands me back to my family, the war he is trying to win will escalate into a full-on nuclear disaster.

But then there's the other half of that comment. *What I want.*

He wants me.

This should fill me with dread. But instead, like a little kid pulling petals from a daisy and chanting, he loves me, he loves me not, it sends a frisson of excitement traveling through me.

I knew what would happen today. Or at least, I half expected it when Leonid told me he wanted more than a kiss. I entered the maze knowing how it felt when he'd cupped my naked breast with his hand, and the part of me that is still throbbing between my legs was excited to find out how far he would go.

I could've refused to go for a walk. I'm sure it would've made Tamara happy. But I pulled this dress on with a thrill of pleasure knowing that I was naked underneath.

"Printzessa?" Tamara's voice jolts me back to reality.

Pushing myself off the hedge wall, I straighten my dress and ball my hands into fists in case she smells my sex. I turn around to find Tamara watching me inside the maze with her brow furrowed.

"Time's up." She gestures for me to head outside first.

My legs carry me back to the house using muscle memory. My pulse is still racing. My heart is doing its own thing. My head is filled with the kind of images that have only ever existed between the pages of a book until now.

But for the first time since Leonid's men brought me here, I can't wait to be alone in my room, so that I can relive what happened inside the maze.

The next day, Tamara brings me breakfast as usual along with a jade green dress made of the kind of material that clings to every inch of my body. I spend twice as long in the shower and then moisturize my body from head to toe, imagining Leonid's fingers sliding along my smooth legs and hesitating outside my pussy.

I don't know if he will expect to continue the game inside the maze. But the dress suggests that he will, and suddenly, rather than praying for Xander or Seamus to rescue me, I feel like I'm counting down to my release and the last time I'll set eyes on Leonid Ivanov with mounting dread.

I'm running out of time. Fuck going to Seamus as a virgin. I've had a taste of what I'm missing—just like Mika and Cartier said I would one day—and I can't leave here without knowing more.

So, when I find Leonid waiting for me outside the maze, my heart starts doing a strange hypnotic dance, squeezing the breath from my lungs, at the promise of what today's walk will offer.

"This is becoming a routine," Tamara mutters under her breath. She keeps her gaze fixed straight ahead when Sergei tries to catch her eye. "People might start to question whether the Pakhan is a leader or a groundman."

"People? Or you?" I sense the tension in her spine, but Sergei warns me to keep walking when what he really means is *keep your mouth shut*.

Unfazed, Tamara retorts, "Maybe I'll accompany you today. We will see how much you enjoy the maze with a chaperone."

She knows. Her expression gives nothing away, but she knows exactly what is going on between me and Leonid, and I don't trust her.

SAVAGE BRATVA KING

Regardless of the pakhan's orders, she is a woman, and I'm spending too much time alone with the man she loves. I try to imagine how Mel would react if Xander was going into a maze alone with a young woman every day, and my eyes water just thinking about what Mel would do to her.

"I could lose you inside the maze as easily as I lose Leonid."

It's as much of a threat as I dare to toss her way without risking her dragging me back down to the dungeon. I'm just hoping Leonid will order her to wait outside. He's a mafia pakhan. He will soon tire of this game and then, not only will I never find out what it is he wants from me, but there is no guarantee that he will allow my exercise sessions outside the house to continue.

For now, perhaps, I have piqued his curiosity. But men like Leonid Ivanov can snap their fingers and have any woman they want. Any woman who knows what they're doing.

"Tamara wants to join us today," I blurt out at the entrance. Because why change a habit of a lifetime and allow her to speak first.

We'll let Leonid decide.

And somehow, I feel a little less like a prisoner in this moment, than a boxer sizing up their opponent from opposite sides of the ring. I thought that Ivana was the dangerous one, but now, I think I might've been wrong.

My pulse seems to slow, and my blood turns cold in my veins while I wait for Leonid to answer.

"As you wish."

And just like that, a huge gray cloud seems to hover above my head in the clear blue sky. I thought... I feel like such an idiot.

A foolish, naïve teenager who still has everything to learn and has just realized that her future husband will only teach her what he wants her to know.

Whereas Leonid would've taught me everything. He would not have held back. I don't know this for sure of course, I'm simply going by how he has made me feel so far. If he can keep me awake at night after one kiss, my pussy throbbing to feel his finger inside me again, imagine what else he can show me. Okay, so I might not be able to close my legs ever again, but oh the dreams I'd have.

Might have had. Past tense.

Because Tamara stands aside and gestures for me to follow Leonid into the maze while she walks in behind me.

The fun has been sucked out of the day. I study Leonid's straight spine, the neatly groomed line where his jet-black hair meets his neck, the broad shoulders and narrow hips, and I realize with a jolt of reality that the excitement was never about trying to find my way out of the maze before him. It was about being inside the maze with him.

My captor. The man whose balls will be served up for breakfast by my father when he finds me. The same man who can set my skin on fire with the slightest touch of a fingertip.

He follows our usual route, but today he goes deeper still into the maze. The familiar heavy silence settles around us, the shadows provided by the dense hedges raising goosebumps on my arms. When he finally stops in a clearing with four potential pathways, I suddenly find that I lost my bearings a while ago.

But Leonid's face remains impassive. "Gianna, you can choose which direction you wish to take first."

Tamara's eyes narrow briefly, but she remains silent while I choose my pathway, which I'm not entirely convinced is the way we came.

"Tamara." He inclines his head.

"What about the printzessa? She is going alone?"

"She has a one-in-three chance of completing the maze before we do, and Sergei is waiting for her."

"That way." Tamara points to the path behind Leonid.

Her shoulders have lowered a fraction; she wanted to chaperone me, to stop me from being alone with her boss, and now she finds herself competing in a race that she's uncertain of winning. I'd bet she's a sore loser too.

"Which path will you take?" She watches Leonid closely.

"I haven't decided yet."

He doesn't meet my eyes, but a shot of excitement pulses through my veins.

I don't wait around. Maybe he was lying when he said that he didn't know the layout, but I have the overwhelming sensation that he will find me whichever way I go or however many wrong turns I take.

Despite the cool soothing atmosphere created by the hedges, sweat is soon beading on my upper lip and between my breasts. I stop momentarily, my breath hitching in my throat when I feel something trickle between my legs, and clench my pussy, forcing the image of Leonid sliding his hand beneath my dress from my overactive imagination.

I don't know how long I've been running around the maze when I turn a corner and spot Tamara at the other end of the pathway. I quickly reverse behind the trimmed bush and pray that she didn't see me. Then I run in the opposite direction. I might not bump into Leonid, but if I do, I'm going to try my damnedest to make sure that I'm alone.

The thing with mazes is that every direction looks the same. This coupled with the oppressive silence is disorienting, and I have no idea if I'm going around in circles or getting closer to the exit. I can feel the heat in my cheeks, the dress clinging to my body, and the thump-thump-thump of my heartbeat.

Then I round another corner and stop so abruptly that my feet skid across the grass.

The entrance is just ahead, and no one else is there.

I should want to win. It won't gain me my freedom, but it will give me a one-up against Leonid in whatever strange captor-captive game we're playing. But walking out of the maze will mean that I've chosen winning over being alone with him, and my stomach twists at the thought of standing out there with Sergei and waiting for him to find me.

So, with Mika's voice in my head reminding me that we only live once, I back away from the exit, heart thumping, and my brain shaking its head in despair.

Around the first corner and I collide face-first with Leonid.

He raises his finger to his lips, warning me not to say a word. Like I need to be told. We only go a few steps though, just enough to not be seen from the exit should Sergei peer inside, but not so far that we both get lost again.

Before I can breathe a word, his lips are on mine, and his tongue is filling my mouth, and my hands find their own way around the back of his head, pulling him closer to me. I feel his hand in my hair, his other hand cupping my buttocks. He glides me against him, and the bulge in his pants is even larger than before if that's at all possible.

"Leonid..." My voice is swallowed whole by his mouth. "What about..." I was going to say what about Tamara, but his kisses are demanding, greedy, insatiable, and I can't even hold on to my train of thought.

"Do you want me to stop?" His lips barely leave mine long enough to pose the question.

It feels like an ultimatum. Now or never. And the tingling between my legs answers for me. "No."

"You know what I want."

I don't know how, but he has parted the top half of the dress, exposing my breasts. He lowers his head, pushes my breasts together and sucks on both nipples at the same time. He nibbles them between his teeth, and I reflexively arch my spine, thrusting them deeper into his mouth.

I swear he has grown an extra pair of hands.

One hand is around my back, and the skirt is up around my waist.

I try to remember why we shouldn't be doing this. Why I shouldn't be practically naked in the outdoor maze. Why I shouldn't even be here.

"You're so fucking beautiful, Gianna." His lips are pressed up against my ear, and who knew that could feel so goddamned sexy. "There are so many things I want to do to you."

A shudder travels down my spine. "Like what?"

"I want to fuck you till you can't walk." He pushes his tongue into my ear, and I groan out loud. "I want to fuck you till you scream out my name. And then I want to bend you over and fuck you some more."

"I..." I don't know what I'm supposed to say, and my brain is struggling to form a coherent sentence anyway with the nerve endings sending electric pulses through my body.

"Has anyone ever told you how immensely fuckable you are?"

It should be an easy question to answer, but his tongue traces a line from my ear to my collarbone and down between my breasts, sucking on the skin as he goes. All I can do is pant.

He sucks my nipples, and they grow pink and swollen, while my pussy throbs for some attention.

His face reappears in front of me. "I told you what I want, Gianna." He nibbles my bottom lip, sucks on it, his tongue flicking in and out of my mouth while his finger slides inside my sex. "I want this. I want you. I want all of you."

Our eyes lock, and I hold onto the golden flecks while my heart races.

"Tell me you want me, or I'll stop."

"I want you..." I breathe the words without even thinking about what this means.

But Leonid is about to enlighten me anyways. "Be warned, Gianna, I hold onto what's mine." He slides a second finger inside my sex, and I gasp. "So, fucking tight. How does it feel?"

I try to answer, but no words come out.

Leonid sucks my bottom lip until I feel the blood pumping around it. "How does it feel?"

"It feels ... good."

He pulls away and lowers his eyebrows. "Tsk. Tsk. You can do better than that." He probes my sex, exploring me with his fingers, his palm rubbing against my clit and causing my breaths to come in ragged gasps.

"It feels ... sexy."

"Better." His warm breath tickles my ear. "Do you want more?"

"Yes." My neck is arched, my face tilted towards the sky.

He grips my chin firmly with his left hand and lowers my face so that I'm gazing directly into his eyes. "Tell me you want more."

I can barely move my lower jaw, but I whisper, "I want more."

"I want you, Leonid. Say it."

"I want you, Leonid."

He smiles. "Good girl. You can have me, but then you will be mine, Gianna. No fucking around. You will be mine to do with as I please, and in return I promise to make you feel special."

I'm not really listening because he had me at '*good girl*'. He must feel my sex tighten around his fingers because he smothers my mouth with his, and it's hard to breathe, but I couldn't stop him even if I wanted to.

Then, without warning, his fingers slide out of me, and the emptiness makes my heart clamor against my ribcage. But before I can react, I'm clutching the skirt in both hands, and Leonid is on his knees in front of me.

He spreads my thighs wide, and licks my sex back and forth, rasping over my clit, taking his time so that I can feel every part of his tongue. I tilt my head backwards and lean against the hedge. It's the only thing that keeps me on my feet when he opens my pussy with his fingertips and inserts his whole tongue inside me.

Then his fingers are inside me too. On my clit. Rubbing, teasing, flicking, while he licks and sucks and licks some more.

My orgasm explodes onto his tongue. My body is writhing and bucking like he just sent a million electrical pulses through me, and I can't even think about the thorns scratching my scalp, or the sound of Leonid's name being called from somewhere nearby.

He hears it though.

In one easy casual movement, he picks me up, throws me over his shoulder, and carries me deeper into the maze. He stops around the next bend and sets me down. He lowers the skirt and straightens the bodice with apparent ease as if nothing just happened between us.

"Take your time. You can't come back looking like you just had the best orgasm of your life." Then he turns around and walks away without a backward glance.

My pussy is still clenching and unclenching in the aftermath of my explosion. My inner thighs are saturated. My nipples are stinging. And my legs feel so weak that I sit down on the grass and hug my knees to my chest.

I replay what just happened on repeat inside my head.

And each time I get to the part where he tells me not to come back looking like I just had the best orgasm of my life, my stomach twists.

Is that it? Was it just a game to him? Did he say all that stuff about not being able to have what he wanted just to persuade me to give in?

I squeeze my eyes shut. He used the oldest trick in the book—telling me what I wanted to hear—and I fell for it.

14

LEONID

I DON'T WANT to walk away and leave her like this, but I don't have a choice. I can't afford Tamara to find the printzessa with her skirt around her waist and my face buried between her legs. It would not look good for either of us, and besides, I still have Tamara's comments about everything changing since Gianna's arrival niggling away inside my head.

So, I leave Gianna safely out of sight, rearrange the bulge in my pants, and make my way out of the maze to find Olga approaching with my dog Marvel.

Tamara tracks my movements with narrowed eyes. Sergei, as always, waits with his feet firmly planted at shoulder width, and his hands clasped behind his back. I give them a brief nod, and smile as Marvel comes hurtling towards me.

He's an all-black Belgian shepherd. Another rescue, like the twins. I discovered him filthy and starving wandering around the port one day, his fur matted with blood, his tail tucked between his back legs, his eyes hunted and wary. Despite the cruelty he had previously suffered, he accepted food from me and, in return, offered his unwavering loyalty.

The instant he notices me he lowers his head and slips his leash easily. He bounds towards me, leaping about like a kangaroo, his front paws almost reaching my shoulders. He would be intimidating if he wasn't such a big softie, but I pity anyone who tries to attack me in front of him. He cries and barks at me playfully, always vocal, until I rub his back and his belly and stroke behind his ears. It took Marvel a long while to accept affection at face value, but even now, I am the only person he ever kisses or accepts a hug from.

"Hey, boy." I nuzzle his face and wrap my arms around his neck. I'm buying myself some time to reassemble my thoughts while he licks my face as if he hasn't seen me in months. He communicates through whines and playful barks in a language that only we understand.

I want to see Gianna's face. What happened inside the maze was … not what I expected to happen. She gave herself to me so freely, so trustingly, that making her come was the only thing on my mind. I wanted to pleasure her. I needed her to know how I could make her feel, how I could make her explode all over me because it was what I wanted.

Because I was the one in control. I will always be the one in control.

But it was what she wanted too.

And here is where my thoughts become misty. Dangerous. No one has ever wanted me the way Gianna wanted me today. Not even Elena.

Elena only wanted the promise of what I could give her, of the life she thought she could have with me, of the woman she would become as Mrs. Leonid Ivanov. She said all the right things, pressed all the right buttons, spread her legs wide and begged me to fuck her senseless. And I believed her. Until I caught her on one of my own cameras fucking one of my men in the utility room of my mansion.

Looking back, it's hard to believe that I didn't see straight through her, but I was young, and she rode me like a fucking cowboy.

But I never once saw Elena come the way Gianna did with complete and utter abandon, losing herself in her orgasm until she was left limp and exhausted. I never knew how excited it would make me feel, watching Gianna's orgasm ripping through her. Or how it would leave me desperate for more. Would she explode that way a second time? Or a third?

In the moment, Gianna felt to me like a rare and precious creature, someone to be nurtured, cosseted, adored. *My printzessa*.

I dismiss Olga, my housekeeper. I know that she is wary of Marvel; I also know that my dog takes advantage of this wariness, breaking out of his leash whenever the whim takes him, and chasing birds around the garden until he wears himself out. Only then, does he allow her to lead him back inside.

I straighten to find Sergei and Tamara watching me from just outside the maze's entrance. If I wasn't so preoccupied, I'd remind them that being besotted with a dog is not a sign of weakness. If anything, it is proof that I understand loyalty and trust and friendship, something that many people would benefit from learning.

Involuntarily, I lick my lips and realize that I can still taste Gianna. I can still smell her juices on my face. If it wasn't for

Marvel, I'd march straight back in there and finish what I started, but I remind myself that it's better this way. Gianna will come to me again when she is ready.

My heart beats a strange tune when she finally emerges from the maze, her dress uncreased, her hair pushed back over her shoulders and secured into a messy ponytail. The only giveaway that anything sexual happened between us is the flush on her cheeks and her swollen lips, but an outsider might attribute this to the sun's heat and the maze's difficulty.

Her eyes barely skim mine before settling on Marvel.

She blinks. Her mouth opens into a round 'O' of surprise, and she doesn't move.

"He's friendly." I wait for her to look at me, but she has eyes only for my dog. "Provided you show no animosity towards me."

"It must be a lonely life for him then."

I'm not sure I heard her correctly until I catch the brief smirk on Tamara's face, and disappointment settles on my shoulders like a heavy cloak. Gianna thinks that I've used her the past couple of days and walked away as soon as I'd gotten what I wanted. My hands ball into fists. Does she not understand that if I'd wanted to use her to satisfy my own desires, she would've crawled out of that maze on her hands and knees with my cum trickling out of her swollen pussy?

If she wants to resort to the feisty printzessa role, I can step back into the dangerous captor persona just as easily. And I can make life a hundred times more difficult for her than she can for me.

Before I can think of a suitable retort, Marvel pulls away from me and goes trotting over to Gianna where he promptly licks her hands and face, and sniffs behind her ears to make quite sure that she's a friend. I've never seen him react this way with anyone and it's a pleasant surprise. Even if it is Gianna.

I approach them, trying desperately to keep my eyes off the swell of Gianna's breasts beneath the fabric of the dress and the curve of her ass. "He likes you."

"Of course he does." Her eyes meet mine briefly before she aims her smile at Marvel. "We're kindred spirits. I'm not allowed to run away either."

"The difference is, printzessa, that Marvel would not choose to run away even if the opportunity presented itself."

"Maybe he doesn't know any better."

She gazes at me now with those beautiful turquoise eyes and heat rises in her cheeks. Whether this is caused by the banter or the knowledge that I was able to make her groan with pleasure is unclear. But I am already imagining ordering Sergei and Tamara to leave us alone and fucking her right here in my grounds to prove that I am not done with her yet.

"You might be surprised."

Perhaps something in my tone catches her unawares. She cups Marvel's face in her hands and peers into his eyes as if they are communicating telepathically.

"Where did you come from, huh, boy?" she murmurs.

"No one knows." I stand beside them, so close that I can see Gianna's erect nipples through her dress and smell me on her. "But if I ever find out who was responsible for trying to break his soul, they will wish they'd never been born."

Gianna nuzzles Marvel's neck. Her face is turned away from Sergei and Tamara, and she allows herself this brief respite to hold my gaze. Perhaps she is looking for an acknowledgement that something has changed between us, or perhaps she is looking for something more, something that I can't offer her.

Then she nods briefly as if she understands, and my stomach plummets.

I should feel elated that my plan is falling into place. Gianna Sedric wants me. She is not the same woman who boarded the flight in Montenegro to return home to marry a man she doesn't love. But the plan is already turning sour in my mouth.

"Why did you name him Marvel?" The question breaks through my reverie.

"Because he is my superhero." I have never told anyone this before, mainly because no one has ever asked.

"Marvel, sit." Gianna stands up and offers the dog her hand. "Paw."

He complies almost before the command has even left her mouth.

She glances at me sideways. "He's obedient."

A smile tugs my lips upwards. "He isn't afraid of me if that's what you're thinking."

"I wasn't. It seems that you have a very different image of yourself to the one you present to the rest of the world."

"Meaning?"

"Meaning, you act like you're a demon in an expensive suit, but Marvel can see right through you. You see, Mr. Ivanov, dogs can't smell guns. They smell love and fear and hate and they share their affections accordingly."

"What can he smell on you, Miss Sedric?" I can tell when her eyes widen momentarily that the innuendo isn't lost on her.

"Something that you might not understand. Kindness and honesty."

Movement in the corner of my eyes claims my attention, and I find Ivana striding towards us across the neat lawn. She wears her customary black leathers, the green flicks at the corners of her eyes elongating them and giving her an air of intended wickedness.

A low growl rumbles somewhere deep inside Marvel's chest, and he stands, placing his body between Ivana and Gianna.

"Down, boy."

The dog doesn't even acknowledge my command. His ears, usually large and proud, are flat against his head, and his haunches are lowered, ready to attack. He starts barking before Ivana is within touching distance.

She glares at him. "Shut the dog up, Pakhan."

I bristle. "He is simply doing his job. What is it?"

"You should come." Her eyes roam from Marvel to Gianna and finally settle on me. Then she turns around and heads back to the house.

"I should go." I have no idea why I'm explaining my movements to Gianna, but I guess a small part of me wants her to know that, given the option, I would stay. "Come, Marvel."

The dog doesn't move. He sits down at her feet and watches me with his mouth open in what is unmistakably a wide grin.

"Can I have a bit longer?" Gianna's eyes are wide and clear. "Please?"

"I'll bring the dog back inside." Tamara joins us, and Marvel immediately springs to his feet again, protecting his new friend.

"Fine."

I follow Ivana inside, leaving the dog to settle the logistics of getting him back to the house. I can't help smiling. It's obvious who is going to win, and it won't be Tamara.

Ivana is waiting for me in my study with my sister Victoria. She doesn't sit down. "The Irish are retaliating."

Another piece of the plan sliding into place. Not long ago, I *'persuaded'* a member of the Irish clan to defect to my team; he proved himself useful by orchestrating Gianna Sedric's abduction, while I made certain that Xander Amory would be able to trace his sister-in-law's disappearance back to them. Now, I can sit back and watch this little distraction from the comfort of my own business, while the asset is in my garden playing with my dog.

"Is that all?" My mind is still outside; this is the reason why I have people like Ivana to see that my orders are carried out.

"The shipments." She pauses, watching me coolly. "We have already missed two days."

"We can proceed as planned with tonight's shipment. I'll send Sergei to oversee the delivery."

"Perhaps we should postpone," Victoria says. "There is too much at stake with the asset here."

"Everything is under control."

"Everything? Xander Amory hasn't even begun his counterstrike yet."

"And we will be ready when he does."

I know Victoria is only doing her job, making sure that the lines I cross in the name of the Ivanov business are blurred beyond recognition when the Chicago Police Department comes to look at them. But Gianna Sedric is in my care, and I'm bristling at the thought of any interruptions from anyone... Including my own sister.

"What about the printzessa?" Ivana's voice is all cold metal and barbed wire.

"What about her?"

"When will she be leaving?"

"When I am ready to let her go."

I turn around and walk away, but not without catching the look of comprehension in my sister's eyes.

15

GIANNA

Leonid Ivanov has a dog!

I don't know why this changes everything, but it does. The way his expression softened when he looked at Marvel, the way the dog was with him, totally trusting and affectionate, means that the gun-toting, Armani-wearing, thin-lipped façade is exactly that: a façade.

The problem is that Leonid Ivanov has been wearing the Russian mobster suit for so long that he doesn't know who else to be. Apart from when he is with Marvel. But he doesn't even realize what the dog does to him; if he did, he would never have let me meet him in the garden. Because now that I've had a glimpse of the man who loves his dog, there's no going back.

It opens all kinds of doors, and hopefully one of them will lead to my escape.

I don't want to use Marvel against Leonid, but having the dog on my side will make me feel safer, not that I would risk his life for mine. He's the chink in Leonid Ivanov's armor, and he doesn't even realize it.

That night, in bed, I run through what happened in the maze. It's becoming a regular occurrence, and one that gets my pulse racing when I think of what might happen next. I know what should happen next of course, but if this was just a taster of what Leonid can do to me, I'm not sure my mind—*or my throbbing pussy*—will survive it.

I'm disappointed when, the next morning, Tamara brings me a pair of white Capri pants, a navy-blue cut-off T-shirt, and some functional underwear. She stands by the door and watches me pick up the plain white panties, her expression unreadable.

"Something wrong, printzessa? The clothes not to your liking?"

I turn around and face her squarely. *She* chose the outfit. I don't think she knows what happened between me and Leonid, but she has picked up on the different dynamics and she doesn't like it.

"I prefer lace." I shrug. "But I'm grateful to Leonid for providing me with clothes. I truly am. Without them, I'd be wandering around his house naked, and I'm sure he wouldn't appreciate the distraction, given how busy he is."

Her expression hardens. She steps away from the door and walks closer, holding my gaze. Without warning, the back of her hand slaps my cheek, the rings on her fingers biting into my flesh. I feel warm blood trickling down my cheek, and I cover the side of my face with my hand.

"Just because I wear my hair in bangs, don't be fooled into

believing that I am nothing like my sister. We serve the Pakhan, and he will never choose you over us."

Tears sting my eyes, but I hold them back. "If you're so confident, why do you need to tell me this, huh? What are you afraid of, Tamara?"

She shakes her head, her mouth contorting into an ugly expression that finally resembles her sister. Ivana must live with this permanent fear and mistrust always lurking beneath the confident exterior, while Tamara has learned to hide it well. "I am afraid of nothing."

"I don't believe you. Everyone is afraid of something. Are you scared that the Pakhan might fall in love someday, and that his woman will turn him against you?"

"That will never happen. He is married to his family."

I smile. "But he isn't married to you."

"I am family." Her face has rearranged itself into the beautiful woman I first met, only, like her boss, she too has unwittingly shown me what lies underneath. "Something you will never be."

She leaves the room, and the key turning in the lock sounds more final than it has ever sounded before. She and Ivana wouldn't risk Leonid's fury by disposing of me themselves, but I have no doubts they could make my death look like an accident if I push them too far.

In the bathroom, I splash my face with cold water and stare at my reflection in the mirror. Raised pink welts form a jagged pattern on my left cheek, the skin sliced apart where her rings caught the tender flesh. I soak the corner of the towel and dab the cuts carefully, pressing the cold cloth to my cheek to take down the swelling.

My face stings. Tears spill over my bottom lashes now that I'm alone, and I feel the sharp stab of homesickness in my chest.

I miss Mel and Lucian and my father more than I ever did when I was working in Montenegro because I always knew that they were here in Chicago, a flight away, probably missing me too. What hurts is how badly I miss Montenegro. I miss my friends, my job, and my apartment. I miss being able to make a difference where it's needed most, but more than anything else, I miss my freedom.

I never appreciated the luxury of making coffee in the morning and standing by the window to watch the world go by. Throwing open the closet and choosing my own clothes. Grilling a cheese sandwich and eating it standing up with a family-sized packet of potato chips because I can't be bothered to cook a full-on meal.

Back in the bedroom, I dress in the clothes Tamara left for me and wait for her to come back when it's time for my walk.

Sergei brings my lunch, a grilled chicken and red pepper baguette with a crisp, green side salad. He sets it down on the desk, eyes up the marks on my cheek, but doesn't ask me how it happened.

"Where is Tamara?" I ask when he goes back to the door.

"She's busy."

"I thought… I haven't been outside yet today."

His gaze travels up and down my body, lingering a beat too long on my breasts. "Correct. We are all busy, Ms. Sedric. Some of us do not have the time to go wandering around the maze and walking the pakhan's dog."

I chew my bottom lip and listen to his footsteps receding along the corridor. I was right. Leonid got what he wanted, and now he has no need to charm me with his garden maze based on Hampton Court Palace or his beautiful dog. Why should he care if I leave this room? So long as I'm alive and in his possession, I'm still his leverage against Xander to win this stupid fucking war.

So, what are my options?

I could starve myself, but I've seen firsthand how survival instinct can keep a body alive in the most horrific circumstances. I could try to escape, but this place is patrolled by armed guards, and I'd rather keep both my kneecaps intact.

Besides, as I sit down and take a bite of my baguette, I realize that these thoughts are half-hearted and childish, like a kid trying to get out of completing a homework assignment. Because my captivity could be a whole lot worse than it is. I could be locked in the dungeon with Ivana for company.

I don't even attempt to make conversation when Sergei returns for the tray. I stand by the window with my back to the door, my tiny little bit of control over the situation by not giving into the questions burning my tongue.

Where is Leonid?

Why have I not been allowed outside today?

Does he even know that I've not had my twenty minutes of vitamin D and fresh air? Or is he withholding the one thing that I look forward to because he believes that it will make me want him more?

Well, I've got news for him. I can live without Leonid Ivanov and his wandering tongue.

Heat floods my cheeks. *Tongue?* Why was that the first thing that popped into my head when I thought of my captor?

What the fuck is wrong with me?

I lay down on the bed and close my eyes so that I can't see the blue sky and golden sunlight streaming through the windows.

I'm still there, arms by my side, eyes fixed on a tiny dark patch on the ceiling when Sergei comes back without food. "Coming, printzessa," he says, holding onto the doorknob, "or are you going to pretend to be asleep all day?"

I sit up. "Where are you taking me?"

His expression doesn't even falter. "Outside. Unless you want to skip your twenty minutes today."

"No." I'm already on my feet. I grab my sneakers and slip them on while I walk in case he changes his mind.

Leonid didn't forget about my exercise. That's what I tell myself as I follow Sergei along the hallway and down the staircase, the taste of sunshine on my tongue.

I expect him to be waiting for me outside, but there's no sign of him. There is only Tamara, checking her wristwatch as if she is bored with being kept waiting.

Disappointment congeals inside my foolish gut when I realize that he has no intention of keeping me company today. But then I hear heavy panting from somewhere close by, and turn around to find Marvel galloping towards me, his tongue lolling from the side of his mouth. A gray-haired woman is chasing him, her face pinched into the kind of expression that means she knows she has already lost this race but is obliged to keep running anyway.

"I am sorry." She is breathing heavily by the time she reaches us, bent double and hands on her knees while she catches her breath.

I stroke Marvel behind the ears and nuzzle the silky fur on the top of his large head. "You're okay, aren't you, boy?"

"Bad boy." The woman's voice is harsh as she straightens, the dog-less leash still in her hand. Marvel instinctively nudges closer to me, almost taking out my legs with his weight.

"He isn't bad, he's excited," I snap. The woman's gaze slides across to Tamara and Sergei as if they'll back her up. I ignore them all and hold out my hand for the leash. "I'll walk him."

"It's my job." The woman clings to the leash like I've just announced I'm trying to get her fired. "I'll do it."

I could tell her that the dog was walking her, but I've only just gotten out of the house, and I'm sure Tamara would take great pleasure in cutting my freedom short.

"Twenty minutes." I address Sergei. "It's not like I can go anywhere, and Marvel likes me."

He doesn't even approach the dog, proving my point; they might be able to handle a firearm and follow orders, but they have no clue when it comes to animals.

"Pakhan didn't say—" Tamara begins.

But Sergei cuts her off. "Fine. Nineteen minutes now."

I don't wait around. I know that I'm still being followed by him and Tamara with their steely eyes and guns tucked inside their waistbands, but it feels like a minor victory. I'm outside, I'm with Marvel, and the dog stays by my side even though he has the entire garden to explore.

Looking at his goofy grin and trusting brown eyes, Marvel feels like a knot tying Leonid to me. Or me to Leonid. I'm still the prisoner after all. It just feels so good to have him around, like I could sit on the grass with him and tell him what's been going on and know that he'll be on my side.

I find a stray tennis ball and throw it for Marvel, who gallops off and comes trotting back with it in his mouth. He drops it at my feet and watches the ball, grinning, tail going round and around in circles like a windmill.

I don't count how many times I throw the ball. Sergei is the timekeeper today. But Marvel never tires of running off to retrieve it and dumping it back at my feet, like this is the most fun he has ever had.

"Your dad never plays ball with you, huh?" I bend to pick up the tennis ball, but Marvel pushes past me, tail still wagging, as he performs the kind of leaps a kangaroo would be proud of, crying and barking at the same time.

I turn around to find Leonid standing behind me, Marvel jumping up at him and demanding his attention. "His *dad* plays ball with him when he has the time." He takes in the pants and T-shirt, his eyes almost disappearing beneath his lowered brows.

I realize that he thinks I chose these clothes. Good. Just wait until he sees the practical Sigourney-Weaver-in-*Alien* panties.

Then he notices the marks on my cheek. "Leave us," he says to Sergei and Tamara.

I half expect Tamara to tell him that my time is up, but she walks away without a word. Although, if looks could kill, I'd be buried underneath Leonid's feet with a silver dagger through my heart, and a string of garlic around my neck.

"Good of you to join us." I crouch in front of Marvel who has come back to me now that he's had his daddy fix. "I thought you were busy."

"I am." He kneels on the other side of the dog and tilts my face towards him. "Let me guess, you fell."

"I'm clumsy like that. It's what happens when I don't get a change of scenery."

"I will see that it doesn't happen again." He sounds so sincere that I almost believe him.

"No, you won't. I'm just your prisoner, remember?"

Marvel whines then and licks my face the way dogs do, trying to heal me with love.

"Gianna, I want to apologize for—"

"Don't."

I cut him off and stand up, walking away from the house even though I know I've had way longer than my allotted twenty minutes already. Leonid falls into step beside me, Marvel trotting along in the middle of us.

"Don't apologize for what happened yesterday."

I don't even look at him. I can't. Because every time I do, I can feel his tongue inside me all over again, and this dazzling power that he seems to have over me crashes through my chest and leaves me weak at the knees.

"You gave me the choice, remember?" I remind him.

"I remember."

"You didn't force me to do anything against my will."

He opens his mouth to speak and then changes his mind.

"I'm a big girl, Leonid. It was fun, but hey, I get it, I'm an asset to you. I'll go back to my family soon, and you can erase me from your memory. Forget it ever happened." Pause. "I will."

Fuck, those two words hurt me more than they could ever hurt him. He keeps his eyes fixed straight ahead at a spot in the distance that only he can see, and I wipe the tears from my eyes with the back of my hand, grateful that he isn't watching.

"You'll forget all about me?"

"Yep." My voice shakes, and I pray that he doesn't notice. "Leonid *who*?"

"Are you trying to tell me that yesterday meant nothing to you?"

"Correct again. You catch on quick." Marvel whines by my side and I stroke his head, murmuring to him softly, "It's okay, boy. Daddy isn't in any danger." I glimpse Leonid's stern profile, and my heart starts thudding.

"That's debatable, Gianna."

I don't speak. I've said too much, already. I've let my captor off the hook and preserved my dignity, but I'm sad that I'll probably never get to see Marvel again.

"Are you finished?" His voice is strained.

I inhale deeply. "Yes." It comes out sounding way meeker than I wanted it to.

"Good." He slides his hand into mine and veers left before we reach the tennis courts.

I don't try to pull away. His hand isn't restrictive; it's warm, gentle almost, the way a father might hold his daughter when he wants to keep her close. Marvel, sensing the truce, runs off ahead and I shriek out loud when he pounces on a pigeon and almost catches it.

Leonid chuckles. "He hasn't figured out how to fly, to my knowledge."

But I'm not paying attention. Up ahead is a huge pond surrounded by weeping willows, long-necked graceful swans gliding across the water's surface. There are lily pads and bulrushes and golden fish bobbing for food. A flash of sapphire darts away from the pond as we approach. A kingfisher.

Marvel lowers his head at the edge of the pond and quenches his thirst. Then as if suddenly catching the scent of food, he dashes around the pond and stops at a red and white gingham blanket spread out across the grass. There are baskets on the blanket, a wine cooler, crystal champagne flutes.

"Marvel." Leonid whistles, and the dog raises his head, his ears instantly standing to attention.

"What's this?"

Leonid smiles at me, and I forget, just for a moment, why I'm here.

"Dinner."

16

LEONID

I once prepared a picnic for Elena. I was going to propose to her. My mother said that a picnic would be romantic, the way to impress a woman.

Maybe some women, but it didn't impress Elena.

She complained that she was uncomfortable sitting on a blanket on the ground.

She complained that she could hear a wasp buzzing around the food even though it was covered, and the only insect I saw was a delicate dragonfly.

She complained that the champagne didn't stay chilled in the heat of the sun, and that she didn't bring sunblock with her, and that, if she'd known, she'd have worn something practical.

Gianna squeals with delight when she realizes that I've prepared a picnic. She pulls her hand from mine and runs to the blanket, dropping to her knees and throwing her arms around Marvel's neck before murmuring, "Shall we see what we've got?"

She opens the basket, peering inside at the tiny dishes of caviar and pâté, the triangles of toasted bread, the ripe tomatoes and the sweet tuiles curled into slender rolls and dipped in chocolate.

She looks at me with wide eyes. "Did you prepare this food?"

"Would you believe me if I said yes?"

She smiles. "Probably not."

I open the champagne with a gentle pop and half-fill two glasses, handing one to Gianna.

"Okay." Her expression is serious. "What's this all for?"

"I want to prove to you that I'm not the monster you think I am."

She sips her champagne and watches me closely. "I never said you were a monster."

"You only thought it then."

Her laughter hits me somewhere deep inside. There isn't enough laughter in my life.

"A monster with a sense of humor." She clinks her glass against mine. "You forgot something very important though."

"What?"

"You didn't bring any food for Marvel."

I smile. "He can lick my fingers." It seems that whenever I am with Gianna, all that comes out of my mouth is sexual innuendos.

"Can I?" She slants her eyes at me and my cock responds like a dog sniffing a bone.

"I can give you something better to lick."

She is my prisoner. I'm supposed to be corrupting her so that I can hand her back to her family the tainted printzessa. An experienced woman rather than the naïve virgin who boarded the plane in Montenegro. So, why the fuck do my balls fill up at the image of my cock in her mouth?

This was not part of the plan. But watching her sip champagne with her legs curled underneath her on the picnic blanket, Marvel sitting attentively by her side, I know that the plan is fucked.

New plan. To sample all that Gianna Sedric has to offer and then make sure that she knows how fucking special she is. Because I don't think anyone has ever told her before. Sure, she knows how important she is to her father, how important this arranged marriage to Seamus Mulligan is, but important isn't the same as special.

It's a million fucking miles away from special.

"Is that a promise?" Her cheeks are flushed, and it only makes her look more beautiful. She literally has no idea how goddamned sexy she is, or what she does to me.

"Gianna, I don't want you to do anything that you're not comfortable with."

"Did I look uncomfortable to you yesterday?"

I smile. "You understand what I'm saying. I brought you here against your will."

"I won't tell anyone if that's what you're worried about."

That isn't what worries me. I don't care about her father, Xander, or Seamus. All that matters to me is that she wants me as badly as I want her. This plan is veering wildly off-track, but like an aircraft without a pilot, I'm powerless to stop it.

I lean forward and kiss her, and her lips instinctively part to let me in. Until a slobbery tongue takes out my chin and hers, and we barely rescue our champagne glasses from destruction-by-Belgian-shepherd.

Once we have Marvel back under control, Gianna asks me why I kept him.

"He followed me around. It took about five minutes for me to accept that he was never going to leave my side. So, I gave him a name, a collar, and a bed, and figured that I'd finally found the one who would never let me down."

She averts her eyes, but I've already seen the pity in them.

"This life isn't all bad," I say.

She pops a chocolate-coated tuile into her mouth, starting the meal with dessert. "So, you enjoy intimidating people with weapons and threats and the zeroes in your bank accounts."

"Is that a question?"

"No, it's the name of a pop song. Yes, it's a question."

"Enjoyment doesn't enter into it."

"Why do you do it then?" She puts down her empty glass and scoops caviar onto a triangle of toasted bread. "And before you give me the standard explanation I-have-no-choice response, maybe give it some thought."

I chuckle. "Did you have a choice when you got engaged to Seamus Mulligan?"

"Do you always answer a question with another question? Or are you hoping that I'll shut up and eat?"

"I'm assuming that your answer is no." I refill her glass and hand it to her. Our fingers meet around the stem, burning my skin. "I do it because I'm the eldest son. I can't walk away and watch my father's legacy fall apart. He dedicated his life to building his empire. For me. It's what—"

"Stop right there." She raises her index finger like a child who knows the answer to the teacher's question. "He did not build his empire for you. You know that, right?"

"Is this a trick question to distract me when you take the last sweet treat?"

Gianna shakes her head and ignores me. "Your father built his empire because it was what *he* wanted. He wasn't thinking of you when he gave an order to shoot a member of the Sicilian mob, or the Italians, or the Irish. He wasn't thinking of you when he endangered the lives of his family. Same as my father wasn't thinking of me when he arranged my marriage to Seamus."

Her voice trails off as if she has run out of steam.

Everything she just said is true, I know this. But my reasons remain the same. I do what I do because it is what's expected of me. I wasn't raised to have fun at work. I was raised to get the job done.

"My mom was killed by one of my father's enemies." She confesses.

Her voice has faded to a whisper, and she doesn't look at me. Instead, she tracks the whimsical journey of an insect that seems to have taken a liking to Marvel.

"I know he never meant for it to happen," she continues. "He never wanted his kids to grow up without a mom, but he knew the risks, and he chose the family legacy over the people he loved."

When she turns her face to me, her eyes are large with tears.

"Melissa found her. Can you imagine that? Can you imagine your own daughter finding your dead body? She was never the same again after that. It was like she went from being my sister who loved to dress up and experiment with her hair and makeup to this person who'd forgotten what it's like to play. It's the reason why she doesn't like the color red, because of the blood…"

I don't even think about what I'm doing. I pull her into my arms and hold her close to my chest while the tears flow down her cheeks. We stay that way until the sky starts leaking shades of violet and indigo and our shadows disappear.

Then, I take my jacket off and slip it around her shoulders to stop the shivers racking her body, and we walk back to the house in silence.

My men head discreetly inside the property when they see us coming. They know better than to question my authority with regards to Gianna, but I cannot stop them questioning my authority in general. I might just have to call a meeting to remind them that no man is an island. Isn't that how the poem goes?

No man is made entirely of stone either. I might've argued this point a week ago, before I met Gianna Sedric. But I feel myself softening like butter left in the sun with every day that passes. I'm going to need some serious sessions in the gym when her time here is done.

We stop at the kitchen to hand Marvel over to Olga for his supper. His tail wags for food, and he turns his back on us without a second thought, fickle animal. But I can't blame him for that. He and food didn't exactly get off to a great start, and he will never lose that instinct to eat whenever he can.

The closer we get to Gianna's guest room, the more oppressive the house feels. Like the walls are closing in on me. Perhaps she senses it too because she pulls away from me and puts a respectable distance between us as though she is afraid that someone might see us together.

On impulse, I take her hand and lead her to a different part of the property. The part that contains my bedroom.

"Where are you taking me?"

I don't like the fear in her voice. In fact, fear is the last thing I want to hear or see when I'm with Gianna.

I stop walking and force her to look me in the eye. "Do you trust me?"

"Do you really want me to answer that?" She gives me a lopsided smile.

"I prepared a picnic." Jeez, that sounds lame even to me. "I won't even complain about you turning my dog's head."

This gains a real smile from her.

"So, I'm just going to say this once. I want you, Gianna. I want you in my bed tonight, but I understand if this isn't what you want. Just say the word. Tell me right now that this isn't what you want, and I'll take you back to your room. I won't stop you from walking Marvel, but we'll spend no more time together."

I realize that I'm giving her an ultimatum: be mine or turn around and walk away. But this is as much for my protection as it is hers. It's the only way I can do this. I can't be this close to her knowing that she isn't mine.

"Do you mean that?"

Fuck, fuck, fuck! I let myself get too cocky. After the way she exploded on my face yesterday, I was confident that she would agree. I forgot that she's only here because of me and because of the fucking Sicilian, Xander Amory.

"Yes, no fucking around now, Gianna. This is your last chance to walk away. But if you say yes, there's no turning back. You're mine to do with as I please."

"Yours?" She leans closer, so close that my lips are drawn to hers like a magnet.

"Mine. Be warned, I protect what's mine with my life, but fuck with me and I'll—"

Her lips meet mine. Her tongue finds its way between my lips, and I can taste champagne on her. Champagne and chocolate and the promise of unfettered uninhibited sex.

I swing her up into my arms and practically run to my room. I don't care about the cameras set up high in the corners of the ceiling. I don't care that my security staff will be watching us right now.

Once inside, I kick the door shut behind me and lower Gianna onto my bed. I undress her slowly. She's wearing plain white underwear that I shouldn't even register, but on her they make me pause, sliding my hands up and down her body, devouring her with my eyes.

I push the vest up over her breasts, soak up the sight of her pink nipples. I trace lines down her stomach with my fingertips, hooking them inside the panties, and exposing her sex slowly. I drag them over her hips, toss them aside.

My cock throbs and twitches inside my pants, but I ignore it. Focus on Gianna.

She watches me watching her.

"Te takaya krasivaya. You're so beautiful."

She smiles, and her eyes glitter. I lay down beside her and close her eyelids with my kisses.

"Don't watch, just feel and enjoy."

I start with her ears. I nibble the delicate lobes, push my tongue inside her ear, my cock reacting when her nipples stand to attention. With my tongue, I trace her jawline where the bruises are starting to fade, down her neck, her collarbone, her breasts. Down and down, between her ribs to her flat stomach, leaving her nipples wanting, for now.

It isn't enough for me to have her for the night. I need to claim her. Make her mine.

I suck the flesh around her belly button, creating a band of tiny dots just beneath the surface. Branding her where no one else will see but me and Gianna. She will look in the mirror and she will know.

I drag my tongue down to her sex, teasing her with the tip. She purrs like a cat and spreads her legs, inviting me in.

"Not yet, my printzessa. Be patient."

Holding her legs still, I continue to track my tongue down her inner thighs, to the sensitive flesh behind her knees, and down to her ankles, the soles of her feet. Kneeling on the end of the bed, I raise her right leg and suck her toes, one at a time, licking the flesh between them until I can see the slickness on her sex.

Still, she keeps her eyes closed.

"You like this, printzessa?"

"Yes."

"You want more?"

"Yes." It comes out as a gasp.

"Tell me."

Her eyes fly open. She sees the warning look on my face and closes them again. "I want more."

"More what?" When she doesn't answer immediately, I bark, "More what, Gianna? If you don't tell me what you want, how can I pleasure you?"

A brief smile dances across her lips. "I want... I want you to lick me."

"Where? Where do you want me to lick you?"

My cock is knocking to be set free now, but I need to hear her say it. No one has ever wanted me in this way, and I already know that my orgasm, when I'm done giving Gianna what she wants, will be explosive.

"Between my legs."

I smile. "Here?" I push her thighs open and backwards, kneel between her legs, and lick the flesh on her inner thigh.

"No, not there."

"Where then? Show me, Gianna."

"Show you?" Her eyelids flicker open again, but when she realizes that I'm still watching her, she squeezes them shut. Then she touches her pussy with her fingertips. "Here."

"What do you want me to do?"

"Lick me."

"Like this?" I drag my tongue across her clit and pull away.

Gianna gasps. "Yes."

"You like this, huh?"

"Yes, I like this."

"How much do you like it, printzessa? Show me."

"What?"

I find her hand and guide it back to her wet pussy. "Show me what you want me to do."

"I..." She shakes her head against the pillow. "I don't—"

"Yes, you do, Gianna. You know exactly what you want me to do, and now you're going to show me."

I release her hand, and she inserts a finger tentatively between her flaps. She starts rubbing her wetness around her clit, teasing it, making it engorged. Two fingers. I watch her, my erection still growing.

"Good girl."

When her breathing becomes ragged, I remove her hand and insert my tongue in its place. "You're dripping, Gianna. I can get drunk on your juices."

"Lick me, Leonid..."

"Louder. I need to hear how much you want me."

"Please, Leonid, lick me."

I push my tongue inside her and rub her clit with my fingers. She's throbbing. Spasming. I open her thighs as wide as they will go, needing to get deep inside her, her pleasure fueling my own burning desire.

"Like this?" I gaze at her body. Her back is arched, her breasts thrust forward, her breaths coming in short, shallow pants.

"Yes. Don't stop!"

I insert two fingers inside her and suck her clit until her orgasm explodes. Her body writhes and wriggles, but I grip her thighs tightly and keep right on sucking and probing. Her orgasm keeps right on coming too. She covers her face with a pillow, drowning in the moment.

I pull away and take off my clothes.

Gianna tosses the pillow aside and watches me, a dreamy smile on her face, her body limp. Her eyes widen when my cock springs free.

"It's all yours, Gianna. Come and get it."

She rolls onto her stomach and crawls across the bed towards me, like a cat on the prowl, and my pulse starts racing. She literally has no idea how fucking sexy she is.

Wrapping her hand around the base of my cock, she licks the head, watching me the whole time. Round and around, her tongue licks the precum oozing from me and then she wraps her lips around the head, her teeth biting gently into the sensitive flesh.

"You can take more than that, Gianna." I entwine my fingers in her hair and hold her steady, pushing myself into her gently. She gags, and tears well in her eyes. "Good girl."

She closes her eyes, and I guide her deeper onto me. Her mouth is warm and wet. Her teeth are gentle. But she has my blood simmering through my veins, and I need to be inside her. The need to fill her up is more than I can bear.

I tilt her head backwards, slide my cock out of her mouth, and rub the head around her lips. "Taste me, Gianna." She licks her lips, those wide turquoise eyes holding my gaze.

In one fluid movement, I flip her over so that she is on all fours on the bed and drag her ass towards me. Her pussy is even more goddamned beautiful from behind. I open her velvety folds and lick her again, getting her ready for me, then I lean over her, and ease my cock gently inside her.

"You're so fucking tight, Gianna," I whisper into her ear.

I push further, hitting the wall, my cock throbbing against her. I knew she was a virgin—this is why she was promised to Seamus—but it hits me right now just what she is prepared to lose to me here.

"If I keep going, you're mine, printzessa." My breathing is shallow now. She knows what I want, but it's her choice.

"Keep going, Leonid."

This is music to my ears. I push harder. My cock is dripping with her juices. "Say it again. Tell me you want me."

"I want you." She twists her face around to meet mine, and we kiss, her tongue pushing into my mouth.

I push harder, gripping her hips and pulling her onto me. And then I'm through the wall. I feel a gush of warm wetness, and she groans against my mouth. Then she pushes herself backwards onto me, and my thrusts grow more urgent.

With one hand, I grip her hair, our kisses becoming needy, impatient. She whimpers, and I slam into her, feeling my explosion through every inch of my body. And when I come, we collapse forward into a tangled heap of sweaty limbs on top of the comforter, her pussy squeezing around me as if she is trying to hold me inside her.

17

GIANNA

I ROLL over in bed and stretch my aching limbs, turning my face towards the sunlight streaming through the open curtains. For one brief, blissful moment, everything is right with the world.

Then I remember where I am and why I'm here.

Fuck!

I thought being called back to Chicago to marry Seamus was bad enough but just look at the mess I've made of my life now. Seems I didn't need interference from my family to screw things up; I've done a pretty good job of it all by myself.

I wish Mika and Cartier were here. They might not have all the answers, but they would have a bottle of Tequila and strong shoulders for me to lean on.

I sit up and look around the room.

Leonid's room.

The room where we spent the night exploring each other's bodies and one of us lost our virginity while sucking on the other's tongue and whimpering like a wounded animal.

My cheeks are on fire even though there's no one here to accuse me of letting down the family name. And Seamus.

I can't marry Seamus now.

I can't even think about explaining my reasons why I can't marry Seamus. To anyone. Not even my sister Mel. Although Mel would understand considering she fell in love with Xander Amory when he was still the enemy.

But I'm getting ahead of myself like I always do. There are too many things to think about and if I don't get my brain organized, I'll end up lying here all day in a heap of tangled sheets that smell of Leonid and sex and... Oh my God...

I flop backwards onto the silk-covered pillows and pull the comforter over my face.

All I can see is Leonid. His amber eyes peering right through to my soul every time he said, *"Tell me what you want, Gianna,"* and *"You're mine now, Gianna,"* and *"Good girl. Make yourself come for me."*

What. The. Fuck. Am. I. Doing.

I cover my face with my hands and wait for my breathing to regulate.

I'm going to have a long wait because my body is reliving last night's orgasms, and my pussy is already wet. For him. For Leonid Ivanov. The man who had me kidnapped because he's in the middle of a stupid war with my brother-in-law.

Why couldn't it have been someone else?

Why didn't my friends let me have one night of glorious, mind-blowing sex with the adonis in the nightclub, or with the guy from the grocery store (although my pussy never clenched for him), or with Cartier's brother (who is unabashedly gay).

I could blame it all on Leonid, but that wouldn't be fair either. I could've gone back to my room last night; he gave me the option, and what did I do? I opened my legs wide and begged him to lick me. Multiple times. So, I can't even pretend that it was a moment of madness from which I came to my senses, grabbed my stuff, and ran like the house was on fire.

I wanted this and now I must deal with the consequences.

But first … food. I'm ravenous.

I sit up again, throw the comforter off my tingling body and stand up woozily. I feel like I either drank a bottle of Tequila on my own or lasted three rounds in the ring with Mike Tyson. My body is *sore*... I peer down at my swollen nipples, the marks around my belly button, the raised pink flesh from Leonid's stubble that seems to cover every inch of my body. And I can't even think about my sex.

But if the door opened right now and he walked back into the room, I would turn around, bend over, spread my legs wide, and beg him to fuck me all over again.

Because, it seems, I have a whole lot of catching up to do.

I cross to Leonid's dressing room and gape at the racks of designer suits and coordinating shirts and accessories. The guy couldn't look like a tramp if he bathed in mud and wrapped himself in black sacks. Pulling out a white shirt, I ignore the label stitched inside the collar, shrug it on and button it up to cover my nakedness.

Then, I follow the aroma of bacon, eggs, and coffee back to the bedroom.

He had breakfast sent to his room for me. The thought adds an extra layer of warmth to my already flushed body as I carry the tray to the bed, sit cross-legged on the crumpled sheets, and eat every morsel, washed down with three cups of creamy sweetened coffee. I try not to think while I eat.

Once my hunger is satisfied, I feel armed and ready to face the day.

Or at least, that's what I tell myself.

Because even with my stomach full, the impact of what happened last night settles on my shoulders like a coat made of thorns.

Not only have I destroyed my planned marriage to Seamus, but I've obliterated any potential alliance with the Irish mob and signed Leonid Ivanov's death warrant at the hands of Xander Amory and my family. He knew the consequences though, didn't he? He knew and he still wanted me, and I don't know how to feel about this.

This—*whatever this is*—will inevitably reach its natural conclusion when Leonid allows me to return to my family. And then what...? I told him that I would forget he even existed, but we both know that's a lie. What makes my pulse race and leaves me feeling slightly nauseous after the mountain of pancakes I just ate is: will Leonid forget that I exist?

Was last night a pleasant interlude for him?

Maybe he makes a habit of sleeping with his prisoners, especially the ones who are still virgins.

If I stay here, I know I'm going to chase my thoughts round in circles and get myself rattled, and I can't leave the room wearing Leonid's shirt. So, I quickly change into the clothes I wore yesterday, toss the shirt into the laundry hamper in the ensuite bathroom, and try the door.

I can't believe my luck when it opens.

A guard in a black suit with bulges in his pockets, stares as I step outside carrying the breakfast tray. It's obvious why I'm leaving the pakhan's room and not the guest room assigned to me, but I'll give him credit where it's due, his expression is completely neutral. Leonid's men are well-trained.

"Can you take me to the kitchen?" I suck on my bottom lip. This feels weird; I'm still the prisoner here, and I don't know what I'm supposed to do with the freedom to roam the house, even if I do have a guard one step behind me.

The guy doesn't speak. He gestures for me to walk with him, and I carry the tray feeling suddenly self-conscious, down another staircase that I haven't used before and into the kitchen where the gray-haired woman who looks after Marvel is scrubbing an already spotless marble counter that I can see her reflection in from the doorway.

She eyes up the tray when we enter, stuffs the cloth into a pocket in her apron, and hurries around the breakfast island like I left a trail of muddy footprints on her gleaming floor. "You shouldn't have carried the tray." She takes it from me and shoots a look at the guard like this is all his fault.

"It was no bother." I mean, jeez, if her boss wasn't holding me hostage, I'd be quite capable of preparing my own meals.

A whine reaches me from the far side of the room, and I look around to find Marvel trying to chew his way out of a gigantic crate. "Marvel!" His ears prick up at his name. "Can I?" I ask the housekeeper.

"It isn't time for his walk." The woman is bent over the dishwasher, loading my used plates and cutlery into the tray.

"I only want to stroke him."

I feel sorry for Marvel if he's only allowed out of the crate to be walked. It isn't fair for him to be confined behind metal bars like this; he might be safe, but this is no life. For an animal or human. I should know.

"It's fine, Olga. I'll watch her." The female voice belongs to Tamara. I never heard her enter the room; I swear the woman is a predator, prowling around the house and trying to catch people in the act of doing something they shouldn't.

She has obviously never heard that no one likes a snitch.

Or perhaps Leonid does. Who knows? My knowledge of my captor is limited to his love of dogs and torture and what he can do with his tongue.

She dismisses the guard, and Olga the housekeeper goes back to polishing the marble work surface to within an inch of its life. I don't thank Tamara. She isn't doing this out of the kindness of her heart. She has an ulterior motive, one that will serve her, I just need to figure out what it is.

Instead, I go to the crate and set Marvel free. He bounds out and places his heavy paws on my shoulders, licking my face clean. Maybe he can smell Leonid on me. The mental image of Leonid rubbing the end of his cock over my lips sends a fresh surge of heat to my cheeks.

"Hey, boy," I mutter into Marvel's fur. "It's good to see you too."

Olga brushes past me and drops a handful of dog treats into my lap. Marvel, sensing a reward, sits his backside down smartly and offers me his paw. I can't help smiling. Dogs are the most lovable creatures on the planet; all they want is to love and be loved, unconditionally. Even if their human is a ruthless mafia leader with little regard for human life.

"Don't think this changes anything." Tamara has come closer and is leaning against the breakfast island watching us.

Marvel takes the treats from me, his eyes firmly fixed on the woman wearing tight black pants, red shirt, and a black bomber jacket. His ears are down, his head streamlined to attack should the situation arise. I stroke the fur behind his ears and nuzzle his neck.

"You are still his prisoner."

"I didn't think otherwise."

"Really?" Her eyebrows slide upwards to meet her bangs. "But you think you can wander into the kitchen and pet the dog."

"I returned the tray." Is that like: *I carried a watermelon*? God help me.

Marvel is on his feet. His eyes never stray from Tamara, but his body language is wary. If I ever find out that she or Ivana have mistreated him when Leonid isn't around, I'll torture them both myself and stuff their body parts into a crate, see how they like it.

"You know that this was part of his plan for you, printzessa."

Her words make the hair on the back of my neck stand on end. I straighten and turn around to face her. Marvel presses his body against my legs protectively, letting me know whose side he is on.

"What are you talking about?"

She smiles, but it isn't designed to put me at ease. "I know you spent the night with the pakhan." She takes an apple from the fruit bowl on the counter and bites into it. "I see it in your eyes. To you, it meant something. It was a big deal. He made you feel special, am I right?"

Deep breath. My pulse is racing, but I need to keep my head clear. "Why don't you say what you have to say, Tamara, and take me back to my room?"

She takes another bite from the apple, chews it leisurely, and swallows. "His plan wasn't just to kidnap you. He knew that wouldn't give him the leverage he needed. His plan was to corrupt you. To do things to you that no one else has ever done before."

She climbs off the stool and tosses the remains of the apple to Marvel who catches it easily and promptly drops it onto the floor. A growl rumbles in his throat. A warning.

"You see, the pakhan wanted to send you back to your family a different woman. He wanted to know that no one else would touch you, and you played right into his hands."

She reaches out with her painted talons to stroke my face, and I bat her hand away.

Marvel bares his teeth at her, his lips curled into a ferocious snarl.

"You don't scare me." Tamara stares right back at the dog. "I'm the one with the gun."

"Don't you dare touch him." My voice is low. I can be ferocious too when I'm pushed, and right now, I feel more dangerous than Marvel could ever be.

"Or what, printzessa?"

"Or I'll cut your hand off myself."

She tips her head back and laughs out loud. "Wow, he really did a good job on you, huh?"

"I have no idea what you're talking about."

She steps closer. "Sure, you do. You can't fool me, printzessa. I see it in your eyes. You thought that it meant something to him, that he finds you desirable, that he wants you as much as you want him."

I shake my head, try to keep the tears from welling in my eyes because that will give her exactly what she wants. "That's where you're wrong. I know exactly what he is. Why would I want him?"

Because he makes me feel special. Because he makes me feel like I've never felt before. Because when he looks at me, my insides quiver, and all I can think about is his cock filling me up. All of the above.

"Fine." She shrugs. "Have it your way. You won't need me to help you escape then, will you?"

18

LEONID

"Leonid, are you listening to me?"

I've been listening to Victoria for the past thirty minutes, without paying attention, and my sister doesn't cope well with being ignored. It's the reason why she handles the legal side of the family business—she's the one with the eye for detail, Andrej is the strategist, and I get the job done.

"The warehouse?" Her brown eyes are little more than slits in her beautifully chiseled features.

"Did the cops find anything to pin on us?" I peer at her from across the walnut desk in my office. Even to me, my voice sounds distant.

"You really need to ask?" Victoria places her pen down on the notepad in front of her, measuring its distance from the edges as if her life depends on it being equal. "Is there any point in me being here if you're not going to be present?"

I sit forward in my seat. I recognize that I'm about five seconds away from her storming out of here and refusing to come back until I resolve the matter of the prisoner in my home.

"No, I don't need to ask. Yes, there's every point in you being here. And, yes, I am present."

"Finally." She puffs up her cheeks and releases a steady breath. "Would you care to enlighten us? I mean, we're only family. It's starting to feel like you think you can do this alone."

She shoots a glance at Andrej, who leans back in his seat and links his fingers behind his head. "Suits me. I'll take that vacation to Barbados that I've been putting off since forever."

The truth is, my siblings are as much a part of the family business as I am, but I've spent my life carrying the burden alone, and it's a tough shell to crack. Family always comes first: the golden mantra. Which means that, as the eldest son, it is my duty to protect them. They could sit here and scream until they're hoarse that I'm not responsible for them, but it won't alter the way I feel. The responsibility is all mine, just as our father intended.

"I've never believed that I can do this alone, Victoria." The lies spill from my tongue like water. "We all know that I wouldn't be here if it wasn't for you."

I was four years old when a mafia rival of our father invaded our family home. It was nighttime. Everyone was asleep, apart from Victoria, who has always survived on three or four hours sleep, even as a child. My six-year-old sister was in her room with the curtains open, studying the sky with the telescope that our parents had recently bought her. She wanted to go to the moon. She wanted to be an astronaut, and visit all the planets in our solar system, and bring back souvenirs from each to pin to the ceiling of her bedroom the way other people brought back fridge magnets from vacation.

Catching a glimpse of movement in the corner of her eye, she lowered the telescope to the extensive grounds and realized that the shadows were moving. But what didn't make sense to her was that there were no guards.

At that age, she didn't understand that moles could be people who don't have your best interests at heart. We knew that we never went anywhere without protection. But when armed guards are an intrinsic part of your life, they almost become invisible like the sub-audible hum of the refrigerator or the artwork on the wall or the way the laundry hamper gets emptied and clean clothes reappear in your closet.

But she understood the crushing silence and the missing security lights outside the house. So, she set in motion the process that our mother had instilled in us from the moment we were old enough to walk and talk: If something feels wrong, hide.

She grabbed a flashlight from the desk in her room, tiptoed along the corridor to my bedroom, and woke me up. Andrej wasn't yet born, so she only had to protect one little brother. Pressing a pale finger to her lips, she whispered, "We're going to play hide and seek, Leo." She gripped my hand tightly, led me outside to the unlit hallway, locked my door behind us, and pocketed the key.

Then, we ran back to her room as quickly as we could. We had barely closed the door when we heard a gunshot from somewhere in the house. I still remember the way my heart was hammering inside my chest, but Victoria ... she was so cool and calm as she opened the back of her doll's house wide and made me climb inside with a warning not to make a sound. She messed up her bed and hid inside her closet where I could see her through the crack in the door, a smile on her face so that I wouldn't be scared.

The bad men, finding my bedroom door locked, used force to open it, alerting our father to their presence. They never made it to Victoria's room.

It wasn't until many years later that I understood how my sister's bravery and quick thinking had saved my life. As always, Victoria accepted the praise with quiet humility. I have often wondered if she understood how her life would be affected if she were the only child of a mafia boss and saved me then to spare her own future.

I wouldn't blame her if she had.

"Don't try to deflect the question, Leo." She finally releases the pen, satisfied that it is precisely where it needs to be. "What's going on?"

"Nothing is going on that you're not already aware of."

Her eyes drift across the table to our brother and back again. "You know the police commissioner didn't just turn up at the warehouse on a whim because it's Wednesday, right, or because he's trying to manipulate the figures to earn himself a big fat bonus."

I smile. We all know that the police commissioner has enough handouts from the mafia families to make his legitimate bonus look like a child's monthly allowance.

"I can handle Xander Amory."

"That's good to hear," Andrej chimes in. "Because from where I'm sitting, it's starting to look as if he's the one in control."

"Good." I spread my hands wide. "That's exactly what we want him to believe."

They both wait for me to elaborate.

"I couldn't bring our operations to a complete halt. It would've been too obvious. I needed to give him just enough to allow him the upper hand while he tried to figure out what the Irish were doing with his sister-in-law."

"Ah, the printzessa." Victoria blinks slowly and tucks an imaginary stray lock of immaculate hair behind her ear. "What is happening with her? She's a little like our mother's Faberge eggs, Leo. Untouchable."

An image of Gianna on all fours with her pussy in my face pops into my head, and my pulse picks up speed. If they only knew what Gianna does to me whenever we're alone together, they would drag her onto the back of my brother's motorcycle and deliver her back to her father before I could blink.

Andrej chuckles. "You fucked her, didn't you?"

The tension in the room is as thick as soup. Victoria turns accusing eyes my way and draws in a deep slow breath. "Please tell me you didn't, Leo." Mentally, she is already preparing the paperwork for the legal battle of the century while measuring me up for my coffin.

Andrej scratches his jaw, his mouth twisted into a lopsided grin. "So, this was the great plan? Fuck her before you send her back?"

"Not exactly."

"Not exactly?" Victoria's voice has risen a notch. "Give me something I can work with, Leo, because *not exactly* doesn't cut it in a court of law."

"She was engaged to be married to Seamus Mulligan."

"*Was*? Your use of past tense isn't lost on me, Leo. So, what, we have the Irish on our case as well as the Sicilians now?"

"I don't see the Irish clamoring for my blood, do you?"

"No, because they have Xander Amory offering to deliver your head to them on a silver platter." Andrej's tone is serious. "What's the plan, Leo? We need to know what we're dealing with here."

"We invade Amory territory. Hit them where it hurts along with a ransom note for the printzessa."

Andrej shakes his head. "Then what? We send her back reeking of your cologne and with a signed affidavit that you didn't touch her pinned to her back. You think they're going to believe that their printzessa lost her cherry in Montenegro?"

"I don't care what they believe."

This is an absolute fucking lie. The thought of anyone else touching Gianna makes me want to tear down buildings with my bare hands. It occurs to me then that her family might force her into a medical examination to prove that she's still intact, and that makes me want to ride straight through Xander Amory's front door in an armor-plated vehicle and rip him apart limb by fucking limb.

"Oh, my fucking God." Victoria's face is pale. "You do care."

A smile lights up Andrej's face. "You've let the printzessa get to you, brother. What did she do, promise to be a good girl if you didn't hurt her?" He wrinkles his nose and shakes his head. "No, you'd need a heart to fall for something like that."

"We're done here." I stand up, ending the meeting.

"Leo, sit down." Victoria's voice is calm. "Please." She knows that she is the only person in the world apart from my parents who can give me an order and expect me to comply, but she still softens it with a please. "What have you done?" she asks when I'm seated again.

Where do I begin? I took the printzessa's virginity because there's something about her that I'm powerless to resist?

I refuse to acknowledge Gianna's power over me, even to my siblings. Weakness is like toxic gas, spreading and seeping through walls and underneath floors, unnoticed until it is too late.

"You fucked her, didn't you?" Victoria's glittering eyes hold mine.

I ignore Andrej's chuckles. "It was consensual if that's what you're thinking."

"I don't give a fuck if she swung from a chandelier and fucked you upside down, Leonid. You know what this means."

"Hopefully our brother had the good sense to use protection." Andrej shrugs. "He can throw in a few threats and maybe she'll keep her mouth shut. No harm done."

"No harm done?" Victoria sucks in a deep breath and stares at the window as if she can't bear to look at her two foolish brothers. "It would be no harm done if this was one of our escorts we're talking about. This is Gianna Sedric. Xander Amory's sister-in-law. Daughter of—"

"I know who she is." I cut her off.

I know exactly where Victoria is going with this, but she can't tell me anything I haven't already thought about. What worries me is that she's already figured out that I won't want to let Gianna go when this is all over.

"Okay, so perhaps you would care to explain what you intend to do about it, Leonid?" Victoria sits back and folds her arms across her chest. "I mean, we're only your brother and sister, but we can't protect you if we have no idea what's going on."

"Hold up." Andrej tilts his head backwards, closes his eyes, and raises his palms to the ceiling. "Maybe we can consult with the spirits. They probably know more about our brother's intentions than we do."

"She will return to her family as planned."

The words stick in my throat like dry pasta. Putting Gianna into a car and sending her home is the furthest thing from what I want right now, when all I can picture is her curled up in my bed asleep when I left this morning. Her hair tumbling over her naked shoulders. Her lips plump and moist.

"Okay." Victoria pauses, choosing her words carefully. "Let's assume for now that you're happy to send her back when you're finished with her." She arches a perfectly groomed eyebrow, daring me to protest, and I remain silent. "What do you think will happen to Gianna then?"

"Her family will increase her security detail. She will get married as planned and lead the life that was chosen for her when she was born into a mafia family." Even to my own ears it sounds like I'm reading from a script.

Victoria picks up the pen and taps it on the file in front of her as if the click-click-click is helping her to assemble her thoughts. "You don't believe this, Leonid. You know how it works. You have stolen from her the only thing that a mafia printzessa has to offer. Even if her fiancé agrees to go through with the marriage, and she can convince him that she is still a virgin, she will have to live with that lie for the rest of her life."

For once, even Andrej is quiet.

Victoria has always been the voice of reason, the family member who views our business as a game of chess, the game at which she excelled even as a child, with all our moves mapped out inside her head. The reason she is the best at what she does is because she can see both sides of the coin. But in this instance, she knows firsthand what it means to be a mafia daughter.

Her marriage to Aleksei was arranged by our father. Her husband treats her well, and she has never complained about having the choice taken away from her, but I've always known that something is missing from her life. There is no glimmer of excitement in her eyes whenever she looks at her husband. No sparks fly between them when they touch. I'm sure that she loves him, but it's the kind of love that exists between friends who know each other well. It isn't the love of two people who are unable to resist the magnetic pull of the other.

She's right. I knew what I was taking from Gianna last night even when I gave her the choice. Because I'd made sure that she wouldn't be able to refuse.

"What do you suggest?"

"You could always marry her." Andrej gives our sister a sideways glance, gauging her reaction. "Kill two birds with one stone. Save her reputation and seal an alliance with the Sicilians."

"No." I'm back on my feet.

"Why not?" Victoria asks. "It isn't such a bad suggestion." She pointedly ignores Andrej's wide grin. "Unless you would rather wait to find out who father has chosen for you."

"I have no intention of getting married."

"Ever?"

I can't answer that. I only know that I vowed when I was a teenager never to drag the woman I love into this way of life. If I'm being honest with myself right now, I always envisaged married life as two people madly in love, creating a home with rosy-cheeked children and at least a couple of dogs.

As if reading my mind, Victoria says, "She is already a part of this world, Leonid. She understands the dangers. And you have always prided yourself on being authentic. A man of your word. At least think about it."

I nod once; it's all she's getting. "Now, if you don't mind, I have somewhere important to be."

19

GIANNA

WE'RE ALONE in the kitchen.

I've been alone with Tamara before when she brings my food to the guest room, but this is different. This feels as though it has been manipulated so that she can cause trouble for me while Leonid isn't around.

One thing is irrevocably certain: she knows exactly what has been going on. She doesn't know the details—if she did, I'd be lying on this pristine kitchen floor in a puddle of my own blood—but her feathers have been ruffled, and she wants me out of the picture.

Only, I don't trust her. Why would she help me when the consequences of getting caught in the act are worthy of the kind of horrific news headlines that make people keep their kids inside after dark and their doors locked.

"Maybe I don't want to escape."

She smiles. "I hear you, but the words don't match the look in your eye, printzessa."

Tamara unhooks the dog's leash from the wall and loops it around his neck. Then she offers the other end to me.

"What are you doing?"

"It's time for his walk. The pakhan trusts you with his dog, unless that was simply a ploy on your part to get into the pakhan's bed."

My cheeks grow hot, and I wish that I could erase the feel of him inside me, just while I'm with her, because it feels as though she can see exactly what I'm thinking.

"What do you want from me, Tamara?"

She shrugs. "Isn't it obvious? I want you out of the pakhan's life."

"Why? Because you want to be in his bed?"

"It wouldn't be the first time."

The mental image of Tamara lying on Leonid's bed with his face between her legs makes me feel physically nauseous. She's lying, I tell myself. She wants a reaction; she's goading me into trying to escape, and I mustn't fall for it.

I scan the room, checking out the ceiling and the cornices for cameras, and realizing that Tamara has her back to the ones that I can see. Right now, someone must be watching us on a TV monitor somewhere in these grounds, maybe even zooming in so that they don't miss anything. Can they hear us? Instinct tells me that Tamara wouldn't be so reckless if there were microphones tapping into our conversation. But it wouldn't stop the guards from lip-reading everything that we're saying.

Everything that *I'm* saying. Because it's obvious now that she intentionally positioned herself between me and the cameras.

Is she scared? She should be; Leonid won't reward her interference with a slapped wrist and her verbal confirmation that it won't happen again. Which means that she is more afraid of me staying here than of me leaving if she's prepared to risk all to help me escape.

My head is screaming at me that this is a ruse. Convince me to escape and then have me shot before I even reach the property's boundary. But now that the suggestion is out there, part of me is already running home, back to where I feel safe.

I take the leash from her and cross the room. Marvel walks alongside me, big brown eyes peering up at me as if this is going to be the best walk of his life, and I can't help smiling back at him.

Tamara follows me through the house and outside. The guards close in on me when they see me with Marvel, but she must dismiss them with a gesture that I don't see, because they stand aside and let me pass.

She can't be trusted. She can't be trusted. *She can't be trusted*.

The words keep playing on repeat inside my head, but still my legs keep carrying me forward, past the decking and the pool, past the maze and the Japanese garden and another walled area that I haven't noticed before. Marvel doesn't slow his pace; he's perfectly comfortable walking with me, stopping often to relieve himself over stones and flowers and anything else that lures him with a scent that only he understands.

Past the tennis courts, and I can see the edge of the woods surrounding Leonid's land. Tamara still hasn't spoken. But she hasn't tried to stop me from walking too far either.

My ears strain for the sound of a loudspeaker voice ordering me to turn around and walk back to the house. Or worse, a gunshot. A tiny part of me is praying for heavy footsteps to come thumping up behind us, and for Sergei to take the decision away from me, yelling, "Stop right there!"

But he doesn't.

Nothing happens, and we're so close to the woods now that I can smell dew and tree sap and hear the birds announcing our impending arrival to the animals on the ground.

I'm torn. I feel like a ragdoll wrenched by her arms into two jagged pieces straight down the middle. I don't want to leave Leonid. After last night, it feels wrong to run away. It's like I'm treating it as a one-night stand when all I really want is to experience a repeat performance when Leonid comes home.

The thought of never feeling him inside me again or his tongue lapping up my sex or his teeth nibbling my nipples leaves a gaping hole inside me that I don't fully understand.

But worse than this is wondering how he will react when he finds out that I'm gone. Will he be disappointed? Angry? Relieved? Will he try to find me himself, or will he send Tamara and Ivana to drag me back kicking and screaming?

There will be no more leniencies. No more games inside the maze. No more kisses or nice clothes or walks with Marvel. He'll probably lock me inside the cold room in his dungeon and throw away the key, and I have to smother this thought to keep me from turning around and sprinting back to the house with Marvel a few paces ahead of me.

Because, despite the way I feel about Leonid and my fears that this is a trap, I'm still walking towards the woods. He might've turned my legs to Jello-O with his tongue the night before, but there's still the little matter of me being his prisoner. He had me abducted because of Xander. He sat behind his fat over-polished desk in his runway-worthy suit and gave the order for me to be drugged and locked up in his basement.

Somehow, I'm struggling to align the ruthless monster with the amber eyes that smiled at me when I could barely move my orgasm-drained limbs. But if I was free to leave, why would he have me followed around by armed guards who are most likely trained to shoot first and clear up the mess after?

"Stop!"

I'm so trapped inside my head with images of Leonid sliding his cock inside me that I do as I'm told without even questioning the reason why it was given. Marvel whimpers and leans against my legs like I'd be able to support him if he decided to give me one good hard shove.

Tamara stands in front of me, arms by her side. From this position, I can't see the back of the rambling house, but I'm still not convinced that there aren't cameras hidden inside tree trunks and monitoring our every move.

"You don't know where you're going." Her eyes harden.

"But you do."

She glances at the trees, her eyes flitting from one to the next as if she is counting them. "On the other side of the woods is a wall. It is patrolled. There is razor wire along the top. But if you follow my instructions, someone will be waiting to help you."

"Who?"

My heartbeat is thudding, a strange tune that I don't recall ever hearing before. When Tamara offered to help, I assumed that she would deliver me safely outside the boundaries of

Leonid's property herself, and now that I know she isn't coming with me, I'm not sure that I can see this through.

"No names. You will have to give your family something, but you will not be foolish enough to give them my name."

She doesn't threaten me with her sister; she doesn't have to. I can already picture Ivana appearing in my bedroom at night, fangs and talons bared and dripping with the blood of previous victims.

"I..." I shake my head. "I don't think—"

"No turning back, printzessa. The guards saw you walking with me. If you come back with me now, Pakhan will never believe that we were enjoying some bonding time."

Click. It is like a key turning in a lock inside my head, setting in motion the first part of her trap, and a shudder travels down my spine.

"He will know that you helped me then."

She smiles and her eyes are almost filled with pity. "I will tell him that you attacked me."

"I-what?"

"Hit me, printzessa." She slides a gun from her pocket, flips it around and offers it to me, then taps her cheekbone with a tapered scarlet fingernail.

"You want me to hit you with your gun?" I don't take it.

"You won't shoot me. The gunshot would alert everyone on the property to your location, and you would be dead before you reach the first tree." She pushes the weapon into my hand. "It has to be convincing or Pakhan will never believe that you overpowered me."

My heart is screaming at me not to do it.

Will Leonid even believe her? What if she's lying about someone waiting at the wall to help me? I'll have no choice but to come back and pray that last night meant something to him too. Perhaps, in another world, one in which mafia wars and power struggles don't exist, we might've met under different circumstances and had a chance to get to know one another like regular people. But we don't. And there is no chance for people like me and Leonid.

I take the gun from her, ignoring the bite of cold metal against the palm of my hand, and jab it into the side of her face before she can prepare herself.

An involuntary groan escapes her lips. She clutches her cheek with her hand, blood oozing between her fingers from the split skin.

I hand the gun back to her and walk towards the dark shadows of the trees lined up like sentinels protecting Leonid's kingdom.

But she calls me back. "Wait, printzessa."

I turn to face her, and she gestures to the dog whose leash is still in my hand. I didn't even realize that I was taking Marvel with me, and I reluctantly hand him over to Tamara.

Crouching beside him, I cup his large face in both hands and talk to him softly. "Go back to the house, Marvel. Good boy. She won't hurt you." Then I kiss the top of his head and address Tamara. "If I ever find out that you or your sister have hurt the dog, I will come back and finish what I started."

I stroke her bleeding cheek and run into the woods.

I've no idea if I'm doing the right thing. I want to go home to my family, but something is telling me that I'm not done with Leonid Ivanov. Not yet. Maybe this is for the best though. If I can convince my family and Xander that he didn't hurt me, perhaps they can reach a truce over this relentless war.

I might even meet him again someday. Who knows, we might find that our attraction is even stronger when one of us isn't being held against her will.

Blurry eyed with hot stinging tears, I protect my face with my arms from the branches clawing at me, stumbling over exposed roots and boulders, and dodging clumps of thorny nettles.

I'm so focused on my footsteps and the heavy thump-thump-thump of my heartbeat that I don't even hear the thundering paws behind me until Marvel leaps up, his front paws hitting me square in the middle of my back and sending me sprawling forward. I hit the ground face-first, my arms taking the brunt of the fall, the air leaving my lungs with a whoosh.

Marvel is all over me, licking my face and my arms and covering me with slobber. I try to sit up, but he must think me lying on the mossy ground is part of the game because he straddles my torso and sits on my lower body, preventing me from going anywhere.

"Marvel, stop," I manage between slobbery kisses and the hysterical giggles threatening to erupt from somewhere deep inside me.

But the game is irresistible, and how do you push a fifty-kilo dog off you when you can't even draw a breath?

Then I hear voices, and the implications of being discovered in the woods with Leonid Ivanov's dog hits me like a wrecking ball.

"Marvel, enough." I manage to inject enough authority into my voice for the dog to back off and sit smartly by my side, panting, his tongue lolling out of the side of his mouth.

But before I can haul myself back onto my feet, the voices come closer, and I hear the low hum of a drone hovering above the dense canopy of trees.

"Marvel, run."

I don't need to repeat myself. The dog runs with me, his panting providing the backdrop to my heavy breathing and the blood gushing in my ears. But I've lost my bearings, and I don't know if I'm heading away from the house or towards it. Did Tamara raise the alert to catch me out or were we followed?

Then a bullet whistles past us and blows a hole in a tree trunk up ahead, sending splinters flying in all directions.

Marvel yelps, and my heart almost leaps out of my rib cage as I kneel beside him. "Are you hurt?" Tears streak my face as I check him all over for a bullet wound and blood, sobbing with relief when my fingers come away dry. His tail is between his legs, and he is quivering with fear, but unharmed.

I wrap my arms around his neck and rest my face against his thick silky fur, letting him know that I won't let anyone hurt him.

We're still in the same position when heavy footsteps come crashing through the trees. Marvel tries to pull away from me, but I hold on tightly to his leash, murmuring to him, "It's okay, boy. I'm here. You're safe with me."

"Marvel. Come here, boy."

The voice as cold and hard as granite slices straight through my chest and leaves me trembling more than the Belgian Shepherd wrapped up in my arms. It's Leonid. And he isn't happy.

Marvel whimpers but doesn't move.

"Good boy," I whisper before standing slowly and turning around to face my captor.

His eyes are dark and stormy, his lips set into a grim line as he watches me draw myself to my full height and wrap Marvel's leash around my wrist.

This isn't the man who guided my hand to my pussy and watched me touch myself. This isn't the same man who lifted my skirt inside the maze and made me come all over his tongue, or the man who carried me, shivering, from the dungeon to his guest room and shared his body heat with me to help me heal.

Nonetheless, the butterflies which, until now, have been dormant all my adult life, wake up and start beating those fragile wings against my ribs.

I can't tell what Leonid is thinking, but I can sense the anger emanating in red-hot waves from him. So can Marvel who shuffles closer to my side and places a paw protectively on my foot as if warning me to stay where I am and let him do the negotiating.

Before either of us can speak, Tamara appears beside Leonid. Her cheek is swollen and bloody, the purple bruising already leaking into her eye giving her the macabre appearance of a Halloween mask.

"That's my dog," Leonid growls.

"I wasn't going to take him." My voice sounds pathetic and weak, and I think of Hope and the other women at the refuge, and how they stood up to their abusers. I refuse to let them down. "He followed me."

I slide my eyes across to Tamara whose expression is neutral. She is looking out for herself, and if that means throwing me under the bus, that's exactly what she'll do.

Sure enough, my stomach twists when she says, "She refused to hand over the dog."

A tic appears on Leonid's temple, and his hands ball into fists.

I lift my chin and look him squarely in the eye. "Marvel followed me. He was trying to protect me, and I... I thought I could use all the protection I could get."

He keeps his eyes on me but addresses Tamara. "Tell me what happened."

"We were out walking the dog. You left no orders to keep her inside so—"

"I want to know what happened," Leonid cuts her off.

"The dog ran off. We followed him to the edge of the woods. The printzessa started asking questions about what's on the other side." She pauses, and I think I see a flicker of uncertainty in her eyes. "I told her about the wall. I said that the perimeter is patrolled, and that's when she stole my gun and hit me."

"Where is the gun now?" Still, his eyes don't waver from mine.

"Here." Tamara slides the weapon from her pocket.

Leonid doesn't even look at it. "Empty the bullets."

"Pakhan, I don't understand." The uncertainty dancing behind her eyes morphs into something that looks remarkably like fear from where I'm standing. "Why do you—"

"Empty. The. Bullets."

Tamara does as she is told and tosses the unspent bullets onto the ground at her feet.

"Count them."

"There are five bullets."

"How many did you use trying to stop her from escaping?"

Tamara's eyes flash my way briefly as though daring me to contradict her. "One bullet, Pakhan." The tic in his temple continues to pulse, and she adds, "You warned us not to harm the printzessa."

A gush of warmth spreads through my chest. He warned them not to hurt me.

I wish that we could have a moment alone so that I might explain to him why I ran. If I mean anything to him, if our night of passion meant anything to him other than a quick fuck, then surely, he will understand. He is an intelligent man. Ruthless but intelligent.

"Is that what happened?" The question is aimed at me.

I have two options. I can be honest and tell him what really happened in the hope that he will believe me. Or I can go along with Tamara's version of events and convince him that the attempted escape was my idea.

I force myself not to look at Tamara. I've seen what she and her sister are capable of, and I would rather have them on my side than make enemies of them.

So, I look him directly in the eye and say, "That's what happened."

20

LEONID

In my study, I fill a shot glass with vodka and drink it straight.

It's going to be a long night.

I refill the glass. Knock it back. Wait for the burn that doesn't come.

When I left my brother and sister, I got Marco to drive me to the canine rescue center and I wandered around the building, alone, checking out the animals that had recently arrived. Marco is the only person who knows about my regular contributions to the rescue center. I do it for Marvel. If he hadn't found me when he did, he wouldn't have survived another winter, and every time I look into his eyes, I have to force the image of him dying alone and shivering in a dank alleyway from my head.

Sonia, the rescue center manager, introduced me to a German Shepherd puppy they'd recently recovered from a travelers' site. They'd named her Lucky. If she hadn't been recovered when she was, the puppy would almost certainly have died from starvation, and that was without the flesh wounds around her neck and the fleas and ticks covering her little body.

Lucky came to me, curled up into a tight ball in my lap, and closed her eyes, and I knew that she belonged to Gianna. When I looked at her head resting against my chest, front paws tucked in tightly, all I could see was Gianna curled up in my bed.

Loyal. Trusting. Faithful.

I signed the paperwork with Sonia before I left. I could already picture telling Gianna about Lucky, the way her face would light up with pure joy, the way she would throw her arms around my neck and hug me tightly, her body pressed up against mine.

Then, driving home, I got the call from my men that Gianna and Tamara were walking with Marvel towards the woods surrounding my land.

I didn't think about why.

I didn't consider that she might be trying to escape.

All that was going through my head was that I couldn't protect her if she wasn't on my property, and if anyone harmed her, I would serve time for what I would do to them in return.

Because Gianna isn't like other women. At least, that's what I told myself when I was cradling the white and tan German Shepherd puppy in the rescue center.

I down another vodka shot.

Gianna flashed those turquoise eyes at me, spread her legs wide, begged me to fuck her, and this is the result.

What did I always tell my parents? Love is a weakness. Not that I'm under any illusions that this is love, but I let her into my bed, I let her fill my head with her groans of pleasure, and this is how she repays me.

Only something about this whole episode doesn't sit right with me.

I questioned Olga, who told me that Ms. Sedric came to the kitchen with her breakfast tray and gave some treats to Marvel. Olga said that she left the room shortly after Tamara entered, and that was the last time she saw them.

The guard stationed outside the back door confirmed that Tamara had dismissed him when the two women went outside to walk the dog. The men in the control room were still deciphering the video footage of the brief conversation between Tamara and Gianna that took place inside the kitchen, and Sergei, conveniently, had been called away to the warehouse.

But here's where the story starts to become a little fuzzy around the edges.

Two women, one dark and sharp as steel, the other light and soft as butter despite the core of reinforced metal at her center. I see the bruise on Tamara's cheek. I see it, but I don't believe it was inflicted by Gianna who then promptly handed the gun back to the woman who was supposed to be guarding her. Gianna has grown up in a mafia family. She might not be involved in the family business, but self-preservation will be ingrained in her blood. So, why didn't she keep the gun?

Another shot.

Another flurry of images of Gianna's naked body writhing beneath me while I ram my cock inside her.

Another surge of anger directed at my inability to live by my own beliefs.

Women cannot be trusted.

But Gianna wasn't faking those orgasms. She wasn't faking the way she looked at me with those huge eyes when she kissed me. I'm no expert when it comes to women, but I know how it feels to be played—I still have the Elena scars tattooed across my heart—and Gianna wasn't playing me. The scene over breakfast the morning after she arrived was her idea of using my own testosterone against me, and we all know where that got her.

I've no doubts at all that if Gianna Sedric wanted to escape, she would not be locked up in one of my guest rooms right now. She'd be at home with her family, giving them enough information to take me down within the next twenty-four hours.

So, what the fuck happened this morning?

Between leaving Gianna in my bed, rosy-cheeked, serene, and smelling of sex, and receiving the call from the guards, something snapped. Like a light being flicked on. My gut is telling me that this is down to Tamara, and my gut has never let me down yet.

But I don't like where this is leading.

One of them is lying to me, and I don't tolerate being lied to. Tamara knows this. She has lived with me long enough. Gianna doesn't know me at all, but I can't figure out why she is lying to protect Tamara when it creates more problems for herself.

Two more vodka shots, and I stop overthinking the situation, instead, allowing it to unravel and present itself to me in all its technicolor glory.

Gianna lied because she understood the consequences of Tamara's betrayal, and because that's the kind of person she is. She works at a women's refuge for fuck's sake. She won't see another woman suffer through her actions, so she took the blame instead.

But where does this leave Tamara?

The familiar icy sense of duty crawls through my veins, putting up a heroic battle against the hazy effects of the half-bottle of vodka I've already consumed.

Duty first. Duty to family. Duty to my people. Duty to Gianna.

While she is under my protection, I will not allow her to come to any harm. I stand up too quickly, my brain cells taking a beat to catch up with the movement. It's obvious that I can't trust anyone else to protect her, and while she might be locked inside a guest room with Dmitri standing guard, anyone can get to her.

My blood is pumping around my veins. I can't leave Gianna alone. No one will dare touch her while she's with me or in my quarters, so this is in her best interests. I'll sleep on the couch if that's what she wants, but from now on, she doesn't leave my sight.

I open the door.

Voices coming from the kitchen sober me up instantly, my thoughts immediately ganging up on me. What if Tamara is telling the truth? She has never lied to me before; I trust her and Ivana as much as, if not more than, I trust my own family because they stick with me through choice not through blood.

It's feasible that Gianna stole Tamara's revolver, hit her with it to slow her down, and deliberately handed it back to make it look as if Tamara was lying. The timing is impeccable. She waited for me to fuck her first, she gave me a taste of what it's like to slide in between her open legs and then wham! She hit me with an escape attempt almost before I'd washed her cum from my cock.

There's only one way to resolve the fireworks exploding in my head: speak to Gianna.

Laughter. It sounds like there's a party going on in my kitchen, and the mood I'm in, I'm going to be the biggest fun-sucker the world has ever seen.

I hear Andrej's voice from the hallway. He's telling a joke using a clipped British accent, his voice rising as he builds up to the punchline. He's one of the few people I know who can tell a joke and have people crying with laughter, and he has the uncanny ability to pick up accents from all around the world. He lowers his voice so that I miss the end of the joke, but it's obvious from the ripple of laughter around the room that he has finished his storytelling.

I enter, and silence settles around me. "Don't stop on my account, Andrej."

He raises a beer to his lips and takes a long glug. "I would offer to fetch you a beer from the fridge, brother, but it looks as if you're already a few drinks ahead of me."

Tamara and Ivana are sitting on the breakfast island with their feet on bar stools like this is a public holiday, and I realize that business has been slack for too long, thanks to Xander Amory's relentless attacks. Relaxation isn't in the Ivanov vocabulary. Take your eye off the ball for a fraction of a second and the enemy will be performing a victory dance between the goalposts before you can blink.

"Is everything on track for tonight's shipment?" I address the room and wait to see what comes back to me. In his crate, Marvel rests his head on his front paws and his eyes on me.

"Sergei has it under control." This is Ivana.

"I want you to be present, Andrej."

Andrej strokes his chin as though contemplating whether to shave or grow his stubble for another day. "Not my remit."

"I'm making it your remit. Xander Amory has a taste for the blood of our men, it seems. I trust you to make sure that the next blood he samples is tainted with something lethal."

Andrej's mouth contorts into a lopsided grimace. He might be the comedian of the family, but he's also the one without a conscience. He stands up, glugs the rest of his beer, and studies the empty bottle. "Sounds like an offer I can't refuse. Although you do understand that Xander doesn't personally steal our shipments out from under our noses, right?"

"He's a rodent. He'll snatch a poisoned crumb if he thinks it will add some zeroes to his bank account."

I keep my eyes fixed on my little brother, but I sense the sisters following the conversation closely. Bringing Andrej in is a last resort. I was hoping to save it until I was done with Gianna, but after this morning's fiasco, it can't wait. There's a loose knot in my team and I need it tightened.

"Point taken, brother." My brother's gaze slides sideways and settles on Tamara's swollen cheek and black eye. "I was hoping to meet our little printzessa first."

Ivana and Tamara bristle like cats on the scent of a bird, and I clench my jaw. As the youngest sibling, Andrej has always had the luxury of treating life as his latest video game, something I've learned to ignore over the years. But not when it comes to Gianna.

"She isn't a doll to be dressed up and pushed around a pretend house."

"Really?" His eyebrows zigzag across his forehead. "That isn't what I've heard."

I breathe deeply, regulating my heart rate. The fact that he has heard anything outside of what we discussed earlier with our sister is pushing me to my limits; any information being leaked, even within family, is too much information.

"What exactly have you heard?"

"That you let her into your bed and then she tried to escape." The lopsided smile reappears. "You want to win the war, you've got to learn to lock it inside your pants."

I count to three. Slowly. Biting back the retorts that I would fling at my brother if we didn't have an audience.

"I'll be sure to bear that in mind."

"Good. Because I'd hate to see you lose your precious asset when the fun is only just beginning." Andrej tosses the empty bottle into the recycling.

The sisters both hop off the breakfast island to leave with Andrej.

"Tamara stays here."

"But, Pakhan, I—"

"That's an order."

Tamara holds my gaze. This goes way deeper than jealousy of the printzessa. The two sisters might be calculating, ruthless, and even reckless on occasions, but one thing they are not is careless. She knew that I would question this morning's events, so she's either trying to play me against Gianna, or she isn't the person I thought she was, and there's only one way to find out: process of elimination.

I don't hang around. My brother can show himself out. Tamara can wait.

I want to hear what happened from the printzessa first.

I dismiss the guard stationed outside the guest room where Gianna is being held, but I hesitate before barging in. Now that I'm here, I'm torn between demanding the truth and leaving her to stew on whatever is going on between her and Tamara. I know that when I'm alone with her, I'll struggle to 'lock it in my pants' as my brother so eloquently described it.

This is what she has done to me.

I don't believe in witchcraft, but she has somehow bewitched me to the point where I close my eyes and all I can see is her smile as she opens her legs and hooks a finger at me to come inside.

Deep breath. I rearrange the bulge inside my pants; I don't want her to believe that she has the advantage the instant I walk into the room.

Gianna is lying on her back on the bed when I enter. Awake. She stands up when she sees that it's me, but she keeps her distance, and that rips a hole in my heart. We had trust. She had the option to walk away from me and forget that the kiss ever happened, and she chose me before duty.

She chose me.

"Is Marvel alright?" Her eyes lock onto mine, gauging my reaction before I speak.

"He is fine. No thanks to you."

I see the hurt flicker behind her eyes and the way she juts her chin. Defiant. "I would never hurt him."

"But you knew that he would protect you with his life."

She swallows and looks away. I don't consider it a win.

"I-I didn't take Marvel with me."

I lean back against the closed door, afraid to get too close to her. Afraid of what will happen if I'm close enough to touch her.

"Yet you were caught running away from my house with him."

"He followed me."

"Why didn't you shoot Tamara while you had the chance?"

I'm giving her the opportunity to tell the truth. To snitch on Tamara if she convinced Gianna to lie on her behalf. To choose me again.

"I didn't want her blood on my hands."

"Did she offer to help you escape?" My jaw is so tight I can feel my back teeth grinding.

She peers directly into my eyes, and says, "No." But it's all a little too forced for my liking. Gianna knows that I don't believe the story, same as she knows that avoiding my gaze will make her look guilty.

I step closer. "What did she offer you?"

"Nothing. I overpowered her. She didn't shoot because you'd warned her not to hurt me. She knew that I'd be captured before I made it to the perimeter."

"But still, you didn't turn back. You might've been killed."

"Killing me isn't part of the plan though, is it, Leonid?" She narrows those beautiful turquoise eyes just enough to let me know that she isn't defeated. Yet.

"No," I concede. I can't expect her to be honest with me if I'm not prepared to give her honesty in return.

"But fucking me was."

I hear the tremor in her voice and step closer, reaching out to cup her face in my hands. But she pulls away.

"Fucking you was never part of the plan, Gianna." I lower my hands and keep my voice steady. Because right now, getting her to believe me is all that's important.

Xander Amory can go fuck himself. All I care about is making sure that Gianna Sedric doesn't get caught in the crossfire.

"So, then what was, Leonid, huh? What was part of the plan? Getting me to kiss you? Getting me to spend the night in your room or the part where I showed you what I wanted you to do to me?"

I can feel the heat emanating from her cheeks, but she isn't finished.

"Introducing me to Marvel was a great strategy, I've got to hand it to you. You knew I wouldn't be able to resist your dog, and it made you look less like a monster and more like a regular human being in my eyes."

I suppress the smile that's aching to spread across my face. "What did Tamara tell you?"

"That the great master plan was to seduce me and send me back home unable to go through with the marriage to Seamus." She blinks hard, tears making her eyes appear twice their normal size.

I want to fold her into my arms and never let her go. I want to catch her tears on my tongue and kiss her better. But touching her right now will only lead to me ripping her clothes off, pushing her back onto the bed and eating her till she screams my name, and I can't bear the thought of her rejection.

"You got what you wanted." She pushes her shoulders back and faces me squarely. "So, why am I still here?"

"Here's the thing, Gianna. I didn't get what I wanted." I reach for her hand which feels cold and frail in mine, but at least she doesn't snatch it away. "I got way more."

She blinks again, her tears finally collecting on her lashes. "I-I don't understand."

"You're still here because I'm not prepared to let you go. I can't lie to you. My intention was to get under your skin, to make you want me, and send you home even less inclined to marry the Irish *pank*. But you gave yourself to me so freely..."

I raise her hand to my lips and kiss her palm.

"So openly..."

I kiss her wrist and trail my tongue along her arm to the crease inside her elbow.

"And with such utter abandon..."

I pull her close to me and kiss her damp eyelids, holding her body against mine with my arms wrapped around her.

"The plan was scrapped the instant you agreed to come to me, Gianna." My voice is husky with desire for her, my lips brushing hers.

But I still see the uncertainty in her eyes, and I wish I could take back the plan, make Xander Amory and this never-ending war go away, and start afresh. Perhaps meet her at a nightclub in town or at the airport or a taxi rank or any one of the regular meet-cutes two people destined to meet might have.

"Why should I believe you?" Her breath is warm against my lips.

"Because you're still here. You didn't escape when you had the chance."

I pause, uncertain how far to push it. I've never had to convince a woman that I find her desirable. I've never even had to fight for a woman before, not even Elena. But I already understand that Gianna Sedric is worth fighting for.

"And because I think that you want me as much as I want you."

I wind her hair around my fingers and crush her lips with mine. And Gianna doesn't resist. She stands on tiptoes, head tipped back to meet my kisses hungrily, her hands sliding around my neck.

My cock responds by wedging itself between our bodies.

Tiny heart-wrenching whimpers escape her lips as I hoist her up into my arms, and she wraps her legs around my waist. I turn around and sit down on the bed with Gianna on my lap. I drag her T-shirt over her head and fumble with the buttons on her pants while she tugs my shirt open, her kisses hot and hungry and greedy. My shirt follows hers onto the floor.

Gianna pushes me back horizontally across the bed, tugs off her pants and straddles me naked. She drags her tongue across my jawline and nibbles on my earlobes. Down to my collarbone, between my ribs, and then she finds my nipples, nibbling them between her front teeth.

My cock throbs at the wetness between her legs that's seeping onto my skin, and she drags my pants over my hips, her eyes widening as it springs free. Cupping my balls with one hand, she grips the base of my cock with the other and teases the head with her tongue.

But I grip her wrist and her hips and pull her around so that she's straddling my face. "You're so fucking ready for me, Gianna." I open her up with my fingers and tease her clit with the tip of my tongue.

Gianna's body immediately spasms, and she grips my cock tighter. "Leonid..." She breathes my name huskily, brushing my chest with her erect nipples.

"Do you want me to stop?" I rest my head back against the comforter and insert a finger inside her instead.

"No." She wraps her lips around my cock and slides her tongue back and forth across the slit.

"Good girl." I work her with my finger, matching my movements to the flicks of her tongue. "You're so wet, Gianna. Did you start without me?"

"I-no." She stops licking and turns her head to look at me.

"Don't stop. You're not allowed to come before I do."

Her pussy clenches around my fingers, and she tries to pull away, but I don't let her. "Leo, I won't be able to stop it."

"You can try for me, can't you?" I drag my tongue across her clit, still working her with my finger. I slide in a second finger. "I can't hear you."

"I... I don't know."

Her pussy is already spasming, and I haven't even gotten started yet. "Wrong answer." I suck her sweet pussy, flicking her clit with my tongue.

"I'll try."

I would smile, but this is game on. "You'd better make me come then, Gianna."

She grips my erection in her fist and slides the head into her mouth. I give her a couple of beats to get into a rhythm before I slide my fingers out of her and slide my tongue in. She tastes so fucking sweet I want to make her come on my face all night. I want to wake up with her pussy in my face so that it's the first thing I taste in the morning.

Her pleasure eclipses my own. My balls are full for her, but this is one game she'll never win. Even when she takes all of me into her mouth.

"Fuck, Gianna." I stop sucking on her. My breaths are rapid, my pulse racing. "That feels so good."

She slides my cock out of her mouth and supports her upper body on her arms either side of my hips. "Only good? Surely, you can do better than that."

I bounce my cock back to her mouth. "It feels fucking awesome."

I sense her smile as she crushes my length between her breasts and rubs them up and down me.

"So, the printzessa is playing to win, huh?"

I pull her hips down onto my face and push my tongue into her as far as the hilt, rubbing her clit with my dripping wet fingers. Her explosion is almost instantaneous. But she isn't getting away with it that easily. Each time her orgasm starts to fade, I hit the spot again with my tongue until finally, she admits defeat and releases my cock, unable to focus on anything but the pleasure rippling through her body.

21

GIANNA

My orgasms leave me feeling weak and limp, like I could sleep for a month. But Leonid turns me around and eases me onto his cock so that I'm facing him.

"Ride me, Gianna."

I can't look away from him. He doesn't allow me to feel self-conscious about being a novice at this. The gleam in his eyes makes me feel like the most beautiful woman alive. Like a ... princess.

"Good girl."

It isn't meant to be patronizing, and it's what I want to hear. Each time he calls me his good girl, I get a surge of adrenaline through my veins, and any shyness I felt the first time he kissed me in the maze evaporates a little bit more.

He squeezes my breasts, and I lean into him, our skin slamming together as I thrust my hips back and forth, then pausing to grind in circles. I slide off him and lick my taste from his cock. Then, I guide him back inside me and kiss Leo, sharing my juices with him.

It's hard to believe that I'm doing this. Me. The twenty-three-year-old virgin promised to a mafia boss. Ex-virgin, I remind myself. Because Leonid is like a rare dish that, once tasted, will never be beaten.

I want him. I want him with every fiber of my being. I could no more walk away and forget this ever happened, than I could stop breathing. He, this, our bodies coming together, has become my oxygen. Leonid Ivanov is the fix that I need to keep me functioning, and I want to spend whatever time we have left together exploring every part of him.

"Fuck me, you little minx." He pulls my hips above his face and lowers my pussy onto his tongue. "Fuck my tongue, Gianna."

And I do. Using the wall as support, I ride his tongue, my orgasm shuddering through me again and again.

Leonid sits on the edge of the bed, and I sit on his cock, riding him from behind. He grips my hips, making my thrusts more powerful. I hold onto his thighs, back arched, and head tipped backwards, my breasts bouncing with each movement. When he comes inside me, his hand wraps around my neck, he tilts my face towards him and fills my mouth with his tongue.

I feel him inside me, his body jerking with his own orgasm, and I never want to let him go.

We collapse into a sweaty heap on the bed, and he pulls me to him, his arms wrapped around me almost tenderly. He smooths my hair away from my face and smothers me with kisses.

"You're so beautiful, Gianna. Don't ever let anyone tell you otherwise, do you hear me?"

Tears prickle my eyes, and I try to blink them away.

"Hey, what are these for?" he murmurs, catching them with his fingertip.

"I don't know." The lie is spontaneous.

Of course, I know. It sounded so final, *don't ever let anyone tell you otherwise, do you hear me*? A reminder that this thing between us has an end date. That one day soon, I'll go back to my family and be expected to return to a way of life that no longer exists now that Leonid Ivanov is a part of it.

I'm not the same person I was when I arrived. Whether it was intentional or not, I will never be the same person again, but I don't know what the new me is supposed to do now. Perhaps Leonid did intend to corrupt me, but there isn't a chance in hell that he considered his actions might have such a devastating effect on me.

"No one ever told me that I'm beautiful before."

His eyes darken momentarily. Then, he grips my chin between his thumb and forefinger and kisses my lips. "They must be blind. But perhaps I should be grateful to them."

"Why?"

"Because this beauty is all mine." He kisses me harder, his lips crushing mine, his tongue forcing my mouth open. "You're all mine, printzessa, and I guard what's mine with my life."

"But—"

"No buts." His face is so close to mine I can see the brown and gold flecks in his amber eyes. "Do you trust me?"

Do I? I know what Tamara said, but his actions say something entirely different. He took my virginity already, he didn't have to come back for more, and although he knows that Tamara and I lied about my botched escape attempt, there have been no repercussions. For me at least.

And when he says that he will protect me with his life, I believe him.

"Yes."

He pulls away just enough for me to see his smile. "Good. Because I promise that I will always look after you, Gianna. I won't let anyone hurt you."

More tears spill over my bottom lashes. "You shouldn't make promises that you can't keep."

"I don't."

He settles my head on his shoulder, pulls the comforter over our naked bodies, and closes his eyes. He falls asleep almost instantly.

I watch him sleeping. Supporting my upper body on one elbow, I study his face, the lines fanning out from the corners of his eyes, the dark stubble on his jaw, the narrow scar that slices his left eyebrow in two, the tattoos covering his torso, neck and arms. Even in slumber, he is like a coiled spring waiting to be released, and I wonder if he ever truly relaxes.

I eventually fall asleep in his arms to the tune of his steady heartbeat.

He is gone when I wake up. I sit up and stretch, the comforter sliding off my naked body revealing swollen nipples and faint marks across my pale flesh from the stubble on his chin. I trace the marks with my fingertip down to my sex and the raised marks on my inner thighs.

This beauty is all mine.

Maybe it shouldn't make me smile, it's possessive after all, but it does. It fills me with a sense of contentment that I don't think I've ever felt before. Is this how Mel felt when she met Xander? Mel changed too when they first met; it was as if a light had been ignited inside her, and she glowed whenever Xander's name was mentioned.

I wish I could talk to Mel. I know now that I'm not ready to leave Leonid, but I just want one conversation with my sister so that she can tell me she felt the same way about Xander. So that I can start to figure out what this is.

I shower and towel-dry my hair. When I hear voices outside the room, I barely have time to pull on the clothes that have been left in the closet for me before the door opens and Leonid appears with a wide grin on his face.

"You didn't lock the door." I didn't even think of checking when I woke up, but from the voices I heard outside, it's obvious that Leonid didn't leave me unguarded.

"It can be arranged." He half-turns back towards the open doorway. "But I have a surprise for you."

"A surprise?" My eyes flit back to the door expecting Mel to walk in at any moment and tell me off for not calling her sooner. But no one comes in.

Despite the immaculate suit and freshly shaved jaw, there's a lightness to Leonid today, like his aura somehow turned from midnight-black to sunny-yellow overnight. Okay, so maybe not sunny-yellow, but the hazy colors of a summer dawn instead.

"Are you coming with me to find out what it is, or do I need to send it back?"

"I'm coming." I cross the room, stand on tiptoes, and kiss him on the lips, heat spreading from my chest and into my face when I spot the guard watching us from outside the doorway.

Leonid doesn't react. He turns around and escorts me from the room ignoring my sideways glances and the excitement oozing from my pores.

"Stop looking at me like that. If I tell you now, it'll spoil the surprise."

"Is my sister here?" I blurt out before I can stop myself. "Is Mel here?"

Leonid's expression is impassive. Even when we reach the kitchen, and he opens the door wide for me to enter first, he still gives nothing away.

Then I hear the bark that sounds nothing like Marvel, and my heart somersaults as a fluffy, tan-and-white puppy comes skittering across the tiled floor towards us. I crouch and scoop the puppy into my arms, while she climbs up me, placing large front paws onto my shoulders so that she can lick my face.

"Her name is Lucky."

I giggle in between sloppy kisses and give up trying to deter Lucky from her public display of affection. "She's ... so ... cute," I manage, narrowly avoiding her over-enthusiastic tongue. "Who does she ... belong to?"

"She's yours, Gianna." His voice takes on a serious tone. "If you want her."

My chest aches at the unexpected gift. I squeeze Lucky so tightly that she squirms and wriggles out of my clutches, skidding back across the floor and colliding with the bowl of water that has been set down for her.

I stand up and slide my hand into Leo's. "Why did you...?" I don't even know how to finish the question.

"I saw how easily Marvel warmed to you, and I didn't want to lose him."

I try to ignore the reference to me leaving again. I don't want anything to spoil this moment. "Thank you. She's beautiful."

"Like you." He takes my chin between his thumb and forefinger, but before he can kiss me, Marvel barks at us from his crate on the other side of the room.

I pull away, grinning. "How does Marvel feel about his new companion?"

"He's already in protective big-brother mode."

I slant my eyes at him. "Maybe I should try to escape more often. You have room for a few more dogs at least."

Leo's kiss is demanding, and I feel the air leaving my lungs as he presses his body against mine. "Next time, you might not be quite so fortunate." His amber eyes lock onto mine. "Promise me that you won't do anything foolish."

"I promise." My heart is thudding inside my chest. It's an easy promise to make.

I spend the next few hours playing in the garden with the dogs while Leonid goes to the office. He was right, Marvel is already acting like the doting big brother, refusing to let Lucky out of his sight, while the puppy masters the art of wrapping everyone around her little finger.

In typical puppy-fashion, she finds everything an adventure. She darts towards the edge of the pool and would dive straight in if she doesn't catch a glimpse of a butterfly flitting around the buddleia bushes. She chases a ball around the lawn, tumbling over it and face planting the grass. She tries climbing up Marvel to kiss him and isn't deterred when, every time, he shrugs her off and sideswipes her with his hind legs.

"Lucky." I pick her up and nuzzle her fluffy face. "You're a determined young lady. I think that you and I are going to be best friends."

Leo didn't mention what would happen when I return home, but he said that she's mine, and whatever happens, I'm not leaving her behind.

When both dogs are exhausted and napping in Marvel's huge crate, Lucky tucked between her big brother's paws, I go back to the guest room. It feels wrong to be hanging around the house when Leo isn't here. But the guard is waiting for me, and the door is open.

"What's happened?" I ask, trying to peer inside. I've had no conversations with anyone other than Tamara, but my pulse is racing too quickly at the prospect of a repeat performance of yesterday's escape bid.

"The pakhan asked that you be moved to his quarters." There's no hint of emotion or judgment in his tone; he's simply stating a fact.

"He did?" I try to quell the excitement gurgling inside my chest.

I want to ask what this means, but Leo isn't back yet, and he didn't give me any warning that this was going to happen. Is he worried that Tamara might try to help me flee a second time? Or does he feel, like me, that the air he breathes isn't the same when we're not together?

The guard, whose name I still don't know, waits outside while I enter Leo's room. I don't know what's expected of me, but I feel like an intruder, until I see the small dog bed in the corner of the room. Braver, I enter the walk-in dressing room and find one side filled with clothes that all appear to be my size. Does Leo keep a selection of outfits just in case the need should arise, or did he send Tamara shopping for clothes this morning? I can imagine how well that would've gone down and make a mental note to check the clothes for strategic rips and sharp objects hidden inside the seams.

I haven't eaten yet today, so I walk back to the guard and ask him to escort me to the kitchen. I don't know if it's my imagination, but there seems to be more security staff than usual positioned around the house. I instinctively glance up at the ceiling and catch a glimpse of the flashing red light of the camera.

Tamara and Ivana are in the kitchen, seated at the breakfast counter with their lunch and a couple of cans of soda, and my stomach twists. I hoped that the room would be empty. I get the impression that Olga doesn't particularly like me, but she's less abrasive than the two sisters, and keeps her opinions to herself while she gets on with her work.

I feel awkward helping myself to food with them around, so instead, I find the dog treats and sit on the floor with Lucky, trying to teach her to sit and give me her paw.

The guard who accompanied me sits with them, and the three speak in hushed tones. I try not to listen, but the atmosphere in the room is oppressive, like the calm before the storm clouds start rolling. Each time there's a lull in their conversation I feel their eyes boring into the back of my skull. Lucky is oblivious, and I try to be more like her, but it's difficult when the only person who is happy about my presence in the house isn't around.

Marvel keeps one eye on the group sitting at the counter behind me, and lies with his haunches poised ready to spring him into full-on attack mode. More guards appear in the doorway and walk away again once they've accounted for everyone present.

Something bad is going down. I sense it. I know what it's like to live with the constant threat of danger hanging over my head, and I can feel the tension emanating from the other people in the room.

"Who's handling it?" the guard asks.

There's a pause before Ivana answers, "Andrej." Her voice is rougher around the edges than her sister's, a heavy smoker's voice.

"He was here yesterday," Tamara adds. "Pakhan said it was time."

Time for what? And who is Andrej? I shouldn't be eavesdropping, but there's no mistaking the bitterness in Tamara's tone.

"We hit them last night." Ivana drops her voice a notch, but either she wants me to hear their conversation, or she never learned to be quiet.

Either way, she can only mean one thing: Leonid's men hit Xander Amory's mob last night while Leo was in my bed. Something cold and slimy slithers down my spine. Was I a distraction to take his mind off what was going on outside? Or had he not intended to spend the night with me when he came to my door?

Before I can think about what this means for me, I hear the screeching of tires outside the house. The two women and the guard are on their feet in an instant, guns in their hands.

Panic solidifies inside my stomach.

Has Xander come for me? Where is Leonid? Will the guards try to stop him from taking me or will they hand me over. What if someone gets killed...?

Without thinking, I scoop Lucky into my arms and put her back inside the crate with Marvel, locking the door so that they can't escape. Then I stand in front of the crate, shielding them with my body as best I can.

My heart beats erratically when Tamara and Ivana place themselves between me and the door, while the guard presses his back against the wall behind the door, both hands wrapped around the handle of his revolver which is raised to chest height. They're expecting trouble. Despite everything, the sisters' instinct is to follow orders and protect me, and for once, I'm grateful as no one is likely to hand me a gun to defend myself.

Footsteps inside the house.

A voice calls out, "Don't shoot. It's Marco."

A glance passes between the sisters and the guard, but no one moves. Until a short, stocky man enters the kitchen carrying a sturdy box in front of him, followed by several more armed security staff all dressed in black. He knows his way around, and they obviously know him. Tamara and Ivana wait until he places the box on the island counter and steps away, then they sweep in and peer inside.

Their faces are turned away from me, but I watch their spines stiffen. The temperature inside the kitchen seems to drop a few degrees.

"Who?" Ivana asks.

"We don't know yet," Marco answers.

"Has anyone told Leonid?" Tamara slides a phone from her pocket.

Marco nods. "He knows."

"Andrej worked his magic last night." Tamara again. I still don't know what's in the box, but she sounds disappointed that she missed whatever magic display Andrej put on.

"Maybe the printzessa will recognize it." Without warning, Ivana removes the object from the box and turns around to show me.

My stomach churns, and I have to cover my mouth with both hands to stop myself from being sick when I see what she's holding. It's a hand. It only takes me a beat to understand that this isn't some Halloween prop for a costume party, and that the blood and flesh clinging to the wrist is real.

Did Xander send this to Leonid? What kind of grisly warning is this supposed to be? Why didn't he just track me down and set me free? Why did he have to kill someone and deliver their hand to his enemy in a box?

What kind of man did my sister marry?

It's late when I sit up in Leo's king-sized bed and switch on the lamp on the nightstand. My sleep has been fitful; it feels like it should be almost dawn but it's only a little past midnight. Still, Leo's side of the bed is untouched.

I lean across and breathe in the smell of his pillow. It's cold to touch even though I catch the lingering scent of musky cologne that sends a shiver traveling through my body.

He didn't come home after the macabre delivery earlier today. He didn't get a message to me, and no one would tell me where he was or what he was doing; I guess it's on a need-to-know basis, and I don't fall into the right category.

But I can't stay here knowing that he might be in danger.

I get up, pull a bathrobe on and fasten it around my waist before heading to the door. As expected, the guard is instantly alert.

"Where is Leonid?" I don't give him the option to tell me that he can't answer the question, but he remains silent. "Is he in the house?"

"Yes, ma'am."

"Take me to him."

"I'm sorry, ma'am, but I—"

"Take me to him or I'll tell him that you entered his room unannounced while I was sleeping in his bed." His expression tells me all I need to know—Leonid would kill anyone who dared to approach me without his knowledge.

He inclines his head and walks off, and I follow him along the softly lit corridors and downstairs to a room that I haven't yet been inside.

"Thank you." I offer him a smile that goes unacknowledged. Perhaps he will be in trouble for bringing me here, but I'll fight his corner if I must and tell Leo that I insisted.

I knock softly and enter the room.

This must be Leo's study. Lamps are lit on a bureau behind the wide mahogany desk, casting a golden glow across the room that doesn't quite reach the corners. Leo is sitting in a high-backed leather seat behind the desk, a bottle of vodka and a shot glass in front of him. His suit jacket is hanging from a coat stand. He has removed his tie and opened the top couple of buttons of his shirt, but it is the weariness in his eyes that makes me gasp.

"Leo?"

He rises, swaying unsteadily on his feet. "Gianna? What are you doing here?" His eyes instinctively drift towards the closed door.

"I made him bring me to you. I was worried about you."

He shakes his head, a small smile appearing and vanishing in a fraction of a moment. "You shouldn't be here."

"Here as in your study or do you mean here in your house?"

"I shouldn't have dragged you into this, Gianna." He sits back down heavily in his seat, refills his glass with vodka and knocks it back in one.

I walk around the desk, his eyes following my every move, and kneel in front of him, spreading his legs wide so that I can shuffle in between them. "I'm here now. Will you tell me what's going on?"

"I'm sorry you had to see that." He makes no move to touch me. When he speaks, his voice is slurred. "I wanted to keep you out of it. I wanted to protect you from it, from seeing the kind of man I am."

"You didn't deliver someone's hand in a box." His eyes linger on mine and something melts inside me. "You can't protect me from reality, Leo. I'm a Sedric, remember?"

"You don't understand…" His hand drifts towards my face and I grab hold of it, pressing his knuckles to my lips.

"I understand more than you give me credit for." I push him back in his seat and unfasten his pants. "I understand that you want me as much as I want you."

"Gianna." He tries to push my hands away, to stop me from touching him, and I move his hands down by his sides. "Stop."

I smile. "I'm not one of your men to be ordered about. And we both know that if you really wanted me to stop, you'd be on your feet and dragging me back to the guard waiting outside the door."

His eyes snap towards the door and back again.

I tug down the zip of his pants, slide my hand inside, and free his cock. "Now tell me that you don't want this."

In response, he raises his hand to the back of my head and guides my mouth onto him.

I watch him closely as my lips close around his erection and I lick the head, already sticky with pre-cum. In the glow of the table lamps, his cheekbones appear even more chiseled than usual, his eyes so dark they're like bullets. But his features soften as I slide him deeper and deeper into my mouth fighting the gag reflex because being his 'good girl' is what we both need tonight.

His hands fist in my hair, and he holds me still, sliding my mouth on and off his erection until tears trickle from my eyes. "Make me come, Gianna." He sounds so vulnerable that I grip the base with one hand and squeeze tightly while I suck until my cheeks ache, the fingers of my other hand trailing over his balls.

I feel the pulsing through his length a moment before he grips my hair so tightly my scalp burns. Then his cum spurts down the back of my throat and coats my tongue and the back of my teeth. I swallow.

But before I can react, Leo lowers me backwards onto the floor and opens the bathrobe, ripping open the buttons of his shirt that I was wearing in bed. He studies my naked body like I'm a priceless painting, and I already know that no one else will ever look at me this way.

He gets down on his knees and raises my feet so that they're over his shoulders. "Hold on tight, printzessa. I'm going to make you come like you've never come before."

He raises my hips off the floor, supporting my lower body with his thighs, giving me an unobstructed view as he buries his face in my pussy. His tongue is hot and wet, and my pussy constricts around it welcoming the first orgasm almost immediately.

But Leo doesn't stop. He licks me inside and out, his tongue hitting the spot every time. I reach behind me, holding onto the legs of a sturdy seat pressed up against the wall, and ride the crest of an orgasm that just keeps on coming. Then he's inside me, his body crushing mine, his fist gripping my wrists behind my head so that I'm pinned to the floor.

"I've never seen anyone come the way you do," he murmurs, grinding his cock so deep inside me there isn't a part of me that doesn't feel it. "You love coming for me, don't you?"

"Yes."

His hips slam against me, driving his cock even deeper. My knees are almost touching the floor behind my head, and I can feel the burn of the carpet on my back, but if I could suck him in deeper I would.

"Say it."

"I love coming for you."

"Come for me now, Gianna. Show me how much you want me."

He grinds his cock into me, round and around and ever deeper until I can't think about anything else but the pleasure exploding inside my body.

"There's my good girl." He smothers my mouth with his kisses until our bodies finally stop shuddering.

22

LEONID

Victoria's eyes follow me as I enter the boardroom, walk around the table, and take my seat. She's wearing her customary pantsuit, today's color choice: black. Appropriate. She has a cup of steaming black coffee in front of her alongside her tablet.

Andrej sits across the table from her, chair pushed back, one leg crossed over the other. He smells of perfume and last night's liquor. The smudges under his eyes are like fading shadows compared to the bruise-colored pouches that circle our sister's eyes. Everything is just a job to Andrej; he doesn't take his work home with him.

"The printzessa keep you awake last night, brother?" He swallows a mouthful of creamy coffee and smiles.

I fill my cup with freshly brewed coffee and add a spoonful of brown sugar. No cream. Andrej is closer to the truth than he realizes, but for the first time, a hangover is squeezing my brain in a vice-like grip, and I need the caffeine to hit my veins. Quickly.

Victoria begins. "You know it makes my life easier when you keep me in the loop. I had to deal with our parents last night, and where were my brothers?"

It's a rhetorical question. She could probably hazard a fair guess as to what we were both doing and would rather be spared the sordid details.

Andrej chuckles. "And this is exactly the reason why some things are best left unsaid. If anyone can cope under pressure, it's you, sis."

"I think what Andrej is trying to say is thank you, Victoria." I'm in no mood for my brother's childish humor this morning.

He did what I asked him to do. He planted the seed for Xander Amory when he had the head of one of his men delivered to him in a velvet-lined casket with an apple in his mouth like a stuffed pig. He opened the floodgates, showed the Sicilian a way in, and waited for him to bite.

Which he inevitably did. In typical Amory style, the severed hand delivered to my home belonged to the future son-in-law of the Chicago police commissioner. The same police commissioner who raided my warehouses a couple of nights ago on a tip-off from the Sicilian mob. The same police commissioner who is determined to clamp down on organized crime in his city commencing with the Ivanov family.

"We had no choice." I down the liquid in my cup and refill it. The buzz is nowhere near strong enough yet.

"Bull-fucking-shit, Leo." Victoria's eyes harden. "You had plenty of choices, but you can't see beyond this ridiculous vendetta against Amory. You don't even care that an innocent man was murdered last night."

She's angry, I get it. When our parents call in Victoria, we all know that shit is going down. But this is what she's paid to do: keep us looking visibly legal, keep us on the right side of the police commissioner, and clear up the mess. My sister is the only person in the world I can trust with this, but Andrej is right, no one can resolve issues on the spot the way Victoria can, which is why I kept her in the dark.

"Firstly, the guy wasn't innocent."

"True." Andrej inclines his head. "No one ever is."

Victoria inhales deeply and flashes him a warning look to keep quiet if he knows what's good for him. "Go on, Leo."

"He wasn't receiving handouts from the Italians for no reason."

Her expression remains neutral. "And secondly?"

"Secondly..." Fuck, I've lost my train of thought, and I can't tell if it's the hangover or the mental image of Gianna watching me lick out her pussy on the floor of my study last night.

"Please don't try telling me that you do care." Victoria is still waiting for me to give her something she can work with, and until she gets it, she'll be in full-on Rottweiler mode.

I rest my elbows on the table and lean forward. "Xander Amory knows that I'm holding Gianna, but what has he done about it?" I don't wait for my siblings to respond. "He's biding his time. All Andrej did was give him a little push in the right direction."

"Which direction is that?" Victoria asks.

"Straight into a blackout tunnel. Now all we have to do is block both ends and trap him inside."

"Wonderful imagery there, brother," Andrej says. "Anyone would think you've been reading the classics in your spare time."

"Andrej!" Victoria snaps. "If you've got nothing constructive to say then keep your fucking mouth shut."

"Whoa, sis." He raises his hands in mock surrender. "If I'd known you were going to be this antsy, I'd have brought the swear jar. I could be on my way to Vegas now with a pocket full of cash." At Victoria's pursed lips, he draws an imaginary zip across his mouth.

"Leo, please continue."

"Xander will try to pin the murder on us. It plays straight into his hands if the commissioner takes us down. The war will be over, and he'll declare himself the victor."

"Okay." Victoria stares at a spot behind my left shoulder while she processes the information so far. "That would never work. He's not exactly Mr. Innocent; he wouldn't risk bringing the spotlight down on his own head at the same time."

She's intelligent, my sister. She graduated from Harvard with the highest honors in her year, but it's her natural intuition that sets her apart from her peers. This is why I could never run the family business without her.

"The victim wasn't his intended target." That gets her full attention.

"Who was?"

"A mole."

"A mole?" She shakes her head. "Come on, Leo, you've got to give me more than this."

"I will when I've figured it out."

Victoria addresses Andrej. "Did you know about this?"

Andrej makes an exaggerated display of unzipping his mouth. "I don't know who it is either, if that's what you're asking."

Victoria's shoulders slump. "What the fuck, Leo. Why didn't you mention this sooner? What are you going to do about it?"

Her tone has lost some of its abrasiveness. She is the only person I have ever told about what I witnessed in our father's study when I was five years old.

"I'll sort it."

Andrej is about to mention Gianna's failed escape attempt, but I shoot him down with a barely perceptible shake of my head. The second coffee is starting to hit the spot, and this game of chess with my rivals is what I do best.

"Fine." Victoria's tone makes it blatantly obvious that everything is far from fine, but she knows when to stop pushing. Another quality that makes her the best. "So, how did the police commissioner's future son-in-law got caught in the crossfire?"

"Let's just say that it was a case of wrong place, wrong time. It was too late for Xander to pull out, so he went with Plan B."

Victoria steeples her fingers on the table. "So, now what?"

I refill my cup a third time, taking my time. I need Victoria on board with what I'm about to suggest. It doesn't matter what Andrej thinks; we've both learned to work around him over the years.

"Xander has never gotten the police commissioner on his side. They tolerate each other while the Amory Corp funds the commissioner's vacation homes. Xander is too volatile for the relationship to go any further."

"Our mother however…"

I smile. "Our mother is close to the commissioner's wife. They've come to respect one another through their philanthropic involvement. He won't want to hit us if he can find a way around it because his wife will make his life a living hell."

"So, what do you propose?"

"We're going to build and fund a women's refuge in the city."

Silence. Victoria hasn't immediately quashed the idea which is a good start.

"Have you discussed this with Gianna Sedric?" she asks eventually.

"Not yet. She was working in a women's refuge in Montenegro before her family requested her presence back in Chicago."

Victoria unlocks her tablet, and I give her time to do whatever research can't wait until the meeting is over. "So, you want our mother to sell the idea to the commissioner's wife."

"With your assistance and expertise."

"Don't flatter me, Leo. It doesn't suit you." Victoria looks up from her tablet. "And you think this will sway the commissioner's attention in our favor."

"I know it will."

"That's it?" Andrej's voice slices through the air in the boardroom. "That's your master plan? Throw a fucking refuge into the mix and convince the cops to look the other way?"

I bristle at his choice of words. I haven't seen Gianna at work, but I've seen how she is with Marvel and Lucky, and it doesn't take rocket science to figure out that helping people and animals less fortunate than herself is her passion. I want this to work for her sake as well as to get Xander Amory off my case.

"Andrej." Victoria doesn't care for his tone either.

"What?" He uncrosses his legs and swings his seat around to face the table. "You're not buying into this shit! You know he's doing this for the little printzessa, right?"

"So, what if he is?"

Andrej narrows his eyes. "You don't think it is out of character for our big brother to suddenly announce that he has a caring side? What next, huh? He'll take a sabbatical and go set up a gorilla sanctuary in Rwanda?"

"I revert back to my initial observation, Andrej." Victoria stares him out. "If you have nothing constructive to say, then please zip it."

"Fuck this." Andrej stands up, scraping his chair backwards across the polished wooden floor, and goes to the door. "I'll be sure to come and visit you when this all comes crashing down on your heads."

He leaves the room, slamming the door behind him, and we wait for the dust motes to settle silently before we resume the conversation.

"Talk to me, Leo. What does this have to do with Gianna Sedric?"

"She has hands-on experience of working in a refuge. I want to involve her from the planning stage right through to completion."

"And then what?"

I know Victoria needs to see the finish line before she can start the race, but I haven't thought beyond seeing Gianna's face light up when I tell her what I've planned.

"I want her to run it."

"Okay." She stares at the window without seeing what's on the other side. "You know that her family will never agree to this."

"Gianna isn't her family."

Victoria shakes her head like this is going to be more painful for her than it is for me. "I can see that you want to believe this, Leo, but you know that isn't how it works. She'll do whatever her family orders her to do." Pause. "What do you think would've happened if I'd refused to marry Aleksei? You think our father would've helped me set up my own law practice and given me his best wishes?"

"Gianna is different. She wants to make a difference. *She cares*, Victoria."

"I care. You care. We all care, Leo. We just care about different things."

"She hasn't been involved in the Sedric family business. She'll stand up to her father for this opportunity."

"Like she stood up to him when he arranged her marriage to Seamus Mulligan?"

This stabs me straight through the chest, but I'm not giving up that easily. "She didn't have me to fight in her corner then."

Victoria closes her eyes briefly while she chooses her next words carefully. "You can't fight in her corner from where you're sitting. Do you think she'll forgive you for your part in this war against Xander Amory?"

"She knows what I am, same as she knows what kind of man her sister married."

She smiles, and when she speaks, her voice is gentle. "What's this really about, Leo?"

"I need to end this war. I can't keep doing this forever."

"And what about Gianna?"

"What about her?" I'm stalling. I know what she wants me to say, but I haven't figured out what it is about Gianna Sedric that has me wanting to do everything in my power to make her happy.

"Where does she figure in 'I can't do this forever'?"

"Honest answer: I don't know." I wouldn't even reveal this much if Andrej was still in the room, but Victoria has always been able to see right through me.

"Okay, here's what I think. You have feelings for Gianna Sedric." I go to protest, and she raises a finger to stop me. "Hear me out. I know you better than you know yourself, Leo, and since you met her, you've softened. Why do you think Andrej is so angry? It suits him being the youngest sibling. You shoulder all the responsibility while he spends his time messing around and reaping the financial rewards of being an Ivanov. The last thing he wants is for you to step down."

I know she's right but admitting that I have feelings for

Gianna is like cutting open my own chest and inviting my enemies to come and take a piece of me.

"It was going to happen one day. You're only human."

I can't help smiling. "I always believed I was part monster and part automaton."

Her expression crumples. "It's what this life does to us, Leo. Look, I think the refuge idea will work. I'll speak to Mom when I leave here."

"But…?"

"What makes you so sure that Gianna will want to get involved?"

"I'm offering her a lifeline. A way out of her arranged marriage, and an opportunity to be happy."

"Are you happy?"

The question catches me by surprise. "I will be."

She casts her eyes to the ceiling and mutters, "Thank you, Lord. You'll be happy when she's happy, right?"

I don't answer.

"Stop being such a cold-hearted moron, Leonid. Admit it. You're in love with her."

"I got her a puppy."

"Of course you did." Victoria releases a heavy sigh. "And I bet you've never experienced a feeling like it when you saw her reaction."

I smile and I know how goofy I'd look right now if I could see my reflection in a mirror.

"You spoke about trapping Xander Amory in a tunnel earlier. I get it now. The refuge will block him in at one end when the commissioner's wife tells him what upstanding citizens we are. But if you were to marry his sister-in-law, there'd be no way out for him."

Andrej joked about me marrying her at our last meeting, but Victoria is serious.

"When I get married, I don't want it to be a strategic move to take down my enemy."

"It won't be. You're looking at this totally the wrong way."

"But you just said—"

"Jeez, Leonid. You've got it bad. Did you not hear me when I said that you have feelings for this woman? You're in love, my silly little brother. You might end a war, but you'll get to spend the rest of your life with someone you care about. If she'll have you."

If she'll have me?

That's the million-dollar question.

Gianna is playing with the dogs in the garden when I get back to the house.

I stand on the decking and watch her for a while. When she's with the dogs, she loses the strained air of a prisoner who doesn't know when she'll be released, and instead, becomes the Gianna Sedric she would be if her life choices were hers to make.

She wears no makeup. Her hair has been fashioned into a messy bun on top of her head without the use of clips or bobby pins, stray curls framing her flushed cheeks and broad smile. She's wearing denim cut-offs, a plain black T-shirt, and her feet are bare. She's comfortable in her own skin without the pressures of the family she was born into, and I try to convince myself that this was my gift to her. By holding her hostage, I unwittingly gave her the freedom to exist outside of family constraints.

But marriage is a whole different ball game.

She wants me. Her desire and passion for me is as violent and powerful as mine is for her. I'm no expert on love, but now that Victoria has spoken the words out loud and opened my eyes to my feelings, I know that a world without Gianna Sedric in it will be a world without sunshine.

Sweat beads on my forehead and trickles down my spine as I crick my neck from side to side. I feel like my world is teetering on the edge of a precipice. If I'm not totally deluded, and Gianna agrees to be my wife, my life will land on an even plain, one that I'll have to learn to navigate with her by my side, but it will have a bright dawn on the horizon, and a glorious sunset to match. But if she refuses...

I might as well walk naked into Amory territory with a target on my exposed back and ask him to shoot me with my own weapon.

And I haven't even considered what my parents will say about it.

At least I have Victoria on my side. Her love for Aleksei may not set off fireworks whenever she looks at him, but there is no jealousy or bitterness in her heart; she still wishes happiness on her siblings.

"Leo?" Gianna smiles at me as the dogs come bounding my way, and heat spreads through my chest. "You're back." She studies my face closely, her eyes filled with concern.

"I-I have something to discuss."

She chews her bottom lip. "Is it my family?"

Her eyes drift to the back of the house as if her sister might suddenly appear in the doorway, arms open wide to welcome her back into the fold. Is this the best parting gift I could give her: a reunion with her family?

Suddenly, I feel way off track here.

Maybe this, us, our nights of unrivaled passion, has just been a learning curve to her.

Her parting gift to me: *Thanks for the ride, Leo, it was fun while it lasted*.

I almost turn around and head back inside the house to call Victoria and call off the refuge plan. Almost. But then Gianna is standing in front of me on tiptoes, and smiling at me with those turquoise eyes, and my lips meet hers.

23

GIANNA

LEONID CROUCHES ON THE GROUND, and Lucky throws her little body at him while Marvel washes his face with his tongue. It's like a scene from a cheesy Hallmark movie where the guy without a heart finally thaws when he discovers that all he ever wanted was the daughter of his rival and a garden filled with dogs.

"Do you have a stash of meat treats in your pockets or have you been training them in secret to come to you?" I ask.

"I think it's my allure. Dogs just love me."

At the mention of the word 'love' I feel the heat spreading up my neck and into my face. After last night, I woke up to find Leonid gone again, and tears immediately welled in my eyes like he was never coming back. What is wrong with me? I'm his prisoner—he can't just disappear and leave me here with the wicked witch of the west and goth-Glinda for company.

I realize that he's dodging the furry bodies clambering all over his once-immaculate suit and watching me closely. I hope he wasn't planning on wearing it outside of the house again today.

"Is that right?" I toss the tennis ball I'm holding from one hand to the other and deliberately throw it away from the decking. "Go get the ball."

Both dogs follow the ball's trajectory and bound after it without so much as a backwards glance.

"It's a shame your allure doesn't quite live up to a tennis ball."

I chuckle, and Leonid comes over to me and kisses me on the lips, gripping my chin in what I'm starting to think of as his signature move.

"What do you want to talk about?"

When I found him in his study last night, he looked like a shadow of the man he is today, the man in the designer suit with his well-groomed hair and the kind of broad shoulders that Atlas would've been proud of. I never expected to see Leonid Ivanov looking anything less than perfect, like he was crafted from marble and steel. But last night … it was as if something had broken him.

Or perhaps that's how he looks with the polished veneer stripped away, and his guard lowered.

Now that I've seen it though, I can't unsee it, and I still have the overwhelming urge to wrap my arms around him and cradle him to sleep the way a mom would cradle a baby.

"Let's walk." He whistles. The dogs come running over, and I fall into step beside him.

There are still guards positioned strategically around the property, but it feels bizarre to stroll across the lawn with Leonid and the dogs like this is a game of happy families. At what point will he come to me and say that it's time for me to leave? It's inevitable. This isn't real, and people like me and Leonid will only ever be game players even if I'm just a lowly pawn and he's the king.

I should have kept him at arm's length. I saw what he was capable of that first morning and promised myself that I would make him pay, and here I am walking beside him and counting down the hours until he slides between my legs in his bed tonight.

We keep walking, past the maze and the tennis courts, and I'm hit with a strong sense of déjà vu. This is the same route I walked with Tamara when she offered to help me escape.

Is this some kind of trick? Does he expect me to reenact what happened or is he going to give me a second opportunity to run while he looks the other way? If that's the case, what will I do? Can I leave Lucky behind and pick up my life where it left off?

And what about Leo? To never feel his arms around me again, or his lips crushing mine, or to hear him call me his printzessa... Is that what I want?

I already know the answer.

We approach the edge of the woods, and my pulse starts to race. This is it. This is where he tells me that I get a head start if I want to reach the perimeter of his land before his men hunt me down.

He tosses the ball for the dogs to chase and turns to face me. "I have a proposition for you, Gianna. Well, two propositions. Although they're connected so perhaps it is only one after all."

Is he *nervous*? Leonid Ivanov, Russian mafia boss, casino owner, and enemy of Xander Amory is actually sweating.

"Are you going to tell me what it is?"

"Gianna, what happened yesterday—"

"That was yesterday." I intertwine my fingers with his to stop him from pulling away from me as fresh tears collect on my bottom lashes. He's letting me go, and he doesn't even realize that this isn't what I want. "And today is another day. It's what my mom used to say when I was a little girl."

"She sounds like a wise lady."

"She was."

What would she have thought of Leonid? It makes my chest ache to think that I'll never get the chance to ask my mom's opinion, but I think that Mel would approve. She would want me to be happy, and to experience the kind of love she has for Xander, no matter how difficult it might be.

"I want to build a women's refuge in the city."

I blink. I think I must be delusional because it sounded like he just said that he wanted to build a women's refuge in the city.

"Which city?"

He grins at me like I just told him he has ketchup on his tie. Not that Leonid probably ever eats ketchup. "This city."

"Chicago? Why?" I hear him, but the words aren't computing inside my head.

"Why not? There aren't enough places to go around."

The dogs run back to us, and I throw the ball for them on autopilot. "But ... a women's refuge? I mean, it's a wonderful idea but..."

"But not the kind of project a man like me would undertake."

His eyes grow dark, and my chest grows heavy with guilt. This is exactly what I was thinking, and I should know better than to judge people on what the rest of the world sees. He rescued Marvel, something that I could never imagine in a million years Xander Amory doing.

Something I could imagine though, is my brother-in-law getting hold of this information and using it to his advantage.

"I'm sorry." I suck on my bottom lip, and I swear I can still taste Leo on it. "I didn't mean it to come out like that."

"Gianna, you don't have to apologize to me. Ever." He holds my gaze, and I couldn't look away even if I wanted to. "Perhaps it isn't a project that I would have accepted, until now. But you've opened my eyes."

My heart does this funny skipping thing. "I have?"

"I see your passion, and your conviction, and your determination to make the world a better place, and I know that if anyone can succeed, it's you."

"What are you saying, Leo?"

"The refuge is yours... If you want it?"

"Mine?"

"Yours." Leo tilts my chin towards him and kisses me on the lips producing more tears. "I told you I look after what's mine, and I've never wanted to protect anyone more than you, my printzessa."

"I could fly my friends over from Montenegro to help me."

"You can fly the Pope in to help you if that's what you want."

"I don't know how to run a refuge, but I can learn."

"Anything can be learned, Gianna." He folds me into his arms and holds me close. "Anything."

My thoughts are spiraling out of control. I can already picture me, Mika, and Cartier in our own refuge, helping vulnerable women to rebuild their lives while keeping them safe. I can imagine Lucky dividing her affection between the women like a therapy dog, listening, loving, and teaching them to trust again.

It's a dream come true.

But these idyllic images shatter when I think of my father's reaction to me rejecting Seamus to, instead, manage a refuge with Leonid Ivanov.

He will never allow it. He would rather send me back to Montenegro than have me flaunt his orders in his face right here in the city.

My fragile dreams are already turning sour on my tongue as Leo holds me at arm's length and lowers his face to peer into my eyes. "What is it, my printzessa?"

I swallow the solid lump in my throat. "It's a lovely idea, Leo, but it will never work."

"Hey, that's not the reaction I expected. You're a fighter, Gianna. If anyone can make it work, you can."

"It isn't that." Adrenaline, disappointment, the looming prospect of returning to reality, these things are all rushing through my veins and making my heartbeat feel like the dull thud-thud-thud of heavy stones inside my chest. "It's my father. He would never agree to me working with—"

"With me?"

Of course, he already thought this through. But not even Leonid Ivanov will sway my father on this one.

"He would have no say in the matter if you were running the refuge with your husband."

"Seamus?" I shake my head and pull away from his strong arms. It feels wrong to mention my fiancé while my body is pressed up against Leo. "Seamus would never... Why would you even suggest it?"

Does he want me to go through with the arranged marriage? Is this Leo's way of getting rid of me, by bribing me with my own refuge when I can still feel him inside me from last night?

"No, Gianna, not Seamus. I'm talking about me."

"You?" It comes out as a high-pitched squeak, and I wish I could take it back, but my brain has given up trying to keep up with this turn of events. "I-I don't... I mean... I don't know what ... is going on here."

Leonid takes my hands in his. "I realize this is probably the most unromantic marriage proposal in history, and this isn't how I would've wanted to propose to you. I mean, I don't even have a ring, but well, like I said, the two propositions go hand in hand and..." His voice trails off when the look of utter shock on my face sinks in. "You could manage the refuge as my wife."

"Your wife?"

Excitement and joy and more excitement ripples through my veins, being quietly tampered down and suppressed by the fear that he is doing this for all the wrong reasons. I come from a mafia family. I know how these things work, especially for the daughters. And I'm frightened to acknowledge the very real probability that love hasn't played even a tiny part in this unexpected proposal.

"I know I've sprung this on you without warning," he continues, "and I don't expect you to give me an answer immediately. But I know it would make you happy, and I want to make you happy, Gianna."

I avert my eyes. I get a rush of warmth from these words. I know that he wants me as much as I want him; I'm not completely naïve. But he still hasn't mentioned the word 'love'. My head is yelling at me to ask him outright: do you love me? But my heart is counter attacking with *I shouldn't have to ask.*

If he loved me, he would tell me, right?

"I don't know." I swallow the tears clogging my throat and behind my eyes. "I need time to think about it. My father..."

"Once we're married, there's nothing he can do about it, Gianna. You'll be mine. You'll be free to run a refuge or travel around the world or rescue dogs if that's what you want. I will never stop you from doing whatever makes you happy. I promise."

I'm not paying attention. I'm stuck on the word 'free' because I'm not free to do whatever I want. Whatever Leonid says, I'm still a prisoner in his house. I'm not even allowed to call my sister—the one person who could give me the advice I need right now.

"I'll think about it." I don't meet his eyes. "I'm going to stay in the guest room tonight."

I walk back to the house, and I don't look behind me.

I toss and turn all night. I eat supper in my room, brought to me by Tamara, and curl up beneath the comforter imagining Leo lying next to me. How is it possible to miss someone you hardly know so much? I miss his heat, his kisses, his tongue between my legs. I feel as though I've instinctively raised a barrier between us, and it breaks my heart to think that the dogs, and the maze, and picnics by the pond are all on his side of the wall.

Marrying him without my father's permission would be like sticking a middle finger up at my family and all that my father has done for me since my mom died.

Marrying him without Mel would feel like an even bigger betrayal.

Mel knows everything there is to know about me. Apart from this. But I spend the night alternating between Mel's disappointment when she discovers that I married a mafia boss in secret, and my disappointment that my family hasn't tried to free me.

Even if I don't agree to marry Leo, though, how can I marry Seamus now, or anyone else for that matter? Seamus is expecting to marry a virgin. It's part of the contract.

But more importantly, I can't imagine being married to anyone else. I would climb into bed beside my husband and think of Leo. When we kiss, it would be Leo's lips I'm imagining. When we have sex, it will be Leo I can feel inside me. Because the truth is, he set out to corrupt me, and instead, he has left his imprint on me that no one else will ever be able to erase.

My head is fuzzy when I wake up like my brain cells are wrapped in cotton wool. I dress and eat breakfast in the guest room. Alone. It makes me feel uneasy how comfortable I felt sharing Leo's bed and staying in his room; staying in the guest room without him is like sleeping on the floor without a blanket and with all the windows open.

Cold and lonely.

Will he expect an answer today?

Did he go to the office early this morning as usual or did he stick around to wait for me?

I wonder if he slept soundly or if he missed me in his bed.

I contemplate telling the guard outside my door that I'm sick and will spend the day in my room—anxiety is making me feel nauseous, so it wouldn't be a total lie—but Leonid will know that I'm avoiding him, and so will everyone else on his staff. Besides, it isn't like there's anywhere for me to hide. If he wants to find me, he will.

So, I shower and dress, finish the last slice of cold toast on the breakfast tray, and wander down to the kitchen unescorted. I pass several other guards along the way, and no one comments about me roaming the house alone. Has Leonid warned them to give me the freedom of the house?

I smell his woody cologne before I reach the kitchen. Closely followed by voices: Leo's and Tamara's. The hair on the back of my neck immediately stands on end.

She can't be trusted. Who knows what she'll say about me when I'm not around to defend myself, and after my reaction to Leo's marriage proposal and me choosing to stay in the guest room, he might be more inclined to believe her today.

I know what curiosity did to the cat, but what the hell—I stand outside the kitchen entrance and listen to what's being said.

"You know what people will say, Pakhan." This is Tamara. "They'll say that the cracks are starting to show."

"Let them say what they will. You know how I feel about gossip."

"This isn't just gossip though. Xander Amory has been waiting for a reason to discredit you."

My stomach twists as the image of the severed hand pops into my head.

But Leo's voice is calm and steady. "I have already given him plenty of reasons. If he believes that opening a women's refuge with his sister-in-law is a sign of weakness, then he still has much to learn."

He told Tamara about the refuge!

Maybe it's a childish reaction, but the thought of Leo discussing the refuge with Tamara taints it somehow. As though she has seen the completed building before me and has already dismissed it as a novelty that the pakhan will tire of when he comes to his senses.

I'm about to turn around and head back upstairs to the guest room when she adds, "The printzessa has changed you, and not for the better. The sooner she goes home, the sooner our lives can return to normal."

I bristle.

I knew she didn't want me around, but to hear her say the words out loud to Leo drives home what I already feared: I don't belong here.

With tears making my vision blurry, I turn around and run back along the hallway, colliding face-first with a woman I've never seen before.

"Gianna?" She knows me though.

She stands back and reaches for my hand, staring at the tears streaking my cheeks.

"What's wrong? Is it Leo?" Her casual use of his shortened name causes me to sniff loudly and peer at her through my tears.

The woman appears to be around Leo's age with long dark hair slicked back into a tight fashionable ponytail, and large brown eyes. But it's the high, chiseled cheekbones and strong jawline that tell me that she must be related to Leo.

"No." I shake my head and blink away the tears. "It's nothing."

"Okay, it doesn't look like nothing to me. Did Leo speak to you yesterday? Is that what this is about?"

She knows as well. Fresh tears spill, and she ushers me through a doorway and into the dining room where I first met Leonid. She pulls out a seat and tells me to sit, and it's clear that, like her brother, she is used to being obeyed.

A cup of freshly brewed coffee is placed in front of me along with a crisp white napkin that I'm afraid to use to wipe my eyes. She sits next to me and pretends not to notice my streaked cheeks and puffy eyes.

"I'm Victoria, Leo's sister. I handle the legal side of the operation."

I don't know what to say, so I dab my cheeks carefully, and sip my coffee.

"Leo came to see me yesterday. He wanted to discuss the women's refuge." Her eyes flicker across my face, gauging my reaction to see whether her brother mentioned his proposition or not. Satisfied that this isn't a complete shock to me, she presses on. "I told him that I thought it was a good idea."

I feel a 'but' coming on, so I keep quiet, and let her do the talking. I need to clear Tamara's voice from my head before I say something that I'll regret when it gets back to Leo.

"You're worried about your family, aren't you?"

I nod. "My father would never agree to me working for Leo."

"But you wouldn't be working for my brother. The refuge would be in your name, Gianna. Didn't Leo tell you this?"

"I... No, he didn't."

She rolls her eyes, and I can imagine them bickering when they were kids, and Victoria always coming out on top. I wonder if she resents his position as the head of the family, but it isn't the kind of question you ask a mafia family member. At least not if you want to keep your kneecaps intact.

"Typical Leo." She sucks in a deep breath. "He expects people to know what he's thinking."

"Why? I mean, why would he put it in my name? Does he not want to be associated with it?"

"You really haven't figured it out, have you?"

Sniff. My tears are drying up, but emotions are still swirling around my gut like a whirlpool. "Figured what out?" I wish this family would just learn to say what they mean.

"You're really not like the others. No wonder my brother has fallen hard."

My heart chooses this moment to start fluttering like a butterfly on crack, and I can't concentrate on what she's saying.

Victoria tugs a lock of my hair over my shoulder in an action that mimics her brother. "Leo is doing this for you, Gianna. Because, although he hasn't had the balls to admit it yet, he's in love with you."

And just like that, my world flips on its axis, and the sun comes back out with a vengeance.

24

LEONID

Gianna is leaving the dining room with my sister when I go in search of her. Victoria winks at me as we pass in the corridor, and for the first time in my life, I'm left standing in front of a beautiful woman not knowing what to say.

Gianna isn't like any other woman I've ever met. She gives a whole new meaning to the idiom 'beauty is only skin deep' because she is beautiful inside and out. When I look at her, I want to collect all the stars in the night sky and present them to her as a gift fastened with a silver bow. If I could bottle how she makes me feel, I could kiss goodbye to this way of life and live like a king off the proceeds.

"I…" My stomach churns, and my palms are slick with sweat. This isn't me, but then again, perhaps this is more me than I've ever been. "I missed you last night."

Her smile sets her face aglow. "I missed you too."

I don't know what Victoria said to her in private, but I make a mental note to thank her later. When I grip Gianna's hair and pull her to me, her body melds with mine. Our lips meet, and my erection grows inside my pants, rock solid between us.

"Don't ever leave me again, printzessa," I murmur against her demanding lips.

Reaching behind me, I push open the door to the drinks room and, in one fluid movement, we slip inside where we can be away from the security cameras and patrolling guards.

I came to ask if she'd reached a decision on my proposal, but it's forgotten now. At the moment, all I can think about is claiming her, making her mine because I can't imagine a world in which our bodies never get to do this again.

I can't imagine a world in which her smile isn't all for me.

I can't imagine a world in which my heart doesn't know who to beat for.

Gianna instinctively raises her arms, and I drag her thin sweater over her head. I lower my mouth to her breasts, squeezing them together so that I can tease both nipples at the same time, and Gianna arches her back, pushing them into my mouth.

"We have a lot of catching up to do." I slide my hand inside her pants and find her warm, moist sex. Collecting her juices on my finger, I slide my hand back out again and suck my finger. "Were you saving this up for me, printzessa?"

"Yes."

She wraps her hand around mine and sucks her taste off my finger, curling her tongue around my skin and licking me slowly, mimicking her performance at our first meeting over breakfast. If only I'd known how impossibly sexy she was beneath that bravado, I would never have wasted so much time.

"What do you want me to do to you?" I tug her hair backwards, exposing the smooth creamy flesh of her neck. I dip my head and suck on the skin below her left ear, branding her as mine.

"Lick me, Leo." It's barely more than a whisper.

I lift her hair from the back of her neck and brand her again, just below her hairline. "I need more than that, printzessa or I'll keep going."

Gianna's hand fumbles with the waistband of my pants, but I grip it with my free hand and hold it behind her back, trapping her against me, my erection throbbing. My lips move lower down her neck, and I keep sucking.

"Lick my pussy." The words come out breathy and desperate.

"Are you sure that's what you want?" I lean over her, my eyebrows raised questioningly.

"I'm sure."

I release her and tug her pants down over her hips, pressing my tongue gently between her legs. She immediately groans with pleasure, and my cock bobs in response to the siren call. Gripping her hips, I pick her up and set her down on top of the grand piano, and she lays back, legs spread wide for me.

I smile. "This is what you get for abandoning me last night."

Holding her open, I insert two fingers, curling them inside her and rubbing them against the spot. Harder and faster, her juices dripping down my fingers.

"You still want me to lick you?"

She's panting, spine arched, legs already quivering with pleasure. "Yes."

"Say it like you mean it, Gianna."

"Yes, I want you to lick me, Leo!" She sits forward, grabs my head with both hands, and pulls my face onto her pussy, and it's the sexiest thing that has ever happened to me.

"I'm going in." I make my eyebrows dance independently before I lick her slowly, dragging my tongue the length of her sex.

Gianna lies back on top of the piano, her arms stretched out behind her head.

"You taste so fucking good." I raise my head just long enough to see her contented smile as the door opens behind me, and Olga lets out a squeal of horror before dragging it shut again.

"Oh my God, Leo." Gianna tries to close her legs and sit up, but I keep them open with my shoulders. "We should—"

"Lie back and close your eyes. That's an order."

She does as she's told, but I can tell that the moment is lost. I trail kisses along her inner thighs, teasing her pussy with the tip of my tongue. I open her up and lick her clit, gently, luring her back to me, until I feel her relax against me.

"Good girl. You're going to come for me now. Come all over my face, Gianna. Show me how much you want me."

I suck on her clit, nibbling it between my front teeth until her body is writhing and wriggling in my grip. Still, I keep sucking, drinking her up, imprinting the taste of her in my mind, a reminder of what I'm missing when I'm not touching her.

While her sex is still clenching and unclenching from her orgasm, I free my cock and slide it all the way in, feeling her constrict around it.

I pull her into a sitting position on the piano and suck on her breasts while I pound into her wet pussy. Gianna wraps her arms around my neck and pulls me to her, arching her back, thrusting her breasts into my mouth.

"Fuck me, Leo," she breathes huskily. "I need you to fuck me."

I don't need to be told twice. Folding my arms around her, I feel her heart beating in synch with mine as I explode inside her.

I don't know how long we stay like that, Gianna's legs and arms wrapped protectively around me, holding me inside for as long as possible, her head resting on my shoulder. But when her pussy eventually pushes me out, it still hasn't been long enough.

Her face close to mine, Gianna murmurs, "Maybe I'll sleep in the guest room again tonight if that's how you repay me."

"Next time I won't be so gentle."

"Is that a promise?"

Something has altered between us. The first time I made Gianna come, she was shy, innocent, naturally curious about what was happening to her body. But now... Now she knows what she wants and isn't afraid to go for it.

And what she wants is me.

"Did you—"

"Yes." She cuts me off and rubs her nose against mine. "I thought about it, and the answer is yes, Leo."

My blood is gushing through my veins, and I can hardly believe I heard her correctly. "Yes, to which part?"

"To all of it. Yes, I want to open the refuge with you, and yes, I'll marry you."

Nothing else exists right now. I pick her up and swing her around until she giggles and complains that I'm making her dizzy.

By the time I set her down onto her feet, the implications of her decision are already crawling inside my head and battling with euphoria for prime position.

"You know what this means."

My tone is semi-serious; this is Gianna's moment too, and I don't want to drag her back down to earth with a bump. This is a once-in-a-lifetime moment, and she should be able to savor it without the pressures of outside influences. Like family.

She cups my face in both hands. "It means that I get to spend the rest of my life with you."

I smile. "Your family—"

"—isn't here. This is what I want, Leo."

"Are you sure? It's going to make a bizarre anecdote in the future when people ask us how we met."

"I'll tell them that we met over breakfast, scrambled eggs, bacon, and maple syrup, and that you were so serious, it was days before I saw you smile."

"Serious?"

"Yes, serious." On tiptoes, she reaches up and smooths out the lines creasing my forehead. "And grumpy."

I wrinkle my nose. "I am not grumpy."

"Maybe not right now."

We drift into comfortable silence. "We'll tell your family together, Gianna." I'm not letting her handle this alone. "Once this ... feud with Xander has been resolved."

Now, it's her turn to be serious. "How are you going to do that?"

"He tried to set me up, but it's going to backfire on him."

Her expression crumples, and she pulls away. This is why I must protect her from what I do, or it will always be this way. If she ever catches a whisper of what it means to be an Ivanov, it will ram home to her that her husband flirts with danger every day of his life.

"He's my sister's husband." Her voice has shrunk. "Will he... Is he going to be ... killed?"

"Gianna." Deep breath. "I promise that I will do everything in my power to end this amicably. I don't want you to worry about it, okay?"

I could tell her that the plans to open a women's refuge should work in my favor and bring the feud to its natural conclusion, but I want to erase this fear from her eyes, and the only way to do this is to make sure that she remains oblivious. The refuge will be hers. That's all that matters, and if Xander Amory continues to systematically dismantle my operation, he will bring about his own fate.

"Promise me that Mel and Lucian won't be hurt."

"I promise."

"Leo I never wanted..." She sucks on her bottom lip, and I roll it out from under her top teeth and kiss it gently. "...this way of life, I've seen how it destroys families."

"I know, but I won't let anything happen to you."

"My father, I don't know how he'll react when he finds out that we're getting married."

"He won't." I kiss the tip of her nose. "By the time he finds out, it'll be too late. We'll already be married."

"But..." She blinks hard while she processes this latest revelation. "I can't go home and tell him?"

I know what she's thinking. She's been held captive since she arrived, and even though she agreed to marry me, she still isn't free to come and go as she pleases.

"It's too dangerous right now, and I can't risk you never coming back to me."

"I'll always come back to you."

I know that she means it, and this makes my chest swell with affection for her. I'm even more determined to keep her close and never let her out of my sight because she doesn't understand the lengths that Xander will go to, to win this war.

Suddenly, she stiffens in my arms, and I stroke between her shoulder blades with my thumb to try and smooth out the tension.

"Xander wants to kill you, doesn't he?" Her voice sends a chill down my spine because it's true.

"I'll handle it."

"Let me speak to him, Leo." She wriggles out of my arms to look at me. "Let me speak to him and Mel. I know I can convince them to end this stupid vendetta against you. Once they know that we're getting married, Xander will see things differently, and we can all get along the way families should."

In fairy tales maybe. But in the real world, men like me and Xander rarely shake hands and put the past behind us.

"No." I fold her hand between mine and raise it to my lips. "You must trust me on this one. If Xander finds out, he'll do whatever it takes to stop the wedding from going ahead, and I want to make you my wife, Gianna. I want to know that you're waiting for me when I come home. I want to know that you're mine."

She sniffs back tears, but she doesn't argue. "I am yours."

"Even without a ring on your finger?"

She smiles although I still see the concern in her eyes. "Do you need me to prove it to you again?" She slides a hand inside my pants and wraps it around my semi-solid erection.

"I think we should maybe go somewhere more private so that we don't give Olga a heart attack."

She tips her head back and laughs, and it's the most beautiful sound in the whole world. "I'll never be able to look her in the eye again."

"Trust me, Olga will be too embarrassed to initiate eye contact. But she'll never breathe a word to anyone in case they ask her for details."

"They wouldn't." Her eyes widen. "Would they?"

"So long as Olga believes they would, it works in our favor." I slide my hand inside my pocket. "I almost forgot." It's a lie; I was waiting for the right moment.

I go down on one knee in front of Gianna and take her left hand in mine, slipping a ring onto her finger. Proposing to her like this after fucking her on the grand piano in one of the many rooms that rarely get used in my house, isn't exactly a red roses and candlelight moment. But then we're not exactly a red roses and candlelight kind of couple.

"Gianna Sedric, will you marry me?"

She stares at the ring, open-mouthed, and then back at me. "It's … beautiful."

"It was my grandmama's. I went to see her this morning while you were still snoring peacefully in my guest room."

"I do not snore."

I shrug and smile. "My grandmama is in her eighties and is still an early riser. She was already in her garden when I arrived, on her knees pulling straggly weeds from the flowerbeds. She always said that the ring would be mine to give to my future wife, and, well, now I finally have a reason to claim it."

Her eyes tell me all that I need to know.

The platinum band holds a 10-carat, old mine-cut diamond surrounded by antique Russian sapphires that pick out the darker spikes of blue in Gianna's eyes. I wasn't certain if she would like it, but I needn't have worried.

"My grandmama claimed that it belonged to the Romanovs. I believed her when I was a boy, but now I realize that she's a storyteller."

"I would love to meet her one day so that I can thank her personally."

"You will."

"It's so beautiful, Leo. It's... I never imagined..."

"That you would one day be wearing a Romanov ring?"

Her smile lights up her face. "That I would one day be marrying you."

25

GIANNA

I still can't believe it.

My emotions soar and dip between happiness that makes my heart so full I fear I'm going to explode, and disappointment that I can't share my experience with Mel. She would love Leo ... once she got over the fact that he's at war with Xander. And that he's a Russian bratva boss. And that he kidnapped me en route from Montenegro to Chicago.

So much has happened in the short space of time since I met Leo that I'm going to need a month alone with my sister to fill her in on all the gossip. At least a month.

But as soon as she meets Lucky and Marvel, and I tell her about the refuge, she'll understand that Leonid Ivanov is the man of my dreams.

We are going to be married at the house.

Next week.

Because the sooner we're husband and wife, the sooner I can

tell my family. This is when my mood plummets, each time I try to predict my father's reaction.

I'm currently torn between him hugging me tightly and whispering into my ear that all he ever wanted was for me to be happy, closely followed by him agreeing to forge an alliance with the Ivanov mob. Or—and this is the image that brings me out in a cold sweat and anxiety hives around my neck—he'll draw a revolver from his pocket and shoot Leo straight through the heart.

This is why I need Mel. She would convince me that our father wouldn't shoot my husband first and then ask me if I'm happy after.

He wouldn't.

I time my meals for when I'm in full-on soaring-like-a-bird mode. In those moments, my appetite is so great I could out-eat Leo. This morning, I almost polished off an entire loaf of homemade bread spread thickly with butter and marmalade. But when I picture Leo lying in a pool of blood with my father's bullet lodged in his chest, I feel so nauseous, the only thing I can stomach is a can of soda.

Victoria arranged for me to meet with a wedding planner the day after Leonid gave me their grandmama's ring. The woman was tall, elegant, graceful, dark hair swept into an Audrey-Hepburn-worthy chignon. She casually dropped exorbitant sums of money that her previous clients had spent on weddings into the conversation and promised that she would do her utmost to find me a designer wedding gown at short notice.

I smiled and nodded in all the right places.

Then the instant the door closed behind her, I gathered up all the samples and brochures that she'd left behind for me to read and tossed them into the trash can.

Flashy weddings are for flashy people.

They're not for me.

A wedding is a celebration of two people falling in love and vowing to spend the rest of their lives together. For better, for worse. For richer, for poorer. *To love and to cherish.* Leo cherishes me; I'd be an idiot not to see it in his eyes every time he looks at me.

But he hasn't said it yet. He hasn't told me that he loves me, and these missing words feel like a crushing weight pressing down on my chest.

I don't know why they're so important. Actions speak louder than words, right? The puppy. The refuge. His grandmother's ring. But Leo putting the refuge in my name is niggling away at me. I heard Victoria when she said that Leo wants me to be happy, but I didn't pay enough attention to what she *wasn't* saying.

People like Leo and Victoria and my father never do anything unless it benefits them in some way. I only wish I knew what Leo stands to gain from opening a women's refuge in the city.

I try to shove this thought to the back of my mind and smother it beneath a mountain of wedding preparations. It feels surreal to be planning my own wedding, when I spent the last month in Montenegro dreading my imminent nuptials, but Leo has warned me that he'll marry me in an oversized T-shirt in the piano room if I don't get things sorted.

And I believe him.

I find the perfect setting in the Japanese garden behind the house. It will look so romantic strewn with rose petals, and I liaise with the gardener about laying out a rose-petal path from the house to the pagoda.

Back in the house, I swallow my embarrassment and ask Olga if she knows a caterer who will prepare a small banquet for us and our minimal number of guests. Her mouth pinches into a button-hole shape. She doesn't look me in the eye—perhaps because she saw her boss going down on me on top of the piano—when she says, "I prepare the food in this house. You think I don't know how to make a banquet?"

I don't dare argue with her. Olga in a foul mood could make Leonid resemble an angel in a white robe with a halo hovering above his head.

I spend hours sitting at the breakfast island in the kitchen, the dogs at my feet, and Leo's tablet in front of me, scrolling through endless websites for a wedding gown. I haven't seen anything I like, or at least I haven't seen anything that I want to wear, and I'm panicking because I'm running out of time.

"At this rate, it might have to be the oversized T-shirt." I peer down at Lucky who is balancing her front paws on Marvel's chest so that she can get closer to me. "Maybe we could get matching T-shirts, huh? What do you think?"

"Are you asking me?"

I didn't hear Tamara sneaking up behind me—I swear the woman flies in on an invisible broomstick—and I reflexively lock the tablet and turn it over so that she can't see what I was doing.

"I was talking to the dogs." I go to stand up, but she stops me by grabbing hold of my left hand. I try to wrench it free, but her grip is like metal.

"You're wearing Grandmama's ring." She says this as though she has claimed Leo's family for herself, and a jolt of something icy stabs at my heart.

"You knew about the ring?"

"Of course." She releases my hand, climbs onto the next stool, and gestures for me to sit. "It was Elena's before you came along."

Elena?

"W-who's Elena?" I feel numb. The question formed on my lips before I could stop myself. I don't want to know who Elena is.

But it's obvious from the casual smile on Tamara's face that she can't wait to tell me. "Elena was the pakhan's fiancée. I'm not surprised that he hasn't mentioned her. Everyone loved Elena."

"I..." I swallow.

Leo didn't think to mention that he was engaged to be married to someone else. Neither did his sister. It shouldn't matter—it was before he met me—but the twisting, sickly feeling in my gut is telling me that this is important.

This is a big fucking deal.

This isn't like my family arranging my marriage to Seamus. Leo loved another woman enough to propose to her. She probably sat right here with the sunlight glinting off the diamond on her finger, arranging her high-profile wedding to the man I love, and I never knew. I thought I was the first.

No, it isn't even not being the first woman that Leo proposed to that's eating away at me. I thought—*no, I convinced myself*—that he was somehow broken before we met. That he was married to the family business and that I'd woken up something inside him that, until now, had remained dormant.

I feel such an idiot, that my voice trembles when I ask, "What happened to Elena?"

Like Tamara might tell me that she changed her mind and went backpacking around Asia, or she got swallowed up by an earthquake, or she fell off the side of a mountain and her body was never found. Each hopeful scenario more brutal than the last.

"She left the pakhan when she discovered that he was cheating on her."

And there it is, the bombshell that shatters my heart into a million tiny, bloody shards.

"I'm sure he learned his lesson though, and it won't happen again."

She's still talking. Why is she still fucking talking? I look around for something to shove so far down her throat that they'll have to pick the pieces out of her butthole when they find her. But a banana isn't going to do the trick, and I don't know where Olga keeps the rolling pin.

I climb off the stool, narrowly missing Lucky's front paw with my foot, and bend down to pick her up when she lets out a heart-wrenching whine.

"I'm sorry, baby." I nuzzle her face and kiss the top of her head. "I won't hurt you."

Whatever I'm feeling right now is nothing compared to how Marvel and Lucky must've felt when they were mistreated and left to die by the humans they trusted. It's nothing compared to what Hope and the other women I met in the refuge experienced at the hands of their abusers.

I'm not Elena. Leo would never cheat on me; I feel it deep inside my chest whenever I'm with him. He isn't an actor. No one could fake the way he is with me. It's unfair for me to accept Tamara's word that this is what happened without giving him the opportunity to explain.

That's what I'll do. I'll try to suppress the kernel of simmering disquiet settling in the pit of my stomach until I've spoken to Leo. There are only two people who really know what happened between him and Elena, and one of them will be sharing his bed with me tonight.

"We meet at last."

I don't recognize the voice, or the face of the man it belongs to.

He's younger than Leo. He has the same dark hair and brown eyes as Leo and Victoria, but that's where the similarities end. This man's smile doesn't reach his eyes. His gaze slides away from me as he crosses the room and opens the refrigerator door, but I notice the way it lingers briefly on Tamara before snapping to the bottle of beer in his hand.

"I'm Andrej. I thought I'd come and introduce myself as my brother seems to have forgotten his manners." He leans lazily against the counter and stares at me. "Leonid has probably told you nothing about me."

He cranks the lid off the bottle with his back teeth, and guzzles beer, his eyes on me the entire time.

I don't know why, but I have the overwhelming urge to get the dogs as far away from him as possible. Lucky nestles in my arms. Marvel's ears are pressed flat against his head as he leans against me, his eyes on the unexpected visitor.

"Another mutt?" The question isn't aimed at anyone in particular. "My brother's a sucker for a stray it seems."

Heat rushes to my face, but I force myself to maintain eye contact. I sense the naughty child in Andrej waiting for his parents to turn their backs before he causes mischief and blames it on his siblings. Only now, the mischief has way higher stakes.

"We were just talking about Elena," Tamara says.

That's what she's leading with? I'm starting to wonder if this was planned, an unspoken agreement to gang up on me and shatter my illusions of my fiancé while there's still time to call the wedding off.

"Ah, Elena." Andrej's gaze rakes my body, drawing more heat to my face. "She was a stunner."

Okay, so now I know they're deliberately being obnoxious, or in Tamara's case, more obnoxious than usual.

"I'd have taken a shot at her myself given half a chance." Andrej raises the bottle in a mock toast to himself and his missed chances with his brother's ex.

"One brother was enough." There's unmistakable amusement in Tamara's voice.

"Always my fucking luck." Andrej's mouth twists into a sly smile aimed my way. "Unless you fancy trying out the more athletic brother." At my silence, he shrugs like it's no biggie. "No? You don't know what you're missing."

"I think I do." I wish I sounded stronger, more confident, but this is Leo's brother, and Andrej is right about one thing: I don't know anything about him. Leo might be oblivious to his younger brother's charm, or lack of.

His eyes grow wide when he spots the ring on my finger. "Grandmama told me that she'd given Leonid her ring, but I didn't believe her."

"Why not?" I don't like where this is going, but like a fly caught in a spider's web, I'm stuck here waiting for the spider to claim his meal. "It was promised to Leo."

His eyebrows lower, and his face darkens like he just stepped back into the shadows. "It was promised to Leo's future wife. Not to an enemy printzessa."

I set my shoulders back and jut my chin, just like Daniel taught me when we were kids. "You've been misinformed. I'm not the enemy."

"Oh, but that's where you're wrong." He pushes himself off the counter and comes closer.

A growl emits from somewhere deep inside Marvel, and I don't stop him.

"Your sister is married to the enemy, and therefore that places you on the opposite side of the board."

I shake my head. "This war has nothing to do with me. I haven't even seen my family since I came back from Montenegro."

"Oh, but you're the crucial piece in this never-ending game, *printzessa*."

His use of Leo's pet name for me makes my flesh crawl. "If you'll excuse me, the dogs need some exercise." I turn to leave, but he isn't finished, and I wish I'd taken the dogs out when Tamara first walked in.

"Let me enlighten you, Gianna. My brother is marrying you because it's part of the trap to snare your precious brother-in-law. The ring and the refuge. Sounds like the title of a fantasy novel, don't you think?"

"You're lying."

Marvel must sense the panic coursing through my veins. He prowls towards Andrej, ears still back, his tail between his legs.

Andrej spreads his arms wide and sways in front of the dog, top lip curled away from his gums, snarling like a feral animal. "Come on then, Marvel. Try taking me on and see what happens."

"Stop!" I grab Marvel's collar and pull him towards the door, still holding Lucky in my arms. I'm almost there when Ivana appears in her customary black leather.

"Why are you running away, printzessa?" Andrej's voice follows me as I push past Ivana in the doorway. Marvel is still straining to get back to the man in the kitchen and protect me. "We were just getting acquainted."

"What's going on?" Ivana grabs my arm, but the expression on my face must change her mind, because she drops it almost immediately.

"Ask him."

I keep walking, but not before I hear her say, "What the fuck, Andrej. Why don't you fucking grow up?"

I spend the rest of the afternoon in the garden with the dogs, waiting for Leo to come home. I try to focus on Marvel and Lucky, but it's hard with my thoughts whirling around inside my head.

Elena was Leo's fiancée.

Leo cheated on Elena while she was wearing the same ring that's on my finger.

The wedding is part of the plan to trap Xander.

I want Leo to come home and clarify that it isn't how it sounds. Because Tamara might have the hots for my fiancé, and Andrej might be the demon younger brother, but when I remind myself that Leo had me drugged and abducted from an airplane, they all start to add up to a shit-show that I want no part of.

What if he comes home and denies cheating on his first fiancé?

I know I should believe him over Tamara. I can't imagine life without Leo, and when he asked me to trust him, I did so willingly. I know that what I should do is forget about the conversation in the kitchen and think about the wedding gown that I haven't yet found, but it's hard with Andrej's voice playing on repeat inside my head.

My brother is marrying you because it's part of the trap to snare your precious brother-in-law.

What would Mel do? I've hardly spent any time with her since she married Xander, but she's still my big sister. She knows how it feels to be so in love that it consumes every waking moment. Her advice would be to quit over-thinking it and speak to Leo.

The exact opposite of what she did when she was pregnant with Lucian.

Mel couldn't bring herself to speak to Xander about the pregnancy. Then, before she could change her mind, our father and Xander's father convinced her that it was best if she went away to have the baby. To give Xander a chance to focus on being the new head of his family. The new don. No distractions.

So, she went to Montenegro and kept his child a secret from him for six years, bottling up her own pain at the same time.

I don't think I could do that to Leo.

But what if he has been lying to me all along?

Ugh! The questions in my head are deafening.

So, when Sergei approaches me with a travel cup filled with coffee, I accept the distraction gratefully. "You looked like you could do with some refreshments."

I sip the scalding coffee and grimace. This won't help quell the anxiety tearing through my body, but it might help to clear my head. "Is it that obvious?"

He smiles. I haven't spent much time with Sergei, but looking at him closely, I realize that he has kind eyes. His face is round even though he carries no surplus weight, the kind of face some kids might associate with the grandpa in a story book if he grew a white beard and moustache.

"You normally smile when you're out here with the dogs. Today—" he shrugs "—something is missing."

I swallow another mouthful of coffee. I'm not so naïve that I believe I can discuss Leo's brother with one of his men. "When will Leonid be home?"

He turns his face towards the sky that's already showing hints of pink and lilac as the sun melts into the horizon. "Late. He's at the casino."

This sends another surge of panic through me. What does he do at the casino? Does he mingle with the guests or watch them from the comfort of a glass-walled office? Is he a gambler? A slot machine fanatic? Or is poker his game? I know so little about him, but I'm prepared to marry him without my family's blessing.

Am I being played for a fool or is it real?

"He did ask me to give you this though." Sergei slides a phone from his pocket and hands it to me.

My phone.

I haven't seen it since I boarded the flight back to Chicago.

I take it from him and am surprised at how cold and heavy it feels in the palm of my hand, as if my time in this house has stripped me of all my memories of everyday life. This device was my connection to the rest of the world, but living without it has turned it into forbidden fruit.

"He said to tell you to call your sister." Sergei keeps his face tilted upward as though soaking up the remains of the day.

"Mel? I can call Mel?" I don't even try to hide the excitement in my voice. I hand Sergei the cup of coffee and unlock my phone.

"I have to stick around though. You understand."

"Yes."

I don't even care that he's been instructed to listen to my conversation. He'll probably report back to Leo, but he won't hear anything incriminating. I'm not exactly going to ask her to come and get me. I just want to talk to her about Leo and the wedding and Lucky.

My fingers are trembling so violently that it takes me three attempts to locate Mel's number in my contacts app. When I hit the green button, I pray that she'll pick up—it would be too cruel to be given this opportunity only for Mel to be too busy to answer.

My heart is thumping like crazy. Pick up, Mel. Please pick up.

There's a click, and then Mel's voice is saying, "Oh my fucking God, Gianna, you're alive. Where the fuck are you? Tell me now, and I'll come and get you."

Tears sting my eyes. "I'm okay, Mel. Don't worry about me. I'm safe."

"Bullshit, Gi. You disappear off the face of the fucking earth and then call me up to tell me you're safe?"

"Mel, listen to me. I don't have long." I raise my eyes to Sergei, who is discreetly looking the other way.

"Why? Where are you?" Her voice is shrill, and I feel a surge of love for my sister who probably hasn't slept since I was abducted. "Tell me the name of the fucker who's holding you and I'll kill them myself."

I can't help smiling. I've missed my sister.

I've missed her so much that I don't pay attention to the sounds in the background of the call until I hear a gunshot and realize that it isn't at Mel's end.

It's right here in Leo's backyard.

What happens next is a blur. Sergei grabs my hand. We run, not in the direction of the woods, but back towards the house. A bullet whistles past my head. Something hot and wet splatters my face, and still, we keep running, and I've no idea what's going on, but I do know that everything feels wrong.

More gunfire.

A voice yells at us to stop right there. I look around and, through blurry eyes, find Ivana running in our direction with her gun aimed directly at us.

26

LEONID

I know before I answer the call that I'm too late.

I wanted to give Sergei the benefit of the doubt. Time to put things right. He has been by my side for as long as I can remember, and I allowed my own sense of loyalty to misjudge his.

Fuck. Fuck. *Fuck!*

"Pakhan." Ivana's voice travels from the phone to my ear, cold and clinical, beating the blood gushing through my veins into submission. "The asset has been taken."

She doesn't need to say anything else.

I grip the phone so tightly I could crush it in my bare hand.

I didn't want to be here at the casino tonight. I've spent the entire evening thinking about going home to find Gianna in my bed. Picturing her hair fanned across the pillows, her full breasts and pink nipples winking at me to be sucked, her legs open wide and inviting me in. But I lingered out of a sense of fucking duty.

Duty to the family rather than duty to the woman I love.

The woman who has switched a light on inside me and painted the world in vibrant colors I never knew existed until now.

Gianna, who has taught me that blood isn't always thicker.

If Xander fucking Amory so much as touches a hair on her head, I swear to God, I will chop him into tiny pieces myself and send bits of him to every single member of his fucking Sicilian family.

The casino clientele doesn't register in my line of vision. Something in my expression must warn them to keep out of my way, and they part like the Red Sea, giving me an unobstructed route out of the building.

Outside, Marco is waiting by the car, the passenger door open.

"I'm driving." I don't wait for him to object or climb into the passenger seat. The car is speeding out of the lot before the door has even slammed shut behind me.

I don't check out Marco in the rearview mirror, standing where I left him outside the casino. I need to remain focused. I need to keep this red-hot anger burning inside me until I've obliterated the Amory mob from this planet.

I'll deal with Sergei later. If he sticks around. He'll know what's coming to him, and if he has any sense, he won't wait for Xander Amory to offer him protection, he'll get his sorry ass out of this country and disappear somewhere in the back of beyond. Even then, I'll still find him. I'll hunt him down to the fucking Antarctic if that's what it takes.

My knuckles are white on the steering wheel.

My jaw is clenched so tightly, I can feel my back teeth grinding.

Good. I've been suppressing everything that makes me Pakhan since Gianna got under my skin, but without this simmering fury, I'll never be able to protect her. I only hope that she can learn to live with this. The real me. Rather than the idealistic image of me that she must have created inside her head.

But first, I have to get her back.

The road belongs to me. I don't stop for traffic signals or pull over to let the emergency services pass me by. Tonight, every other fucker on the road makes way for me like I've got a huge fucking beacon on the roof warning them to move or I'll shoot.

I don't even have to think about where I'm going. I've avoided it for long enough that the route is imprinted behind my eyelids with indelible ink.

I drive straight into Amory territory, and what do you know, the place is fucking deserted. Almost like they were expecting me.

I stop the car in plain sight in the middle of the industrial land occupied by the Amory Corporation. I climb out of the car and start walking towards the first building, a gun in each hand.

A sense of serenity takes hold. I should've done this a long while ago when Xander first started systematically trying to destroy my operation. But maybe I needed Gianna in my life to give me a sense of purpose.

"Come and get me, fuckers!"

I fire a round of bullets into the first warehouse.

When the aftershock settles, there's nothing but silence. Not a whisper of a leaf in the breeze, no birds rustling their feathers, not even an insect buzzing around my head. It feels as if the ground beneath my feet is holding its breath, but not a soul from Amory Corp makes an appearance.

"No? Have it your way!" My voice echoes around the warehouses and bounces straight back at me.

I shoot up the next building. Keep walking. The third building receives the same treatment.

"Stop being a fucking coward and come and get me! This is what you wanted, isn't it? Well, here I am!" I spread my arms wide, exposing my body to the retaliating gunfire I'm waiting for.

Still nothing.

"Pakhan?"

I've been so in the zone of what I'm going to do to Xander Amory when he shows his *zhelty trus* face, that I never heard my own people coming up behind me.

Ivana places a hand on my arm, forcing me to lower my weapon.

She isn't alone. Tamara and Marco are with her, and I don't need to turn around to understand that I'm surrounded by my loyal hand-picked men.

"Go home." I keep my eyes fixed on the Amory Corp sign above the closest warehouse. "This is between me and the Sicilian trus."

"You know we can't do that." Ivana's voice is calm and steady. "We're in this together, Pakhan."

Without warning, I fire another round of bullets into the next building.

"Stop, Pakhan." Tamara this time. "This isn't how we operate."

"No?" I don't look at her. "Tell me, how do we operate then?"

"We're better than this," Ivana takes over. "We hit him where it hurts."

"I'm listening."

My mind is still focused on finishing the man responsible for taking my woman, but I'm not so blinded by bloodlust that I won't listen to what she has to say. Ivana is the most calculating of the two sisters, often two or three steps ahead of me in this game of organized crime. The fact that she's here is all I need to know about her unquestioning loyalty.

"We burn down his territories. Xander Amory is all about money and power. We start here. A warning that we will not lie down and take his shit. Then we move onto the next territory, and the next." She pauses. "He'll know who is responsible, so we target some of our own properties, misdirect the blame. I have men in place, Pakhan. I've emptied the warehouses, moved our assets into storage."

While I've been spending my time with Gianna, Ivana has once again, gotten ahead of the game and manipulated the chess pieces in our favor.

"Talk to me."

She explains which of our territories she has prepared to torch. They have already been targeted by Xander in his relentless attacks, making it easy for us to set the blame at his feet. I don't want to lose more assets, but I have to look at the bigger picture. I can't see a future that doesn't include Gianna, and this war with her brother-in-law must end before I can win her back.

"Where is Andrej?"

Ivana shrugs. "He was at the house earlier today. Before—"

"Before they came for the printzessa," Tamara interjects. "He told her that the wedding was part of the plan to take down Xander Amory. She was a little ... distressed."

My fists clench around the weapons in my hands.

I love my little brother, but his ruthlessness has no boundaries and then it becomes a liability. "I'll handle Andrej." There is still the more pressing matter of what to do about Sergei's betrayal.

"I tried to stop them, Pakhan." Ivana is all coiled energy waiting to be set free. Together, she and I will be unstoppable with the mood I'm in, and I pity anyone that tries to get in our way. "I shot Sergei."

I know how difficult this would've been for her—Sergei is like a father to her and Tamara—but I also know that they will do whatever it takes to protect me and the people I love.

"Then all we need to do is follow the trail of blood."

The industrial estate is still silent. Darkness has settled upon the warehouses like a cozy blanket, and I have the unsettling feeling that Xander was expecting us. Like Ivana, he is sacrificing a territory for the bigger picture. But it will not win him Gianna Sedric.

She is mine, she is wearing my grandmama's diamond and sapphire ring, and I protect what's mine with my life.

There is more than one way to lure a rat from its hole.

I turn around, raise my weapons above my head and fire. Within moments, my men start moving forward in formation from their hiding places and close in on the Amory buildings. I'm confident that the area has been evacuated of people. They've had my warnings. Unlike my nemesis, I'm not here to murder innocent people in cold blood.

Ivana came prepared. Within minutes, the buildings light up like funeral pyres, the angry flickering flames casting an orange glow across our faces. The fires hiss and crackle. The heat is immense; sweat beads on my upper lip and trickles down my face and spine.

But I get zero satisfaction from razing my enemy's assets to the ground.

While he has Gianna in his protection, there isn't enough room in the city for the both of us.

"Pakhan?" The flames are reflected in Ivana's flickering eyes, adding a devilish glow to her serious features. "Do I give the order to proceed?"

I nod once. I trust her when she says that she has moved our assets into storage, but I would destroy everything I own to have Gianna back in my arms.

"Proceed," she snaps into her radio device.

One word.

That's all it takes to set the burning wheels in motion, and I follow Marco back to the car, knowing that, by the end of tonight, both my assets and those of my nemesis will be seriously depleted. Dirty gray plumes of smoke bounce across the rooftops and spread out across Chicago like ancient tribal signals. Xander will already know that I am coming for him.

I don't look behind me as I climb into the passenger seat of the car, and Marco starts the engine.

"Where to?"

"We follow the mole."

Here's the thing about moles: they spend their lives digging underground, but they always surface eventually, and when this one does, I'll be waiting for him. Xander Amory will not put his own neck on the line for Sergei, even if he did orchestrate the attack on my property to kidnap Gianna. Sergei will have served his purpose. He is expendable.

What I don't understand is why he betrayed me.

What did Xander promise him? Money? An escape route from this way of life? Or does their alliance go way deeper than anyone else realizes?

Marco takes the back routes through the city, avoiding the screaming sirens of the emergency services, to the suburbs where Xander Amory lives with his family.

I should've ended the mole's life sooner, and this is something that I will have to live with. But Xander Amory will not get away with sneaking into my home and taking the woman I love.

No matter what it takes.

27

GIANNA

"Let me go!"

I've waited too long. Stunned by the gunfire and Sergei's unexpected reaction to the attack, I follow him in a daze and don't jolt back to reality until it's too late. Until I realize what's happening. Until I spot Xander with a weapon in his hand.

But Sergei is gripping me so tightly I'm afraid he'll break my arm if I try to wrench it free.

"Keep moving," he growls.

Blood is seeping from a bullet hole in his shoulder, black and thick as oil in the fading light. His blood must be on my face. Ivana shot him. She tried to stop him from getting me out of here, and she shot one of her own men.

I feel like I'm watching a movie scene, and I'm the person in the audience yelling at the main character to turn around and go back. "*Not that way! That way is dangerous!*" Days ago, I'd have given anything to escape from Leo's house; I didn't hesitate when Tamara took me to the woods lining the edge of his land.

But now… Everything has changed.

Leonid Ivanov asked me to marry him, and I said yes.

I'm wearing his grandmother's ring on my finger and discussing rose petals with the gardener.

I could no more leave him now than I could stop breathing or loving dogs or wanting to make a difference in this cruel world.

"Sergei, let me go!" I dig in my heels and throw my weight backwards to knock him off-balance.

Where is Ivana when I need her? Where is Leo? Where is Tamara with her sly comments about wonderful-fucking-Elena like the woman was some kind of goddess?

But Sergei is still dragging me along, and instinct keeps me moving so that I don't fall flat on my face. I claw at his fist with my free hand. My chest is heaving with the exertion of keeping up with him and fear that I'll never see Leo again.

"I'm not going. You can't make me leave. *You're hurting me!*"

Tears sting my eyes as he drags me further and further away from Leo. From the man I fell in love with, probably the first moment I set eyes on him in his immaculate dining room.

I can see the armed men surrounding the property. How did they get in? Did Sergei open the door wide and stand back to let them pass through? Or was it Tamara?

Panic hurtles through my veins and bounces around inside my chest.

If I go with Xander, I'm never coming back. It's all I can think about. Never sharing his bed again, never feeling his lips pressed against mine, never playing with Lucky and Marvel in the garden.

Bullets are still flying around us, but I know that I would rather take one right here while trying to stay with Leo than run away from him to save my own life. So, I choose the only option I have left: I allow my body to become a dead weight. I land on my knees, dirt and gravel scraping my skin through my pants, but I ignore the pain. Sergei stumbles over me as I drop to the ground, but the man's fist is still like a metal vice around my wrist.

I roll over as he crashes on top of me, ball my right hand into a fist and aim a blow at his diaphragm. He doesn't even groan out loud as he lands heavily on his knees. He's back on his feet in an instant, and I wish I had a gun to finish what Ivana started.

Armed men close in on us, covering us with the barrage of bullets flying from their guns. I'm sobbing now. They're tears of frustration. No one came to rescue me when I was abducted, and now that I've fallen in love with my captor, Xander is going to take me away again like he's some kind of superhero.

When I'm close enough to see the smug expression on Xander's face, Sergei shoves me towards him like he's done with being the fall guy for the Sicilian boss.

Xander doesn't move. He's so arrogant that he thinks I'll fall into his arms and shower him with my undying gratitude. But the way I feel right now, I want to punch him in the face and scream at him to stay the fuck out of my life.

So, that's what I do.

My knuckles feel like they're on fire when my fist connects with his cheekbone, but it's worth the pain for the look on his face. His eyes widen in shock and then darken when the tender skin beneath his eye splits.

He makes no move to touch me himself.

Maybe Mel warned him not to lay a finger on me, or maybe he's just a yellow-bellied coward who, afraid of what Leo will do to him if he touches me, is hiding behind his reputation and his men.

I'm still hollering and screaming at him, "Leave me the fuck alone," when two of his men grab me from behind and lift my feet off the ground. "Xander! Tell your fucking men to put me down!"

I lash out with both feet, catching my captors' thighs with my heels. But they're far stronger than me, and no matter how I struggle and buck and scream, they carry me off Leo's property and out of his life without even raising a sweat.

I'm still struggling and yelling hoarsely between sobs of frustration when they bundle me into the back of a truck with blacked-out windows. I land on my hip and roll sideways, but the door slams shut behind me, locking me in with the murky gloom. Someone else must be waiting for me inside the truck.

They don't speak. But something cold and wet is held over my face, smothering my nose and mouth and filling my brain with a sinister chemical smell, and the world goes black.

I open my eyes, bringing the room slowly into focus.

I don't know where I am. My limbs feel heavy, and a small smile tugs my lips upwards when I think about Leo, spreading my legs wide and burying his face in my sex. I feel the same kind of lethargy that follows a night of passion in Leo's bed. Only, I can't remember him coming back from the casino or what we did when we went to his room.

I study the neutral walls, the abstract artwork in the minimalist frame, the polished dark-wood floor.

This isn't Leo's room.

I sit up, leaning heavily against the padded headboard as the room slides out from under me. I squeeze my eyes shut and breathe deeply until my pulse starts to regulate. I feel nauseous. Bile rises in my throat, and I lean over the side of the bed retching, grateful when nothing comes out. My head feels hangover-woozy, my brain cells spinning.

Jeez, what the fuck happened last night?

Then it all comes bulldozing back to me like a spooked horse.

The phone call to Mel; Sergei; Ivana with her gun aimed straight at us. Xander-fucking-Amory.

Leo will be worried about me. I need to get back to him, let him know that I'm alright, that I didn't want to leave, that Sergei tricked me into calling my sister. It must've been a trap. Xander must've been tracing the call.

The thought that Mel was part of this fills me with a sick sense of uneasiness. I know she must've been worried about me, but when she learns how I feel about Leo, she'll be gutted that she helped her husband drag me away from him.

Will she help me get back to Leo though, that's the question.

And if it means going against her husband's orders, I already know the answer.

No.

I have to get out of here.

Swinging my legs over the side of the bed, I grip the comforter with both hands until my head stops swimming.

The key turning in the lock grabs my attention. I cast my eyes around the room, searching for a weapon, but just like the guest room in Leo's house, there's nothing close to hand that I can use. My gaze instinctively flits to the camera set high in the ceiling cornice.

I've swapped one prison for another, only no matter how hard I look, I'm not going to find my future in this one.

Grabbing the lamp from the nightstand, I stumble across the room and press my back against the wall so that I'll be behind the door when it opens.

The doorknob clicks. The door opens a fraction, and I raise the lamp over my shoulder with the heavy base facing the door. I'm ready to swing when a familiar voice says, "Gi? Gi, where are you?" and Mel walks into the room.

"Mel?" I drop the lamp and fling myself into my sister's arms, my tears finally spilling.

She hugs me tightly, holds me at arm's length, and then hugs me some more. When we finally pull away and sit on the edge of the bed together, both our faces are streaked with tears.

"Are you hurt, Gi?" Her eyes search my face for signs that I've been abused by my captor as she instinctively tugs my hair forward over my shoulders. "I've been so worried about you. When you didn't get off that flight, I didn't know what to think. I thought... Well... I'm just glad you're alright. You're safe here now."

"Is that why Xander locked me in this room? To keep me safe?"

I feel a stab of guilt at the look of hurt that flashes across her eyes, but my sister needs to understand that I'm not a pawn in her husband's war against the Russians.

"He was worried about you. We both were."

"Not so worried that it stopped him from using chloroform on me." My head spins and my stomach lurches to remind me that I'm still suffering the aftereffects of Xander's brotherly concern.

"You were fighting him, Gi." The expression on her face is unreadable as she narrows her eyes. "Do you remember punching him in the face?"

"Yep, and I'll do it again if he walks in here right now."

Mel covers her mouth with one hand like I just suggested walking naked through the house to fetch some coffee. "What did they do to you, Gianna?" she whispers between her fingers before lowering her hand and reaching out to touch me.

I pull away from her. She doesn't get it yet, and until I can make her understand that being away from Leo feels as if my right arm has been wrenched from its socket, I can't bear for anyone to touch me. Not even my sister.

"They didn't do anything to me. At least not what you're thinking."

She breathes deeply. "Let me get you some food and coffee. Are you hungry? Did they feed you?"

"Mel, I'm fine. They looked after me." I don't mention the incident in the cold room shortly after I arrived—I've practically erased it from my mind with everything that followed. "I-I didn't want to leave."

"What?" She furrows her brow. "Why not? What did they say to you about Xander?" She stands up and paces the room. "Oh, my fucking God, they've been brainwashing you. They've turned you against your own family. No wonder you look so different."

I shake my head. "You've got it all wrong, Mel. Leo isn't a bad person. He looked after me. He would've protected me with his life."

"*Leo?* What the actual fuck, Gianna. The guy fucking kidnapped you, and you're calling him Leo." She turns away like she can't bear to look at me. "Wait till Dad finds out. He'll go fucking apeshit. Xander is going to fucking rip the man apart limb from limb, as if this war wasn't crazy enough."

"That's why you have to help me stop him, Mel." My chest feels like it's been ripped open, and my heart is being pulled in two different directions. "This war has to end. I need you to help me get back to Leo."

It's Mel's turn to shake her head as she backs towards the door, and I'm worried that she's going to call Xander to come and knock me out again. "You don't know what you're saying. Did the Russian put you up to this? Did he turn you against Xander?"

I take a deep breath and set my shoulders back.

"I'm a grown woman, Mel. I can make up my own mind about your husband and he was never my favorite person. To begin with," I quickly add when I see the way her expression crumples. "And *the Russian* has a name. It's Leonid Ivanov, and I'm in love with him."

She swallows hard, steps closer and reaches for my hand. This time, I let her take it. "You don't know what you're saying. You're suffering from a classic case of Stockholm Syndrome, Gianna. We'll get you the help you need. We'll…"

Her voice trails off when she feels the huge stone on my finger. Turning my hand over, she traces the diamond and sapphires with her fingertip and then raises her eyes to meet mine.

"Gi, what the fuck is going on?"

"I told you I'm in love with Leo." I keep my voice steady. If my own sister won't believe me, I don't stand a chance of convincing Xander to end this war and take me back to him. Mel is my only hope. "This is his grandmother's ring. I'm going to marry him next week."

"No." She closes her eyes briefly. "Xander will never allow it. He'll—"

"Listen to me, Mel. Xander isn't my father, and he can't stop me from marrying the man I love." She's about to interject, but I shut her down. "Do you remember how you felt when you first met Xander? You knew he was the enemy, but he kissed you once, and there was no turning back. You were smitten."

"That was different. Xander didn't kidnap me on a fucking flight back from Montenegro."

"No, but he kidnapped me tonight."

Deep breath. I need her to listen, but all she knows about Leo is what she has heard from her husband, and he isn't exactly nominating Leo for the mafia boss of the year award.

"Mel, I know Leo kidnapped me because of this stupid war, but there are two sides to every battle. I'm not condoning what he did. But he isn't the ruthless monster you think he is. I got a fever, and he nursed me better. He got me a rescue puppy—her name is Lucky, and I can't wait for you to meet her. He's going to open a women's refuge in Chicago, and he wants me to run it. And when I'm in his arms..."

"You know that there's nowhere else you'd rather be." Mel finishes the sentence for me. "You know that if you can't be in his arms, the sun might as well never shine again."

I'm smiling despite the groggy pounding inside my head. "Looking at Leo makes me feel alive and like I want to throw up all at the same time."

Mel tips her head back and stares at the ceiling. When she looks at me again, her eyes are large with unshed tears. "I knew you were different the moment I walked into the room. You've got it bad."

"Uh-huh."

She throws her arms around me again, but the hug is fleeting as the implications jolt her back to reality. "Did you...?" She gives me the side-eye. Before I can respond, her shoulders slump. "You did, didn't you? You fucked him already."

I can't lie to my sister. I didn't tell her about the arranged marriage to Seamus, but that was withholding information, it wasn't a barefaced lie.

"I wanted to call you and tell you everything, but Leo—"

"Kept your phone so that we wouldn't trace you." She nods.

She is no longer judging my poor taste in falling for the enemy —I'm only following in her footsteps—she's simply telling it like it is. This is the life we were born into. We both know how it works.

"They're enemies," she's talking out loud. "Xander will want to kill him when he finds out. He already wants to kill him."

"Daniel wanted to kill Xander when he found out about the two of you." I shrug. "Mel, just because this is the way it's always been, it doesn't mean that things can't change. We can make a difference. A new generation that doesn't want to rip each other's throats out."

"If only it was that simple."

"It is, Mel. But I can't do it alone."

"My beautiful little sister." Her fingers are still subconsciously rubbing the diamond ring. "You always were the one who wanted to change the world."

"Leo will come for me, Mel. You know he will."

Mel nods. "Xander would do the same for me."

"I don't want to be the cause of more bloodshed. I need Xander to let me go to Leo. I can stop him, I know I can. But I can't do it without your help."

"Xander will never agree to it."

"Please, Mel."

My sister is almost there. She believes that I'm in love with Leo, but there's a part of her, the part that still sees the images of our mother lying in a pool of her own blood when she closes her eyes at night, that's afraid to interfere in the way Xander runs Amory Corp. I need to give her one final push.

"If Xander kills Leo, I'll never forgive him. I promise you that I'll disappear, and you'll never see me again."

"Gi, please, don't make me choose between my sister and my husband."

"It isn't a choice, Mel. You can have both. All you have to do is convince Xander to let me go before one of us loses someone we love."

She stares at the window, my hand still in hers, pensive.

Have I done enough to convince her? If I haven't, my only option is to try to escape before Leo arrives. I know Xander won't shoot me, even if I did punch him in the face earlier, but he won't sit back and watch me walk out of his heavily guarded property either, not when he went to such efforts to get me here.

"Okay," she says finally. "Let's go."

"Go where?"

"To speak to Xander." She gives me a small smile. "I know my little sister, and when you say you'll disappear, and we'll never see you again if anything happens to Leo... I believe you."

I throw my arms around her neck and squeeze her until she complains that she can't breathe. "Thanks, Mel. You're the best sister a girl could ask for."

"Don't thank me yet. Xander isn't going to know what's hit him."

I flex my fingers on my right hand. "I think he already does."

Xander is in his study when we go downstairs. Mel knocks three times on the door like it's their secret code, and he calls out, "Come in," sounding as if he's a thousand miles away, not just on the other side of the door.

Mel glances at me, eyebrows raised, and I nod.

I can sense the tension emanating from the crack around the door, but we have no choice. Without Xander's approval, I'm a prisoner in his house until this is all over, and this won't be over until at least one of the two enemies is dead.

Quelling the thought of Leo dying at my brother-in-law's hands, I follow Mel inside.

The study is larger than our father's. Xander is sitting behind a solid mahogany desk in a wide leather seat that seems to embrace him like those neck cushions people use on long-haul flights. A bookcase filled with leather-bound books consumes the wall behind Xander giving him the air of a bestselling author who uses it as a backdrop for his social media posts.

Three men dressed in standard mafia black nod to Mel when we enter and leave the room, closing the door behind them with an unobtrusive click.

I look at Xander. There's a shadowy bruise on his left cheek from where I punched him, and his eye is puffy and bloodshot, but that aside, he has aged since I went to Montenegro two years ago. The grooves across his forehead have deepened while I've been away, and the stubble on his chin has a hint of silver in it now that I never noticed before. He's still good looking, just a little more worn than he was when he first met Mel.

His eyes roam over me from top to toe checking, as Mel did, for signs of physical abuse at the hands of my captor. I stand tall and raise my chin, defiant under his gaze, reminding him that I can look after myself.

"You're welcome," he says without a trace of humor.

I instantly bristle. "I never asked you to rescue me. I was doing just fine where—"

"Okay." Mel shuts me down with a warning look. "What's going on, Xander?" She obviously sensed the tension in the atmosphere too, and she knows her husband better than anyone.

"Nothing you need to worry about. I'll handle it."

He looks as if he's in fight-or-flight mode, sitting forward in his seat, ready to either dismiss us and run, or pull a gun from his top drawer and tell us that he's off to kill himself a Russian mobster.

"That's what worries me," Mel says.

She doesn't sit down but stands beside me. Sisters united.

"What's that supposed to mean?" His tone is cold, menacing, and I wonder if he sounds the same when he and Mel are alone or if he softens like chocolate left out in the sun the way Leo does.

"This war…"

"This war that just destroyed fifty percent of my assets?" His eyebrows arch jaggedly. "This war that cost me more men than I cared to sacrifice in order to rescue your sister?"

I open my mouth to protest a second time and change my mind. I need to be patient and let Mel handle it.

"What assets?" Mel asks in a voice that sounds wary.

"Warehouses. Vehicles. Dru-electrical goods." Xander is speaking to Mel but watching me like this is somehow all my fault.

"I never wanted to get caught up in this stupid vendetta if that's what you're thinking," I blurt out before I can stop myself.

"Stupid vendetta?" His eyes become small and dark. "You think you can do better, then go right ahead, and be my guest." He stands, pushes his seat back, and gestures for me to take his place behind the desk.

"This isn't her fault, Xander, and you know it," Mel snaps. "They're just buildings. It's only stuff. Everything can be replaced."

"At what cost?" He remains standing.

"We have enough money to buy more warehouses." Mel squares up to him. "But there isn't enough money in the world to replace my sister."

Xander's gaze flits between me and Mel. He's breathing heavily like he just completed the four-hundred-meter sprint. "What the fuck are you talking about, Mel?"

"I'm talking about my sister, Gianna. She's in love with Leonid Ivanov."

His face has already darkened like the sun just passed overhead throwing us all into shadow.

"If you kill him, she's walking out of here and she's never coming back." Mel's tone is serious but surprisingly calm, so that there's no ambiguity in what she's about to say. "And if she goes, I go."

28

LEONID

The city is covering its ears against the wails of the emergency services speeding towards the ever-growing number of fires. Chicago is sporting a dirty-gray hat made of smoke like a gangster who just walked into a bar and forgot to remove it.

And the rat is still in its hidey hole, cleaning its whiskers and plotting its next move.

I never had Xander Amory down for a coward, not really. I expected him to help me bring this feud to its natural conclusion tonight, one way or another. But it seems that I misjudged him—he is only prepared to fight when he isn't on the defensive.

Or perhaps he believes that I'm done with Gianna Sedric already.

This will be his biggest error yet, and one for which he will pay dearly.

"Why doesn't he come to stop us?" Tamara stands beside me watching as my men set fire to yet another building in yet another territory that is unofficially claimed by the Sicilians.

"He thinks that because he forced his way onto my land and took Gianna, he has the upper hand. But he has learned nothing since he became the head of his family. I will not stop until I have destroyed everything that he owns."

"Pakhan." Ivana flanks the other side of me. "We might not be able to stroll into the next Amory territory quite so easily."

"I think you've made your point," Tamara adds.

"Which point do you think I've made?"

I've yet to deal with her part in Gianna's failed escape attempt, but while I'm cleansing the city of Sicilians, I might as well flush out all the moles digging holes in my soil.

Tamara doesn't flinch. "You've shown him that you're angry about the printzessa's abduction. Now that he has her, he will never hand her over. It's a matter of principle."

"So, what do you suggest I do now?"

"Arrange a meeting. On neutral territory, the way your fathers would've done."

"I disagree." Ivana's voice could be mistaken for her sister's apart from the abrasive edge that grates its way into the listener's ears. "The Sicilians can't be trusted. We might not be able to protect you. I think we should continue to flush him out. It will be seen as a sign of weakness if he doesn't try to stop you; he might as well walk away with his hands in the air and divide the Amory Corp between his enemies."

"So, you think I should fight, and Tamara thinks I should talk."

I stare at the burning warehouse in front of us, the acrid smoke creeping into my lungs and making my eyes feel gritty.

This war has become personal. It is no longer about two families trying to prove that they are more powerful than the other, or that they deserve the largest slice of the city's action. This isn't about money or reputation or respect. It isn't about casinos or weapons or drugs or any other organized crime that takes place in plain sight in the city of Chicago.

Xander Amory has stolen what's most important to me and, whether he realizes it or not, I won't rest until she is back in my life.

Ivana's hand brushes mine to get my attention.. It opens up a tiny hole in my heart for the little kids who reached out to me from that stinking container as if I were an angel in disguise sent from heaven to save them. Somewhere beneath their tough exterior, there are two little girls still desperate for affection.

"I guess it depends on the outcome you want," she says.

"There can only be one outcome." I look at each of them in turn. "I am not going home without Gianna."

"Then you have your answer, Pakhan," Ivana says. "You must let Xander Amory know what you want. His response will decide whether you talk or fight."

"Tamara?"

I know what she did. I don't fully understand her motive, perhaps because I don't love her in the same way she loves me, but I know that she encouraged Gianna to run away so that our lives could return to normal. Perhaps now she understands that what was normal before no longer exists.

She thinks about it, the roaring flames creating golden patterns across her face. "I agree with my sister. Either way, we'll be right beside you as we've always been."

It's all I needed to hear.

"Contact Sergei. Arrange a meeting with Xander and make it clear that if he arrives without Gianna, I'll understand that we are at war until the last man is standing."

Tamara's phone is already in her hand. Ivana is about to protest, either aware of her sister's betrayal or having picked up on the tension between us, but I gesture for her to leave it be. This is Tamara's chance for redemption. The sisters may have been my weakness all along, but I can't turn my back on either of them without first allowing them to prove their loyalty.

"Now we wait."

We are running out of rival territories to invade by the time Xander responds to my request. The delay has done nothing to soothe my temper, which has morphed from red-hot and hellish to the icy chill of a cold-blooded serpent with a taste for revenge. Someone should warn him.

Or not.

I've waited too long to watch him squirm and am almost tempted to kill him anyway. The only thing stopping me is knowing that he is married to Gianna's sister Melissa, and I can't face a lifetime of knowing that I lost the woman I love because I refused to let my enemy live. I will not allow him to have that power over me.

We arrange to meet in neutral territory on the outskirts of the city in a vacant lot of self-storage lockups.

I arrive first with Ivana and Tamara. Against their advice, I send Marco away in the car when he drops us off and warn my men to keep their distance and wait for the order to attack. When, or if, required. Everyone is under strict instructions to ensure Gianna's safety, no matter what happens.

I don't fear death.

When you live with the constant threat of it, death becomes a natural part of life. A stepping stone between this existence and whatever follows it when we pass. I'm not anesthetized to the sight of blood; I've simply learned to compartmentalize it inside my head. It's a coping mechanism that I developed as a child after witnessing my first murder at the hands of my father.

So, when Xander Amory's car rolls into the remote compound with the headlamps killed, the adrenaline rush spiking through me has nothing to do with the fear of losing my life, and everything to do with the alarmingly real terror that I might never get to see Gianna again.

My only consolation is knowing that her sister and my people will do everything in their power to keep her alive.

The car slowly comes to a halt some distance away from where I'm standing with Ivana and Tamara. The engine ceases purring. The night envelops us in balmy silence.

"Wait here." I don't look at the women flanking me.

"No, Pakhan."

I don't glance behind me, but I sense Ivana blocking her

sister's path with her arm as I stride purposefully towards the only car in the vicinity.

I'm a walking target. Xander might have the place surrounded by guards with their weapons aimed directly at my head, but I'm unarmed, and I'm trusting him to honor our mutual arrangement.

My heart thuds dully as I stop at an acceptable distance from the vehicle, my hands by my sides. The windows are tinted. I can't see if Gianna is inside the car, but I'm acutely conscious that if she is, she'll be watching me right now. How does she feel? Is her heart racing at the sight of me, so close but untouchable? Does she want to run to me, fling her arms around my neck and beg me to take her home?

Or have Xander and her sister had enough time to convince her that what we feel for each other isn't real? My chest constricts at the very real prospect she might never want to see me again if they've been successful.

The front passenger door opens.

A woman steps out of the car, closes the door behind her with a gentle click, and faces me.

The resemblance to Gianna is uncanny, only this woman is a little taller, her features a little more defined than her younger sister's as though life has filed them down to sharper edges. Her hair, even in the smoky twilight of the unlit compound, is as unruly as Gianna's, and she walks towards me with the same easy gait. A reminder of what I'm missing.

Why is she here? I don't know whether her appearance is a sign that Gianna is waiting for me in the car, or if Melissa came to break it to me gently that her sister wants nothing more to do with me.

The only thing I am certain of right now is that Melissa will have fought dirty to get her husband to agree to this, and there'll be an army of men watching us, just itching for me to make a wrong move. I can't blame Xander. I'd react the same way if this was Gianna meeting with him in my place.

"I'm Melissa, Gianna's sister." Her eyes appraise me, and I wonder what Gianna has told her about me. "Before we begin, I must ask you to swap places with me so that my husband can see my face. I'm sure you'll understand why."

I understand. Xander will have warned her to signal if she feels threatened. It's a fair request, and one that I can't refuse, not if I want this conversation to go my way.

It will also mean that my back is to Xander's vehicle, and I'll have to rely on sound and gut instinct alone to alert me to any movement behind me.

We circle each other and change positions. I'm willingly exposing myself to my enemy, but I hope Melissa sees this as a sign that I will do anything for Gianna. Her faint smile gives me a glimmer of hope that injects warmth into my chest.

"Is Gianna safe?" I ask.

Another smile: Melissa is keeping it light for her husband's benefit. Trying to prove that I'm perhaps not the enemy he expected me to be.

"She's safe. Talk to me, Leo." Her voice is gentle. "Tell me how you feel about my sister."

Leo. She has listened to Gianna enough for her to adopt the shortened version of my name, and I have to believe that this isn't false hope.

"I love her."

It's the first time I've admitted this even to myself. But saying the words out loud only reenforces my love for Gianna, and my chest swells in response.

"I want to spend the rest of my life with her. I will protect her with my life. I will do whatever it takes to make her happy, because my happiness is nothing compared to hers."

Does this make me sound cheesy, like some lovesick teenager?

I don't even fucking care.

I'll scream it from the fucking rooftops so that everyone in Chicago can hear me.

I'll paint the sky with aircraft trails declaring my love for Gianna Sedric if that's what it takes.

Melissa studies me closely, her expression unfathomable. "What would you do if I said that she isn't coming back?"

"I..."

I lick my lips, buying myself some time to reassemble my thoughts, making sure to keep my fists unclenched so that Xander doesn't get the wrong idea. Did I read the situation wrong? Is Melissa here because Gianna couldn't face telling me herself that it was fun while it lasted but now it's over?

"I'd spend the rest of my life without a purpose." I pause, trying to put into words the kind of man I'd become without Gianna Sedric in my world. "I guess I'd become the kind of cold-hearted monster she believed me to be when we first met."

Something flickers behind her eyes. "My brother would've had me believe that Xander was a cold-hearted monster before I met him." She forces a smile for the man sitting in the car behind me. "But he's different when he's with me. I see a side to him that no one else sees. I see what's in his heart."

I nod. I suspect that she isn't finished.

"He would be angry with me for telling you this, but he calls me his sunshine."

"Gianna is my printzessa."

Melissa's smile lights up her face even in the gloom, making her look even more like Gianna. "She told me about the puppy and the women's refuge. I'm going to keep smiling, for Gianna's sake, not yours, but she also told me that your brother claimed the refuge is part of the plan to defeat my husband."

Fucking Andrej!

My jaw clenches, and I can feel a tic pulsing in my temple. I have to put all thoughts of him aside and focus on the present.

"I won't lie. Opening the refuge will earn me some gold stars within the community, but I want to do it for Gianna. I've seen how passionate she is when she talks about her work. I promised her that I would never make her give it up for me. If she's happy, I'm happy, and believe me nothing gives me greater pleasure than seeing her smile."

Melissa laughs then. "That's a little too much information, thank you very much."

I smile right back at her.

"I believe you, Leo. But one question remains: what do you intend to do about this long-standing feud with my husband? Because you see, I'm in love with him, and I can't bear the thought of a life without him."

"Have you asked your husband the same question?"

"Let's just say that I've laid the foundations. He didn't want me to come here and talk to you tonight."

No surprises there.

"So, how did you convince him?"

"My sister said that if Xander killed you, I would never see her again, and I issued the same ultimatum to my husband."

"She said that?" My pulse is racing. Melissa's voice has softened during our conversation; she believes me, and with her on our side… Anything is possible.

"I need his word that he won't try to stop me from marrying Gianna."

"I'll make sure that you get it."

"There is one more condition. If we're to reach some kind of truce, I need him to deliver the mole back to me."

"I'm sure that won't be a problem." Her smile is genuine. She looks as if she wants to shake my hand or stand on tiptoes and kiss my cheek but can't risk getting too close because we're being watched. "One more thing, if you ever hurt my sister, you'll have me to deal with, and I promise you Xander's vendetta will be nothing compared to what I'll do to you."

Melissa walks back to the car.

Before she reaches it, the rear passenger door opens, and Gianna is running towards me. She launches herself into my arms and wraps her legs around my waist.

I kiss her. I don't care who is watching, or who sees it as a sign of weakness. I kiss her and whisper over and over, "I love you, my printzessa. I love you. I love you. I love you."

29

GIANNA

I AWOKE to an overcast sky and wishy-washy light filtering through the windows of Leo's bedroom, but now... Now it feels as if the universe is smiling down on us with big, wide-mouthed sunshine, coating everything in a fine golden film of fairy dust.

"Fairy dust?" Mel peers at my reflection in the mirror from over my shoulder, her mouth twisted into a lopsided grin. "Who are you, and what have you done with my sister?"

"Did I say that out loud?"

"Yes, along with 'Has anyone fed the dogs?' and 'I can see my nipples through this dress.' For what it's worth, I can't see your nipples, so I don't know what you're looking at."

I stare at my breasts in the mirror.

The vintage dress is floaty and ethereal with an ivory lace train over a cream-colored silk skirt studded with tiny gray-white pearls. I knew what I wanted—I had an image of it in my head from a fairy tale that I remember reading when I was a little girl—but it was Mel who helped me find it by trawling through every vintage boutique in Chicago until our legs ached and I had blisters on the soles of my feet.

It's perfect.

Mel, as my matron of honor, is wearing another vintage dress with a scooped neckline and layers of frothy antique-ivory lace spilling from the waistband. She looks perfect too. Like a princess.

Mel has piled my hair on top of my head and fastened it with strings of pearls to match those on the dress, with long twisty curls framing my face. I hardly recognize myself in the mirror.

"You look beautiful, Gi." Mel lowers her face so that our cheeks are touching, and her reflection smiles back at me. "Positively glowing."

She's right. My cheeks are rosy, my skin has a sheen that reflects the sunshine through the windows giving me an almost angelic appearance, and my hair is glossier than I've ever seen it. I mean, it's been polished and curled to within an inch if its life by Mel, but I look like I belong on the cover of a magazine.

I can't believe I'm marrying Leo today.

Every time I think about the Japanese pagoda covered in rose petals, my stomach clenches, and every part of my body squeals silently with joy.

"How did you convince Xander to attend the wedding?"

"I told him that if he didn't, he wouldn't get to touch me for the next twelve months."

"And he believed you?" I grin at her in the mirror.

"He's a man. He couldn't risk not taking me seriously." She arches her eyebrows and slants her eyes mischievously. "Not when I started moving my stuff into one of the guest rooms."

"Mel! You sly fox!"

"I promise I'll get him to smile later too."

I know it's a lot to expect—a week ago, Xander and Leo were prepared to kill each other. But they've reached an amicable agreement to steer clear of each other's territories and have, temporarily at least, accepted that there's room in the city for both families.

Leo's response to my announcement that I couldn't get married without Mel and her family here, including Xander, was a thin-lipped smile and a flicker of resignation behind his eyes. "If it makes you happy, printzessa, then I will welcome him personally with a glass of champagne and a handshake."

I didn't see Xander arrive. Mel assured me that the handshake, while not exactly warm or accompanied by a toothy smile, was enough to satisfy the other guests that they could eat supper without fear of the two men challenging each other to a duel. It's enough, for now. Mel and I have spent too long apart, and I want to share every step of this new chapter of my life with her.

"How's Dad?"

Mel rolls her eyes. "You know Dad. He doesn't know how to express his emotions, but I think he's coming around to the idea of you marrying into a bratva family. He told me that Mom's family was against her marrying him to begin with."

Dad has never mentioned this to any of his children before.

"They sold their house and were prepared to move to the other side of the country until they realized that Dad would've followed them around the world to find her." Mel swallows hard and blinks back tears. "I hope they didn't regret giving them their blessing."

I half-turn in my seat and cup Mel's hand in mine. "They wouldn't have regretted seeing their daughter in love. Mom was happy. She wanted us to be happy too."

Mel scrunches up her face and sniffs loudly. "No tears today, Gi. Tears on your wedding day are a bad omen."

A wave of nausea washes over me like a tidal wave, and when it passes, I have a desperate craving for pancakes and maple syrup. "Mel, will you go to the kitchen and ask Olga to make me pancakes? I'm starving."

"Did you skip breakfast?"

"No. It's nerves. I always eat when I'm anxious."

She flashes a suspicious look my way from beneath lowered brows but goes to the kitchen anyway.

While she's gone, I stand in front of the full-length mirror in Leo's dressing room and admire my dress.

I wonder who wore it before. Did another bride look at her reflection wearing this dress, turning sideways to get a full view of the lacy train, butterflies tracing crazy patterns inside her stomach? Did that bride feel the same way about her future husband as I feel about Leo?

It's hard to imagine anyone else experiencing the kind of crushing, knee-trembling emotions I feel whenever I'm with

Leo, like these feelings belong to us only. Everyone's different, right? But I hope she was happy, whoever she was. I hope that her husband smothered her with love and made her smile and laugh and dance.

I hope that he was the husband she wanted him to be.

Mel returns shortly after she left with a covered plate piled high with steaming pancakes. "Olga must be a mind-reader—she was already preparing food for you when I got to the kitchen."

I laugh. I might not have been Olga's favorite person when I first arrived, but I think she's happy now that I've taken the dogs off her hands. She still eyes Marvel up from a distance like she's worried he could take her whole hand off with one bite, but when she thinks no one is looking, she prepares the best cuts of meat and feeds them under the breakfast island.

"She's a feeder. I ate two breakfasts yesterday, so she was preempting me being hungry again today."

Mel doesn't say anything. She watches me tuck into the pancakes, careful to catch any crumbs with my hand so that I don't stain my dress with maple syrup. I've eaten two before I think to offer her a pancake.

She shakes her head. "I think your need is greater than mine."

"Were you like this on your wedding day?" I lick syrup from my lips, glad that I haven't yet applied my lip gloss.

"No, but I was like this when I was pregnant with Lucian." She tosses the comment into the dressing room like a hand grenade and stands back while she waits for it to take effect.

The food gets stuck in my gullet, and I start coughing and spluttering, tiny particles of food flying from my mouth and splattering the mirror. My eyes water, and Mel hands me a tissue.

Leaning close to the mirror so that I don't have to look at her, I dab my face carefully, trying to salvage as much of my makeup as I can. I'm stalling for time while I mentally calculate dates, and it dawns on me that I'm a week overdue. I lower my eyes to my breasts which choose this exact moment to start tingling, my nipples swollen and prominent underneath the bodice of my wedding gown.

The bodice that is considerably tighter than it was a week ago when I bought the dress.

"It's the extra helpings of toast," I murmur to myself.

"That's what you're going with?" Mel's eyebrows slide upwards. "The toast?"

I nod. I don't trust myself to speak. Not yet.

I'm still trying to figure out what this will mean to us, to me and Leo, with the refuge that we're planning on opening within the next twelve months. We've already found a building. A huge, three-story, red-brick property in a leafy Chicago suburb with a massive backyard and planning permission to extend outwards and upward into the roof. The instant I stepped inside the building, I knew it was the right one; it had such a positive vibe, that I walked around with Leo telling him how I planned to utilize each room.

And how will Leo react to me being pregnant?

I want to believe that he'll be ecstatic about having a baby, but I've seen too often how a child can alter a relationship. Heard too many horror stories from the women at the refuge. But this is Leo, I remind myself. He isn't like other men. He would protect me and our child with his life, I know he would.

"I'm right, aren't I?" Mel's gentle voice penetrates my reverie.

I turn around slowly to face her. I can't even ask Mel how Xander reacted to the news that he was going to be a father, because Lucian was six before he discovered that he had a son.

I throw my arms around her and hug her tightly, wincing and releasing my grip a little when my breasts complain about being crushed. I ignored the soreness when Leo was sucking on my nipples, but it's harder to ignore now that I'm being forced to confront the truth. I wish that I could turn back time and tell Xander that my sister was pregnant with his baby. So much time wasted because he'd just taken over the family business and everyone said it would be for the best that it makes my heart ache to think of Mel going through this alone.

Best for whom?

"Mel, I'm so sorry." I shake my head, fresh tears collecting on my lashes.

She smiles and dabs my face with a fresh tissue. "Raging hormones; you'd better get used to this. But you have nothing to be sorry for. I'm happy for you, Gi. Both of you."

"But you had to do this alone."

"I wasn't alone. I had you, remember?"

"Did I... Did I help?" I peer at her face through my tears, praying that I gave her some small comfort when she was taken to Montenegro to raise Lucian without his father.

"More than you could ever believe, Gi. I couldn't have done it without you. Even if you did refuse to change a soiled diaper."

I chuckle and promptly start choking on the combination of laughter and slowly erupting sobs. "I still don't think I can change a dirty diaper."

"You'd better learn quick then, Gi, because I'm not doing them. It's payback time."

When our tears and giggles eventually dry up, Mel applies another coat of mascara to my eyelashes and watches while I smooth nude gloss over my lips.

"Ready?" she asks.

"Ready."

Tamara and Ivana are waiting outside the door to escort me and Mel through the gardens and down to the pagoda. They've ditched their customary goth look for simple white shift dresses with rows of colored gemstones embellishing the square necklines. Ivana still has the green flicks elongating her dark eyes, but they both appear softer, like watercolor paintings compared to bold abstracts.

Tamara smiles when she sees us, and for the first time, it feels genuine. I'm not sure that we'll ever be best friends, but I hope that we can at least learn to live together. I know how important they are to Leo, and I don't want to be the cause of any animosity.

"You look beautiful, printzessa." Tamara leans in and kisses my cheeks.

"Does that mean that you'll call me by my real name going forward?"

"Nah." Her curls bounce around her face when she shakes her head. "You'll always be the printzessa."

She and Ivana exchange glances, and Ivana averts her eyes. The only time we ever made eye contact was when she tried to drown me in the cold room, and that feels like a lifetime ago. I vowed then to get her back in my own way, but I think I already have. She respects me for standing up to her, and I think this is the reason why I have her approval to marry the pakhan.

Strangely, Tamara is still the one I'm wary of.

"I just want to apologize," Tamara says out of the blue, "for lying to the pakhan about you."

I sense Mel's bewildered frown. I haven't told anyone what happened in the woods that day, not even Mel, and I don't intend to. I don't know what went down between Leo and Sergei after he betrayed him to Xander, but I saw how badly it affected Leo, and I never want to put him through it again. If he believes Tamara, then I'm happy for it to remain that way.

"And I want to thank you," she continues, "for not telling him the truth."

I smile. "I have no idea what you're talking about."

It takes her a couple of beats to catch on to what I'm saying, but the frown lines are still there between her eyebrows. Ivana gives her an encouraging nod. "I apologize too for lying to you about the pakhan and Elena."

This one still stings. Tamara lied to me about Leo cheating on his fiancee, knowing that the situation was the complete reverse. When Leo and I were reunited, he told me that Elena cheated on him, and that he vowed, afterwards, never to allow another woman into his heart.

Until he met me.

"Can you forgive me?" Tamara asks.

Deep breath. "For Leo's sake, I will try."

She nods, and her gentle smile lights up her face. "Shall we?" She offers me her arm, and I take it, while Mel intertwines her arm with Ivana's. "The pakhan is waiting for you."

"It's acceptable for the bride to be late." Mel links her other arm with mine, and I wonder if the irony of her wedding being six years too late is playing on her mind today.

But I don't have a chance to dwell on it.

The garden is filled with the fragrance of loose rose petals, and I can hear the hum of conversation reaching us from the guests already gathered around the Japanese pagoda.

My legs tremble, and my stomach churns as we make our way towards Leo.

When I see him, my breath hitches in my chest. He is even more handsome than usual in a dark-silver suit and an ivory lace cravat that coordinates perfectly with my dress; Mel must've helped him choose it.

His eyes lock onto mine, and my heart swells with love for this beautiful, strong, sexy man. I almost can't believe that he is mine, but his smile is all that I need. His gaze doesn't waver. He watches Tamara hand me over to my father before she and Ivana join him inside the pagoda as his best women.

And then I'm standing in front of him. He kisses my father's hand, thanking him for blessing our marriage. I barely register my father kissing my cheek and placing my hand in Leo's, or saying our vows, or the celebrant announcing that we are husband and wife.

I think that all I'll ever remember of that day is Leo pressing my body against him and kissing me on the lips in front of our families and friends.

"I love you, my printzessa," he whispers into my ear, his breath tickling my neck and sending shivers down my spine.

"I love you, Leo. I always have, and I always will."

EPILOGUE

GIANNA

I reach one of the rooms on the top floor and sit heavily in the rocking chair in the corner of the room. My belly is so large now that even my thighs are screaming at me to get these babies out and give them a break.

"Not long now."

I stroke my belly through my oversized T-shirt and mutter to myself. Or the twins. Or my thighs. At this point, I'm so used to talking to all three of us while I work that it's like a three-way video call without the images on the screen.

This is how it will always be, and I'm so excited to meet the twins in a few weeks even though I'm still not prepared to deal with the diaper situation. I tossed it out there with Leo early in my pregnancy. He immediately adopted his pakhan expression, the one where his lips almost disappear, and he peers down his nose at the rest of the world simply waiting for them to acknowledge his top-of-the-food-chain status, and said, "Absolutely not."

We'll manage. We don't have a choice, and Mel says it's different when it's your own baby; you're not quite so squeamish. She also loves to remind me that I've faced far more horrific situations working at the refuge in Montenegro, so how can I let a bit of baby poop floor me.

"Here she is." Mika bounds into the bedroom, still clad almost head-to-toe in leopard print, and perches on what's left of my thighs. "Thought we'd find you playing hooky in one of these gorgeous rooms we've worked our butts off to finish before you pop."

"I'm not playing hooky, I'm resting."

A baby foot pokes her in the back for getting too close, and Mika sprawls across the floor like the drama queen she is.

"How do you live with that punishment, Gi? Your insides must be black and blue."

I smile and cradle my belly with both arms like I can protect my babies from her insults. "I'm going to miss them wriggling around after they're born. It's the best feeling in the world."

Soon Cartier comes in carrying a heap of fairy lights. "This is the last room to decorate." Her eyes are already on the ceiling, figuring out how many lights she'll need. "Don't mind me. You two just carry on lazing around and chatting about babies. I'll work around you." To prove the point, she strolls between me and Mika trailing strands of tiny bulbs over our friend.

"Sorry, that last flight of stairs killed my legs." I flash her an apologetic smile. "I might just sit here for a while."

I've been on site every day since Leo and I signed the deed to the red-stone mansion. I've knocked down walls with a sledgehammer, scraped multiple layers of paint from walls, climbed ladders to catch spiders and de-mold ceilings, and sat on the floor to eat sandwiches picked up from the deli around the corner. And I wouldn't change a single moment of it. Apart from meeting Leo, this has been the most exciting thing that has ever happened to me.

But now that we're ready to open, my body is yelling at me to give myself a break. I feel bone-weary but deliriously happy.

As if reading my thoughts, Mika jumps onto her feet and backs away. "You're not going into labor, are you? I mean, I'm excited to meet our girls too. But man, I don't fancy our chances of cleaning this carpet before our guests arrive if you decide to spill your waters all over it."

I laugh out loud. "Firstly, we don't know that they're girls."

"Yeah." Cartier stares at me from the other side of the room while she untangles the wires. "Why didn't you find out what gender the babies are?"

"I wanted it to be a surprise. And I read somewhere that the final stage of labor goes faster if you don't know what to expect."

"Well, hopefully they'll both be babies and not two-headed aliens." Mika can't help chuckling at her own joke. "Although I'm still on the fence about whether Leo is human, or a creature created from the genes of every hot movie star in the history of time."

While on honeymoon, Leo surprised me with a trip to Montenegro so that I could ask my friends face to face to come and run the refuge with me. They said they'd be sorry to leave behind the women we'd gotten to know so well, but coming to Chicago was a no-brainer.

Part of me still wonders if they agreed so that the three musketeers could be reunited, or if they're here because they couldn't resist Leo. The three stress grooves on the bridge of his nose have smoothed out since we got married, and I still wake up beside him every morning reassuring myself that this sex-god is all mine. Besides, I've seen the way they follow him around with their eyes whenever he comes to the refuge.

But having them here has made my world complete. The grand opening is planned for tomorrow. Our families will be here, and the dogs, who successfully managed to christen every room during renovations. The mayor will give a speech to commemorate the opening, and then we hope to start taking women in immediately.

Mika, Cartier, and I all feel strongly that the women who need us the most will be the women who find us. Our aim is to ultimately help them find themselves. To help them become the strongest versions of themselves, women who will take no shit off anyone, women who will walk back out into the world with their heads held high and a middle finger up to the men who tried to destroy them.

I just need my babies to stay safely cocooned inside me until after I've welcomed our first residents.

"Fair enough." Mika shrugs. "I still think they're both girls though. I can picture Leo with silver hair and a grandaddy beard surrounded by women in his old age."

"God help him," Cartier mutters. "Anyway, what's secondly? The suspense is literally killing me, not to mention these lights might just end up being tossed out of the window if they don't cut me some slack within the next sixty seconds."

"Secondly, I still have three weeks till my due date."

"Which is nothing in twin terms, I might add." Cartier stops untangling wires and stares at me with the same expression as Mika is wearing.

I ignore them. "Thirdly, if my waters break—which doesn't always happen—it's literally impossible for me to choose when this might be."

"Do you feel like this is about to happen?" Mika keeps her distance in case her boots get splashed.

"No."

Cartier tilts her head to one side as if I'm a painting that hasn't been hung correctly on the wall. "You're not moving though. I haven't seen you this still since the night you got hammered on Tequila in our apartment and ended up sleeping with your head out of the window."

"That was a great night," Mika adds.

"I'm pretty sure you said it was the worst night of your life," I remind her.

"That was the next day. The night before was mwah." She kisses her fingers to demonstrate.

"Why aren't you moving, Gi?" Cartier isn't letting it go. "Is there something you're not telling us?"

Mika crouches on the floor and peers underneath the rocking chair. "Nope. No puddle on the carpet."

"I'm fine." Gripping the arms of the chair, I haul myself onto my feet.

Before I can straighten, something seems to click inside my belly, and it drops, causing me to catch my breath and reach out for my friends. Mika and Cartier grab a hand each, gap-mouthed, their eyes wide. I wait for my waters to trickle down my legs, and when nothing happens, I let go of their hands and smile.

"False alarm. Don't panic."

Then, my belly grows rock hard, solidifying into a mountain peak protruding through my T-shirt as pain grabs hold of my body and twists violently. I reach out for them blindly and remember to breathe, in through my nose and out through my mouth, eyes squeezed shut to avoid the look of sheer horror on my friends' faces.

The pain seems to go on and on, relentlessly gripping my belly and tightening its hold. Finally, it starts to ebb, and I open my eyes to find Mika and Cartier both grimacing at how hard I'm clutching their hands.

I'm panting, and there's a dull ache blooming somewhere deep inside me, but I'm fine. I just need to reassure them before they go into full-on panic-mode and call Leo to come get me and take me straight to the hospital.

"What the fuck, Gi." Mika's face is drained of color. "Are you in labor?"

"No," I say with as much energy as I can muster, which isn't a lot apparently, going by the expressions on their faces. "It was just a practice contraction. They can get a bit strong."

"Fucking strong? I thought I was going to have no fingers left by the time you were finished."

Cartier still hasn't said a word; she's just watching me as if she can read all the signs.

"I'm not in labor." It sounds like I'm trying to convince myself as much as them, but I plough on regardless. I peer down at my dry legs. "See, waters still intact."

"Yeah, but you said it yourself: they don't always break." Cartier is still clinging to my hand.

"Don't worry, even if I was in labor, I'm not missing tomorrow's grand opening for anything."

"You're in labor?"

We all jump visibly and turn to face the doorway and the worried lines framing Leo's mouth. Marvel and Lucky bounce into the room and sit smartly at Cartier's feet because she's the one who always carries treats around in her pockets. Sure enough, she slides her hand inside the pocket of her jeans and tosses one each to the dogs who practically swallow them whole.

"Leo? I didn't hear you coming up the stairs."

He crosses the room in three strides and places a hand on my stomach. "Are the babies coming? Do I need to take you to the hospital?"

"No," I say at the same time as my friends both say, "Yes."

"No," I repeat. "It's nothing. I need to be here tomorrow."

But another contraction tears through my stomach. All I can do is focus on the pain as I hear Mika muttering from a million miles away, "They're only a few minutes apart. I think we're going to be aunties by tomorrow."

By the time the contraction has passed, Leo has lifted me easily into his arms and is carrying me down the first flight of stairs. The dogs run ahead, taking the staircase in two or three leaps and waiting for us to reach the bottom like this is the best game ever.

"Leo, put me down." I don't want to admit that my legs probably won't carry me all the way down to the ground floor;

I don't want to add fuel to the fire already burning in Leo's eyes. "I can walk."

"Don't listen to her," Mika yells from the floor above. "You go meet your babies. We'll finish up here."

Leo obviously believes my friends over me. He doesn't stop until he's lifting me onto the back seat of the car and climbing in beside me. The dogs are already in the trunk, peering at us from behind the mesh screen.

Before I can tell him to take me home, another contraction is already building inside my abdomen. This one feels even stronger than the one before, and I'm forced to accept that I'm going to miss the mayor opening the refuge.

There are tears in my eyes when I look at Leo. "I want to be there tomorrow," I whisper.

"Our babies have other plans, my printzessa." He kisses me on the lips. "They didn't want to miss it either."

"But—"

"No buts, Gianna. How lucky are we? We get to meet our babies and offer a safe place for women who need it all at the same time. And it's all down to you."

"I couldn't have done it without—"

"Hush. You could've done anything you wanted Gianna, been anyone, gone anywhere, and you chose me. I will never ever stop loving you for this."

I lean into him and listen to his steady heartbeat.

He is right and wrong. I could've done anything and gone anywhere, but as for being anyone I wanted, I was always going to be his. One way or another.

I stop fighting the contractions and leave the refuge in the capable hands of my friends while Leo and I prepare to meet our beautiful babies.

"Mika thinks they're both girls," I say.

"Three of you?" He kisses the top of my head. "My luck just keeps growing and growing."

Thank you for reading Leonid and Gianna's story, I hope you enjoyed it as I much as I did creating it.
Please leave me a review and share to help me grow.

Would you like to read a bonus chapter and meet Leo and Gianna's babies? click here.

If you haven't read Mel and Xander's story yet...you're in a for treat, start with Claimed By The Mafia Prince.

You're all caught up with the series? Dive into the Ruthless Billionaire Mafia Kings Series, according to reviews Caleb and Victoria's story is "unputdownable."

Here is your next hot read...it's dark, addictive, with a possessive, protective antihero, a smart heroine you'll love and a little girl you'll adore.

Convenient Mafia Vows: A Forced Proximity, Surprise Pregnancy Dark Romance Vows Caleb and Victoria's story.

Here is sneak peek of their spicy meet cute...

Prologue

Victoria

I'm hot, hotter than I ever thought it would be possible to be in New York in the winter. Sweat trickles down the front of my chest from beneath the black silk scarf wound around my neck, and I swear that if the line for the restroom doesn't move within the next three seconds, I'll whip off the blonde, curly wig I'm wearing and use it to fan myself. At this point, I don't even care if it ruins my costume.

I'm Sandy.

Or rather, I'm Victoria Callahan dressed up as Sandy from *Grease* for a costume party in a sleazy basement club in the Upper West Side on New Year's Eve. Scratch that. It's probably New Year's Day now although, if it is, I missed the countdown to midnight beneath the thump-thump-thump of hundreds of people in crazy costumes losing all ability to coordinate their movements into something that resembles dancing.

Beneath the blonde wig, my long brunette hair is pinned to my scalp and trapped beneath a scratchy net that isn't helping. Well, it depends which way you're looking at it, I guess. My best friend, Sienna, was going to come to the party as Sandy, but being the sexy loyal best-friend-a-gal-could-ever-have, she suggested that it might work better on me.

Because Sienna has no trouble getting laid.

Not that I have *trouble* getting laid exactly. I mean, how do you define trouble when it simply never happens?

The problem is, the more time that passes without me finding someone worthy of spreading my legs for, and the older I get, the weirder it becomes. It's like, when a guy finds out that you're twenty-three and still haven't a clue what all the fuss is about they think you're either a lesbian in denial or there must be something inherently wrong with you that has deterred any other guy from scoring a home run.

Is there something wrong with me?

I don't think so. A girl's got to have standards, right?

You've only got to look at a classic fairytale to know that Prince Charming is worth holding out for.

Sienna thinks that I give off stay-the-fuck-away-from-me-unless-you're-prepared-to-go-down-on-one-knee-and-propose vibes.

I don't.

At least, I don't give them off intentionally.

I blame my mom. She read those goddamned fairytales to me and then went and ruined everything with a heroin addiction that made her see charming princes behind a slime-ball with her next fix. She also left me with a little brother to take care of when I should've been fangirling over Zac Eron and Orlando Bloom.

Wednesday Addams comes out of the restroom, glaring at the rest of us waiting in line like we should've had the common decency to give her some space, and we shuffle along a couple of paces.

"Smile." Sienna's mouth lifts at the corners to demonstrate the concept, and I mimic her, knowing that my attempt hasn't quite reached my eyes. "That's better. You'll never bag yourself a stud while you look like you want to murder someone."

It's easy for her to say. After loaning me the costume she'd planned on wearing, she bought a leopard-print mini dress from a thrift store, teamed it with chunky blue beads and bare legs, and piled her naturally red hair up into a messy bun on top of her head. And voila: she's a gorgeously stunning Wilma from *The Flintstones*.

I know it sounds like I'm jealous of my best friend, but I'm honestly not. She's the kindest, sweetest-natured person I ever met, and I don't know where I'd be without her. I wouldn't be in this dingy club for starters, but I mean, I don't know where I'd be in life. Hopefully not chasing fixes around the city like my mom did until she met her new husband.

I peer around the club. Fred and Daphne are making out in a corner and, oh my fucking God, did she come here commando?

Blinking the vision out of my head, I avert my eyes and spot Cinderella strutting her stuff—literally—with Mick Jagger. I can't help smiling at them. I don't know if they arrived together, but it's pretty freaking obvious that they'll be leaving together when everyone else starts running out of steam.

This is what I don't understand, and I think this is the reason why I never 'bag myself a stud' as Sienna puts it. Not that there are any studs here tonight. Not that I've seen anyways. Well, maybe there were some here earlier in the evening, but now that everyone's steaming, including me, all I can see is sweaty upper lips and drooping wigs.

But anyway, it's that easy confidence in their ability to attract a member of the opposite sex. Even in this blonde wig and wearing the tightest latex pants in the history of the world, I draw a blank when it comes to looking sexy and flirting. I must've been last in line—again—when they were dishing out the fuck-me-cowboy genes.

"You're doing it again." Sienna jolts me back to reality.

"Doing what?"

"Overthinking it. Vic—" she places her hands on my shoulders and forces me to look her in the eye "—you look incredible tonight. Any guy that gets the chance to slip inside those pants is going to think he hit the jackpot."

"Only if I pay out."

She tips her head back and laughs out loud, a sound that's contagious. "You will, trust me. You'll know when the right guy comes along."

We shuffle closer to the restroom entrance as a whole bunch of girls come pouring out, and suddenly, we're in, and I have to go through the rigmarole of peeling these pants over my hips.

I can still feel the music vibrating in my bones even if it feels good to have a few moments to myself to breathe while I'm shut inside the cubicle. My head is pleasantly fuzzy. I'm probably more chilled than I've been in months. But still, I feel like something is missing from my life.

Flushing, and then standing in front of the mirror, I touch up my lip gloss, and check that my mascara hasn't run while I've been boogying my butt off out there.

Deep breath.

I follow Sienna outside and realize, a beat too late, and when the space we've just vacated inside the restroom has already been filled, that I left my purse behind.

"Sienna, my purse!"

She doesn't hear me with the bass rocking the club, so I dash back inside, breathe a sigh of relief when I spot my purse next to the basin where I left it, and grab it quickly. I need to find Sienna before she gets swallowed up by a whole bunch of sweaty bodies and is lost to me forever. Or at least until we both sober up tomorrow morning.

Head down, I don't make eye contact with anyone in the line, and instead, collide headfirst with a rock-solid chest who isn't watching where he's going either. I tilt my head back and find myself gazing into green eyes framed by the thickest lashes I've ever seen on a man. His black hair is gelled back into an Elvis-style quaff, and he's wearing a beaten-up leather jacket over a white T-shirt.

"Danny?" I squeal like a teenager.

"Sandy?" His voice squeaks as he catches on quickly.

"Oh my God, I've always wanted to say that." My gaze travels down from Danny Zuko's wide smile and perfect white teeth to the broad shoulders and rippling chest muscles. I don't dare look any lower. Besides, chests have always been my thing.

He leans closer, so close that I can smell cinnamon on him, like he's spent the holidays baking cookies. I can't drag my eyes away. My body is refusing to cooperate, and my heart is going frantic inside my rib cage like I just bumped into the real Danny Zuko, and nothing else exists outside of those dark mossy flecks in his green-green eyes.

"Where have you been all my life?" he murmurs.

Wait. Even my fuzzy brain recognizes that this isn't a line from *Grease*. But I play along anyways.

"Waiting for you?"

It must be the right response because his smile grows, lighting up his beautiful face and crinkling the corners of his eyes, and I feel his hand slide around my waist as his lips press on mine.

His other hand entwines with the blonde curls and tips my head back, causing my brain cells to swim, and the ground to slide out from under me. I squeeze my eyes shut and concentrate on his tongue in my mouth. I taste beer and liquor, and it isn't at all unpleasant because I'm kissing Danny Zuko at a New Year's Eve party, and when my legs give way, he keeps me upright like it's what he was made to do.

He pulls his tongue from my mouth long enough to murmur, "You're so fucking gorgeous," and then it's back again, and I'm not fighting it because tonight, for one night only, I'm the Sandy to his Danny.

I don't know how long we stand there kissing like it's the end of the world. Time has stopped, and I barely even remember who I am or what I'm doing here.

When he pulls away, leaving my lips swollen and still parted, my tongue aching for his, I feel the crushing weight of disappointment. This is it. This is the moment when he realizes his mistake, that I'm not the Sandy he arrived with, and makes an excuse to get away from me as quickly as possible.

But instead, he looks me directly in the eye and says, "Come with me."

It isn't a question, and I don't even have a chance to answer before he grabs my hand and leads me through the club and outside into the freezing New York City night.

This isn't happening to me.

It can't be.

I'm Victoria Callahan, virgin extraordinaire, the girl who gives off all the wrong vibes for bagging a stud, and yet, when I climb into the back of a yellow taxi and Danny Zuko's lips reattach to mine, none of that even matters. He could be a psycho serial killer with a blonde wig fetish for all I know. But the ache between my legs tells me that I'm going to let him fuck me.

The cab pulls up on the curb, and Danny tosses some cash to the driver, his warm hand still in mine. He lets himself into an apartment building without a word. While we wait for the elevator, his tongue finds mine again, his hands roaming my body and touching me in places I've never been touched before.

He pushes me against the wall, the button dinging behind my back, and crushes my breasts with both hands, while he smothers my mouth with his own, his oxygen becoming mine. I'm breathless when we both roll into the elevator.

By the time we roll out of it and into his apartment, I can barely even stand, my legs are trembling so badly. "Danny, I'm—"

He tips my head backward, arching my neck so that it's hard to breathe, and then I feel his teeth digging into the soft flesh around my mouth, and I can't even remember what I was going to say.

"You're so fucking beautiful." His words caress my sore lips as he grips my chin between his thumb and forefinger.

Then, his tongue is tracing a line down my neck, and somehow, my breasts are exposed, and his mouth is closing around my nipples, his teeth nibbling the sensitive flesh. I gasp with the sheer pleasure of the sensation, pushing my lower back against the wall and inadvertently thrusting my nipples harder into his mouth.

His free hand fumbles with the latex pants, and I hear a low growl erupt from his throat as he finally manages to drag them down over my hips.

He slides a finger inside me, and I gasp out loud before I can stop myself. My hands are fluttering around his head, and I shove a fist into my mouth and bite down hard. I can feel his finger working around inside me, probing, exploring, and I instinctively open my legs, knees still trembling, to let him in deeper.

"Stay there." He reappears briefly, kisses my lips, a full-on tongue-down-my-throat kiss, and then drops to his knees, and oh my fucking God, when he spreads my sex open with both hands and inserts his tongue, I swear my eyes must roll back in my head.

Oh. My. God.

I feel... I don't know what I feel... My pussy is throbbing and tingling and writhing like it wants to escape his tongue which is dragging back and forth across my clit, when I know that escaping is the last thing in the world I want to do right now.

I'm almost there, my orgasm about to explode, when he pulls his tongue out. I almost collapse on him and press my spine hard against the wall to keep myself grounded. My pussy is twitching, desperate to feel his tongue inside me again, and I don't know what to do about it.

Danny stands and licks my lips with the tip of his tongue. I can't move. The pants are still around my ankles, and I'm conscious that my breasts and my pussy are exposed, and this is not at all how I imagined my first time would be.

But when he murmurs, "Do you want me to let you come, Sandy?" I find myself whispering, "Yes," huskily.

"Say it again."

"Yes," I breathe against him.

"Hmm." Danny watches me with those green eyes, and when I instinctively try to kiss him, he moves just out of reach. "Yes, what?"

"Yes, I want to come." I don't even recognize my own voice.

"Yes, Danny, I want you to let me come." When I remain silent, he grabs my chin again and nibbles my bottom lip. "Say it, Sandy."

"I want you to let me come."

He smiles, and I melt into a giant orgasmic puddle of wetness.

Danny rams a finger inside me, watching me closely. I keep my eyes on him even though I want to close them and lose myself riding his finger. He drags it out of me, pulling his finger across my clit and eliciting another groan, and then his finger is in my mouth, and I can taste myself.

And maybe this is it after all, everything I never dreamed of because I never knew I could be this freaking sexy.

This time, when he sticks his tongue in me, I don't hold back. I explode in his mouth, and for one scary moment I think he might drown in me because I never want this to end...

I don't know when or how we end up in his bed.

I'm naked, and he climbs on top of me, still wearing the white T-shirt, his cock bouncing in his hand as he frees it from his jeans and rubs it around my pussy.

"Tell me you want me, Sandy," he growls.

"I want you." Since when did I ever start being so meek and compliant?

"Louder."

I raise my voice a notch. "I want you."

He shakes his head and pulls away, withholding from me the one thing I want most in the entire world.

"I freaking want you!" I yell.

He smiles, and I've never seen anything so crazily hot and sexy in my life.

I spread my legs wide, and he studies me for several moments before guiding his length to my sex. I feel him pushing against me, trying to gain entry. Without thinking, I reach down and open myself up, holding his gaze the whole time.

"You're so fucking sexy, Sandy." I can see it in his enlarged pupils, and for once, I believe it.

Then he's inside me, and I start panting as he pushes, gently at first, and then harder, hitting that wall, surprise crossing his eyes. He lowers his upper body onto me and fills my mouth with his tongue.

Continue reading Convenient Mafia Vows now Available On Amazon and Free in Kindle Unlimited and on Paperback.

ABOUT THE AUTHOR

Vivy Skys writes addictive high heat romance where grumpy, dangerously hot alpha males fall hard for sassy, stunning women who bring them to their knees.

From billionaires in penthouse suites to irresistible neighbors next door—and let's not forget the wickedly charming royals, protective SEALs and Mafia Kings—no swoon-worthy bachelor is safe.

Vivy's heroines are clever, confident, and impossible to forget—exactly the kind of women these men would burn kingdoms to worship.

Each scorching, standalone love story promises heart-pounding tension, heat you'll feel in your bones, and the kind of happily-ever-after that'll leave you breathless.

🔥 Ready to get obsessed? Dive into the Vivy's Library—and don't forget to join her raving fan newsletter for sneak peeks, bonus books, and insider-only treats

Follow Vivy Skys on Amazon to be the first to know when her next book becomes available.

Printed in Great Britain
by Amazon